THE
DEVIL'S
WALTZ

JESSI ELLIOTT

INIMITABLE
BOOKS
UNFORGETTABLE STORIES

Published by Inimitable Books, LLC
www.inimitablebooksllc.com

Library of Congress Cataloguing-in-Publication Data is available.

First edition, 2024
Cover design by Keylin Rivers

ISBN 978-1-958607-10-7 (hardcover)
10 9 8 7 6 7 6 5 4 3 2 1

ALSO BY JESSI ELLIOTT

Taken by the Fae
These Wicked Delights

TRIGGER WARNING

Implied and on-page portrayal of torture and murder, attempted sexual assault (not between main characters), portrayal of panic attacks

For the readers who can't help but fall for the villain.

I desire the things that will destroy me in the end.
— Sylvia Plath

ONE
CAMILLE

A blast of steaming-hot milk shoots from the espresso machine, narrowly missing my face. I slam my hand on the top, grumbling under my breath. I swear, making coffee is going to be the death of me.

I've been working at Hallowed Grounds for nearly six months. You'd think in that time I would've learned a trick to stop the damn thing from sputtering boiling liquid at me, but no. Safe to say, being a barista isn't my true calling. Hell, I don't even like coffee. The closest I'll get is a dirty chai latte, and that's only when I'm desperate for an energy boost.

"Are you good?"

I glance over the top of the cursed machine to find my best friend and roommate, Harper. She stands on the other side of the counter with her lips pressed together against a smile, her eyes sparkling pools of blue.

"You couldn't have ordered something simple, like tea...or water?" I shoot back dryly before pouring the steamed oat milk into a to-go cup. The machine continues to hiss at me, but I ignore it.

Harper snorts, tying her brownish blond hair back as she leans against the counter. "When are you going to ditch this place?"

I purse my lips. "Hmm, hard to say. Probably when tuition and rent magically become free."

She shoots me an unimpressed, squinty-eyed look at my tone. I've seen that expression many times in the decade I've known her, but it does nothing to squash my sarcasm.

I shake my head, silently asking her not to push it, before finishing her vanilla oat latte and securing the lid. Walking to the end of the worn butcher block counter, I slide it toward her.

"Thank you," she singsongs, wrapping her fingers around the cup. Lifting it to her lips, she takes a small sip before sighing contentedly. "Do you have a few minutes?"

I wipe my hands on the apron tied around my waist and glance at the other barista working tonight. Harper's been our only new customer in the last half hour, so she's currently scrolling on her phone. "Marie, I'm going to take my break before you head home."

She shoots me a thumbs-up without looking away from her screen.

I make myself a drink and join Harper at a table along the front window, passing one of our regulars on the way. It's an older woman who likes to sit near the counter while she drinks her peppermint tea and solves the crossword in the paper.

It's dark outside, and the weather is unseasonably cool. Something rather unusual for the third week of September in Seattle, which only makes the café feel cozier. I've always adored the old wood floors and twinkling lights hanging from the ceiling. Paired with the rich aroma of coffee beans and the sweetness of pastries, there are worse places I could spend my evenings. And considering my student loan debt is only getting bigger, I really need this job.

Soft rock plays through the space, mixing with the quiet conversation of a couple sipping lattes on the green velvet couch across the room.

"How's your night going?" Harper asks, cradling her latte and tapping her fingers against the side of the cup as the faint scent of her Chanel perfume tickles my nose.

"Pretty quiet," I say as warmth radiates from my cup and heats my palms. "I've been studying between customers." We're not even a month into the semester, but my Political Theory professor is a fan of weekly quizzes, so I'm always studying. I don't mind it, though, and I'm already halfway through my political science degree at the University of Washington. "How was training?" A plume of discomfort hits me as the words leave my lips. I suspect where the question will lead this conversation and I kind of regret asking it.

The corner of her mouth kicks up. "I'm at the top of the leaderboard. Three months and counting, so I'd say it's going pretty damn good."

I find it in myself to smile. "That's amazing, Harper. Congratulations."

Her gaze lowers to her cup. "Thanks. I wish you were kicking ass with me, though. I'll graduate from the academy and get partnered with some dud."

A sigh escapes my lips. We've had this conversation before.

"Sorry," she rushes to say as her brows knit. "I know your parents hound you enough about re-enrolling. Ignore me."

I sit back, wishing my chair would swallow me so I could escape this conversation. My stomach roils at thoughts of the academy—of my parents and what they want for my future.

For as long as I can remember, I've known supernaturals live in the shadows of the mundane world. And while most people our age are figuring out what they want to do with their lives, Harper's learning what both of our parents learned before us—demon hunting.

Graduating from the academy feeds you right into the Department of Demonic Protection, an offshoot of the US government unknown to the public. And my parents are in charge, leading the hunters in protecting humans from supernatural threats.

Since I turned fifteen, I started training. Following in their footsteps. Making them proud.

Until my world shattered when Danielle, my older sister, went on the hunt that killed her.

The morning after her funeral, I dropped out and swore I'd never return to that life.

Of course, my leaving five years ago hasn't stopped my parents from doing everything they can to rope me back into the academy. They refuse to accept I'm dedicating myself to my *own* future instead of the fight against demons. And after losing one daughter, they're desperate for reassurance that I can protect myself. To them, more training means less danger.

Honestly, I never wanted to be a hunter—even before Danielle died. The only reason I didn't resist when our parents enrolled me was because Dani was training, too. Whatever she did, I wanted to do, too. To be closer to her.

I've considered training without intending to become a full-fledged hunter. But there's something stopping me from bringing it up to my parents. Maybe I'm worried they'll think their antics are working and then double down on their efforts. I'm hoping once Harper graduates from the academy this year, she'll train me on the down low. She's currently consumed by training and school—yet another reason I wanted out. Being a hunter takes over your entire life, and I want *more*. Something I choose for myself instead of the life I was born into.

"It's okay," I finally say, tucking a stray bit of hair behind my ear. Most of my brown waves are piled into a messy bun at the crown of my head, but some pieces always seem to escape while I'm working. "I really am happy for you." It's the truth.

Harper lost both of her parents during a demon attack a few years ago. Her response was the opposite of mine. Where I turned my back on the hunter's organization, she dedicated herself even harder. Some days I struggle with the fear of losing her like I did Danielle. She's the closest thing I have to a sister now. We'd do anything for each other—which includes me listening to her talk about the life I didn't choose. I've gotten to a place where I'm mostly okay with it, and having Harper support my decision makes the sting of my parents' lack of it a little easier to bear.

She smiles. "And that is why you, Camille Morgan, are my best friend. Well, that, and because you give me free lattes." She lifts her cup and shoots me a wink before finally taking a sip.

I give a short laugh and roll my eyes, then glance at the clock behind the counter. "I should get back. Are you heading home now?"

Realization seems to dawn on her. "Shit, yeah. That's why I stopped here. I left my keys on the kitchen counter earlier, so I'm kinda locked out."

Shaking my head, I get up and walk back to the counter to fish my keys out of my bag. I toss them at her. She catches them easily and tucks them into her pocket as I add, "You better not lock *me* out later."

She nods with a faint grin, zipping up her black rain jacket as she stands. The rest of her ensemble is also black—leggings, T-shirt, and combat boots. The hunters' unofficial uniform. "Yeah, yeah," she grumbles around a yawn. "Fuck, I need my bed. I have training tomorrow morning before class, and I am *so* not looking forward to the early wake-up. Whoever thought it was a good idea to double up on hunter training on top of getting an English degree is a dumb bitch. Past me really screwed present me."

I offer a sympathetic smile, pausing when my gaze catches a figure in the front window. Before I can say anything to Harper, it's gone. I have half a mind to consider the possibility I imagined it. It was probably just someone passing by or checking out the menu through the glass. I turn my attention back to Harper, who's typing on her phone.

"I'm on the closing shift, so I'll be home late," I tell her. "Try to get a good night's sleep."

She sighs. "Yeah. I probably should have made that latte decaf."

"Then it's a good thing *I* did."

She blows me a kiss on her way to the front door. "There you go again, proving to be the bestest friend ever."

I laugh, returning behind the counter as a few new customers enter.

Harper slips out the door, waving as she goes.

The rest of the night drags after Marie leaves. My eyes burn with exhaustion and my feet ache. By closing time at ten o'clock, I'm beyond ready to go home and crawl into bed. I have a weird feeling I can't shake, along with lethargy clinging to my muscles. Like the hint of an oncoming panic attack. My body is trying to trick me into thinking something's wrong, and I have no idea why.

I make quick work of the normal cleaning routine and finish by grabbing the garbage bags. Hauling them to the back of the building, I shove open the door with my hip and step outside.

The alley next to the café is almost completely dark, save for a faint glow from the light at the end of the street. My sneakers are silent against the dark pavement, still wet from the rain earlier today. I carry the bags around the corner, toss them into the dumpster, then wipe my hands on my apron as I walk back to the shop.

The sound of a glass bottle rolling across the pavement behind me halts my steps.

My breath catches, and I whirl around. Only to find nothing.

The breeze must've caught some loose trash. I exhale slowly, shaking my head, and turn to keep walking, picking up my pace. The streetlight at the opposite end of the alley flickers, and my pulse ticks faster as I close the distance between me and the side entrance to Hallowed Grounds.

A low growl rumbles through the damp air, and my heart lurches. My fingers just graze the metal handle before an ice-cold hand wraps around the back of my neck. A strangled sound rips from my throat a second before I'm yanked backward. White-hot pain flares along the side of my body when I collide with the brick exterior of the building across the alley. I don't have time to catch my breath before I'm grabbed again, and my face slams into the same wall. I cry out, my head throbbing as I whirl around and come face-to-face with the most horrific creature I've ever seen. What should be the whites of his eyes are filled with an endless pitch-black darkness, and he bares his unnaturally white teeth at me, hissing sharply.

Demon.

Alarm bells blare in my head, shrill and entirely unhelpful now that it's too late. Every fiber of my being screams at me to run, but my feet are blocks of concrete. I can't move. I can't breathe.

Two years of hunter training, and I freeze when it matters most. Granted, I left the organization while I was still only doing in-class learning—before I could even gain any fighting skills.

But something in me still clicks on, and I push off the building, setting my sights on the mouth of the alley. One of the first things I learned in training was to never run from a demon—they love the chase—but my other option is having my ass handed to me. And that's only the *best-*case scenario.

My heartbeat trips over itself as my feet pound the pavement. I make it halfway to the the street before the demon snarls, making my blood freeze in my veins.

He slams into me from behind, and we topple to the ground. I yelp as pain lances up my side, and I can tell my elbow is cut up from the dripping blood down my arm. Everything moves in slow motion as the demon gets up and hauls me with him then shoves me into the cold brick wall again. He invades my personal space without hesitation, his lips curling into a cruel smirk as he keeps me trapped against the building.

"Aren't you a snack?" he purrs, his black orbs roaming over my body and making my stomach churn. His features are sharp enough to cut glass, so angular he's hard to look at. Several bits of his shoulder-length, white blond hair have escaped its tie and fallen into his face. He licks his lips before continuing, and the pitch black in his eyes fades into a hungry, blue gaze. One human enough that if I didn't know any better, I might be fooled. It's a dangerous trick that allows demons to go undetected. He lowers his voice and digs his fingers into my shoulders. "I'm going to enjoy devouring you."

Fear grips me, like ice in my veins. A dull ringing fills my ears as my entire body continues throbbing painfully.

I'm going to die. Just like Danielle.

She warned me. Begged me to get out of the world of demon hunting. I held onto her as the life left her brown eyes—eyes that matched mine so closely we almost looked like twins—and promised her I would.

I grit my teeth and fight to shove down the terror clogging my throat.

Demons feed off the fear of humans. They also create it in their victims, usually through nightmares while they're sleeping. Sometimes they do it in visions while the human is awake. But they aren't known for attacking so...openly. They're not conspicuous in their attacks, preferring to stay in the shadows to go undetected. Their stealth also keeps the general population blissfully unaware of their existence. I've been away from the supernatural world long enough that perhaps their hunting tactics have changed, but still—this feels *targeted*. Otherwise, what the hell is a demon doing hanging out behind a café?

Said demon opens his mouth, as if he's going to taunt me some more, and—

"Let her go."

The unfamiliar voice has my lips parting in a silent, hopeful gasp as my attacker slowly turns his head. I follow his gaze, and an embarrassing level of relief fills me when my eyes land on a male figure stalking toward us. His stride is measured, confident, but it's the obsidian-bladed dagger in his grip that holds my attention. He's a hunter.

The demon cackles, and I take the opportunity to throw myself forward, slamming my knee into his stomach, and duck under his arm. Stumbling to the side, my entire body throbs, and I cringe at the warmth of blood dripping down my face and onto my T-shirt.

When the demon's gaze whips back toward me, his eyes are completely black again. A stark reminder that I'm dealing with a soulless monster. "Stupid girl," he snarls, then turns his back to me, advancing on the hunter in a blur of white hair and darkness. Clearly, he knows the stranger is a bigger threat than I am.

I battle with the urge to fight, surprised to feel it at this moment after so long, and the knowledge I don't have the training to do much but get in the way. My head is throbbing to the point dark spots are dancing across my vision and my knees threaten to give out any minute. Frustration makes my eyes burn with unshed tears. I've never felt so helpless as I do watching this hunter who just saved my life take on the demon who would've ended it. Clenching my jaw at the pit growing in my stomach, I tense as the hunter ducks to avoid the demon's fist flying toward his face.

His slate-gray eyes meet mine for a breath before focusing back on the demon.

I can't tear my gaze away from the way they dance around each other. The demon is faster, of course—he has preternatural speed on his side—but this hunter's skills are sharp. He moves smoothly, swinging his fist and catching the demon in the jaw once, twice, *three* times before he jumps back to avoid the demon's snapping teeth.

There's a part of me that recognizes my window of opportunity to escape shrinks the longer I stand immobile. But I still don't leave. Can't. My knees bump together as the muscles in my legs protest, barely keeping me upright.

My pulse jackhammers at the sound of a vicious snarl, and my chest tightens as I hold my breath. Bile rises in my throat and my skin tingles in a way I've gotten too used to experiencing.

The panic attacks started soon after I lost my sister. Facing the same kind of monster who stole her from me brings every awful memory to the forefront of my thoughts. No matter how hard I try to shake the feeling, to force myself to move, I'm completely powerless to the visions and sensations consuming me.

Wrapping my arms around myself, I steal a glance at the door to the café. If I can convince my legs to work again, I can sneak inside and call Harper for backup. I take a tentative step, my limbs heavy and wholly uncooperative, and keep my eyes trained forward. I freeze when the hunter growls in pain, stumbling as the demon swats him sideways.

He hits the building with a grunt, then quickly recovers, tightening his grip on his dagger.

In seconds, the demon moves in front of him again, grabbing him by the throat and lifting his feet off the ground.

The hunter's choppy, dark brown hair sweeps across his forehead and is damp with sweat, his eyes widening as they fall on the demon's face. Death shines in the hunter's eyes, and terror seizes me anew, flooding my veins with more ice.

My mouth opens in a silent scream, my vocal cords too tight to make a sound. I start moving away, but I don't get far before the hunter kicks out, catching the demon hard in the groin.

He snarls in pain and drops the hunter onto the concrete.

The hunter coughs as he fights to refill his lungs with air, then pops back up before his opponent can recover. He strikes with a catlike, deadly grace, slamming his obsidian blade deep into the monster's chest.

THE DEVIL'S WALTZ

The demon's all-black eyes go wide, a vein popping in his forehead, and his guttural scream fills the alley before he disintegrates into a pile of black ash.

Two
Xander

She is not at all what I was expecting.

Her heart is a caged bird throwing itself against the gilded bars, trying to beat free of her chest. But the moment the obsidian blade turns the low-level demon to ash at my feet, her fear swiftly morphs into anger. Her russet brown eyes narrow into an icy glare that has my brows stitching in confusion.

"Are you okay?" I wipe the weapon clean on my pant leg before returning it to the sheath at my thigh. Exhaling a heavy breath, I keep my gaze trained on where the brown-haired girl has pressed her back to the brick exterior of the café.

Her eyes stay locked on the remnants of her attacker, her hands curling into tight balls as she fists them at her sides. "I'm...fine," she grits out, a muscle feathering along her jaw as she tears her focus away from the pile of ash.

I take a tentative step closer to her, tilting my head as I study her face, not missing the way her breath catches or the faster rising and falling of her chest. "You're bleeding," I offer in a soft tone, the coppery scent burning my nostrils.

"Yeah," she murmurs shakily, as if to herself, then reaches to press her fingers to the cut above her eye, wincing at the contact. She curses under her breath before finally looking at me. Her pulse is a jackhammer vibrating beneath her flushed skin as sweat dots her brow and upper lip. She swallows and exhales an uneven breath. "Thanks for your help." Reaching for the door, seemingly about to walk away from this interaction, she sways on her feet.

I move without thinking, steadying her with my arm around her waist. "Easy there."

She immediately tries to pull out of my grasp. "I'm—"

"You're not fine," I cut in smoothly, opening the door while keeping an arm around her. I guide her into what appears to be a small commercial kitchen.

She moves away from me as soon as she has a counter to grab on to.

I glance around, taking in the space that isn't much larger than the alley we came from. The aroma of coffee lingers in the air along with something sweeter. It takes me a beat to realize the soft floral scent mixed with something like vanilla is coming from *her*. "Is there a first aid kit around here somewhere?"

She hesitates, her eyes scanning my face. Calculating. "In the cupboard behind you," she says at last.

I turn, open the small door, and find the white container. Pulling it down, I walk over and set it on the counter beside her before grabbing a barstool from around the high top counter in the middle of the room. I move it closer to her. "Sit."

She blinks at me, then mutters, "I can do it myself," before she turns around and pops the lid off, pulling wound care items out.

Her hands are shaking even worse now, making me frown. The drumbeat in her chest hasn't calmed as it should. The danger from the demon attack is gone. But her breath is still shallow, her pulse uneven.

"Shit." She stops what she's doing, pressing her palms flat against the stainless steel countertop.

I watch her shoulders rise slowly as she inhales a deep breath. Her following exhale is uneven as she keeps her back to me and her shoulders remain tense. I think she's having a panic attack.

"Hey," I say in a gentle tone, shifting toward her again. "You're okay."

Her head bobs up and down in a subtle nod, but she says nothing.

"Will you let me help you?" The challenge of getting her to trust me at this moment is paramount. I keep my voice soft, my movements slow and careful, so as not to scare her.

Turning slowly, she takes a few seconds to meet my gaze. Without answering, she hands me a pre-packaged alcohol swab and sits on the barstool, fidgeting with her hands in her lap.

I carefully open it and remove the disinfectant, unfolding it and moving to stand in front of the chair. "This is going to sting."

She nods silently, her pulse ticking faster as she keeps her jaw clamped shut. When I dab her face, she stiffens but still says nothing. I make quick work of cleaning the cut above her brow and toss the bloody wipe into the trash bin at the end of the counter. Then I rummage through the first aid kit until I find an antibiotic ointment and a bandage. I grab a fresh dish towel from the shelf above the sink, wet it, then clean the rest of her face as gently as I can. Her gaze is trained forward and her breathing evens out as I wipe away the blood that dripped down her cheek and neck. The front of her gray T-shirt is smeared crimson, and I frown before moving on to the cuts and scrapes on her arms, pausing to lean back and look at her as I toss the stained towel away. As I'm smoothing the ointment over the injury above her brow, I ask, "Do you know what happened tonight?"

Her gaze hardens, eyes narrowing. "Of course I do."

I cock my head, trying to decipher the reasoning behind her tone. I need to tread carefully here. "Not your first demon attack, then?" I set the tube aside and cover the cut with a bandage. Luckily, it's not deep enough to need stitches and has stopped bleeding.

She laughs, though the sound holds no humor. It's short and bitter. "No. Clearly not yours, either. You wielded that obsidian blade like it was an extension of yourself."

I purse my lips, grabbing a roll of gauze and wrapping it around her elbow to bandage the deeper lacerations there. Her fingers brush my ribs as she holds her arm out for me, and I ignore the way that simple, brief touch makes my skin tingle. Fuck. I need to focus on why I'm here. I can't waste this opportunity—or fuck it up by getting caught up in human urges of...intimacy. "Is that meant to be a compliment?"

"Not really."

I lower her arm slowly so it rests in her lap. "Care to tell me why you seem more upset than grateful that I just saved your life?"

She sits up straighter and sighs. "Besides the obvious?"

I arch a brow, fighting the pressure in my jaw to grind my molars. *What angle is she playing?* "I'm not sure what you mean."

With a scoff, she says, "Are you really going to stand there and pretend you weren't sent here on purpose?"

I stiffen. There's absolutely no way she knows the truth. And yet, the tightness in my chest clamps down harder as I stare at the distrust in her eyes. I need to turn this around, flip the script and regain control of the narrative. I recover with a short laugh. "Sent here?" I shake my head, feigning confusion. "I happened to be in the right place at the right time."

She crosses her arms over her chest, clenching her jaw briefly at the discomfort the movement must've caused her injuries. "Hmm. What's your name, Mr. Right Place, Right Time?"

"Xander," I say, offering her my hand.

She eyes it suspiciously before uncrossing her arms and sliding her hand into mine, giving it a brief shake before pulling back. She doesn't recross them.

I hope it's a sign I'm making progress with her. "And yours?" I ask.

"I don't believe for a second that you don't already know it."

My brows lift at the certainty in her voice. Despite the underlying warning that causes, I find myself intrigued by it. This back and forth with her, while dangerous, is quite entertaining. "Why's that?"

"Well, Xander, from what I saw tonight, you're good at what you do. Considering that, I'm sure you're well known in the organization. Which, of course, means you're well known to my parents. The very same people who have been trying to rope me back into training since the day I walked away from it."

Part of me relaxes at the confirmation she doesn't know why I'm truly here. She thinks this was a setup arranged by her parents.

Rachel and Scott Morgan are something of a legend in the world of demons and hunters. From what I've heard, even after their divorce, they continued training and working with hunter recruits as a team. Married more to their work than each other. Perhaps that has something to do with their daughter's reluctance to join the organization. Of course, the main reason comes from losing her sister during a demon attack five years ago. But I'm sure the complicated relationship with and between her parents doesn't help.

"Look..." I pause, holding her gaze as I wait for her to give me her name. She needs to think I don't already know it.

After a beat of silence, she offers, "Camille."

"Camille," I echo before continuing, "Your parents didn't send me. You have no reason to believe me, considering we just met—in the midst of a demon attack, no less—but I'm telling the truth."

"You're right," Camille slides off the barstool. "I don't believe you."

I nod but don't move away. "Fair enough."

The top of her head is level with my chin, and she tips her head back to meet my gaze. For a moment, we stand there silently. Her eyes roam over my face, studying me, and I soak up the warmth that comes with her attention. I'm enjoying it.

"Are your parents also hunters?"

My lips twitch, though some of that warmth fizzles away. "No." *Far from it.*

She arches a brow. "What's funny?"

"Nothing. I'm just thinking after learning who your parents are that we may have more in common than either of us realizes." I note the confusion on her face and continue, "My mother wasn't around much while I was growing up, and I've never met my father."

The hardness in her eyes softens, and she drops her gaze, her lashes fanning her high cheekbones. "Oh. That's...I'm sorry." Her voice is gentle, and I can't help but notice the tinge of pink in her cheeks.

Reaching out, I touch her shoulder so she'll look at me again. "We don't choose our family," I say. "I'm sorry your relationship with your parents isn't what you'd like either."

Camille nods, seeming to relax a little. "Thanks. Mostly for saving my ass, but for this, too."

I give her shoulder a gentle squeeze before lowering my arm back to my side. "You need a ride home?"

She lets out a breath, putting space between us as she walks to the other side of the kitchen, grabbing a jacket and purse off a hook on the wall. "No. My car is a few blocks away, but thanks. I was about to finish closing up and head out for the night."

I nod. "Do you want me to stay? I don't mind."

A hint of a smile touches her lips as she shoulders the purse and folds the jacket over her arm. "I'm okay. You can go. I'm sure you have someplace else to be."

"On a Tuesday at almost midnight?" I remark in a teasing tone. "Yes, I am overwhelmingly busy."

She offers me a dry look. "Funny." Glancing toward the doorway leading to the café, she sighs. "If you really want to hang around, I can only offer you bottom-of-the-pot coffee or a day-old blueberry muffin."

I close the distance between us in a matter of a few steps. "How about your phone number?"

A surprised laugh escapes her lips. "Yeah, that's not on the menu."

My lips curl into a grin as I hold her gaze. "No?" Leaning toward her, I add, "Come on. What are you so afraid of?"

Camille lifts her chin—as if she's triggered by the challenge in my tone. "Why do you want it?"

I don't miss a beat. "Because I want to see you again." No point in beating around the bush. "Despite this not exactly being a meet-cute from a romance novel, I've had a nice time talking with you tonight. I'd like to do it more, preferably in a less hostile environment." My lips twitch into a faint smirk, and I add, "Though I'll take what I can get."

Her cheeks go pink and her pulse jumps. "Hmm...You're quite the smooth-talker, Xander."

I decide at that moment I enjoy her saying my name. Probably too damn much. "Thank you," I say in a low voice, laced with mild amusement.

Camille blinks at me before exhaling a deep sigh. She holds out her hand, waiting.

I pull my phone from my jacket pocket and set it in her open palm.

"If you text me even once about demon hunting, I will block your number," she warns, tapping on the screen for a minute before handing my phone back. Her tone is stern, but there's a lingering tiredness beneath it.

The adrenaline from the attack is likely wearing off, and I wouldn't be surprised if her muscles were getting heavier with exhaustion by the second. She's trying to project an air of strength, but I see her false bravado for what it is. I admire her for it—it also tells me I have a lot of work to do.

"Understood?" she presses firmly.

I don't bother trying to hide my grin as I return my phone to my pocket. "I don't think that'll be a problem."

THREE
CAMILLE

"You came in late last night," Harper comments from behind her mug with a suggestive grin as I walk out of my bedroom. The apartment smells of freshly brewed coffee and her favorite cinnamon-raisin bread.

I pause at the counter that separates the kitchen from the living room, grabbing a banana from the fruit bowl. "Yeah," I say, sleep clinging to my voice. I've never been a morning person, but nine a.m. was the only Global Communications time slot this semester.

My eyes shift toward her as I debate how much I should share.

Once I finished closing the café last night, Xander had insisted on walking me to my car, where I thanked him again before taking off. My thoughts spiraled the entire drive home, and it took me over an hour to fall asleep. I dreamt of demon eyes and what would've happened if Xander hadn't shown up.

"Hello? Earth to Cami." Harper waves a hand in my face, arching a brow at me.

"Sorry," I mumble, blinking back into focus. "I, uh...There was a demon attack at the café. Well, in the alley beside it."

Her eyes widen, her posture straightening. "What the hell happened?" she demands as her breakfast pops from the toaster. She doesn't take her gaze off me, waiting for me to answer.

I rehash what went down, my stomach twisting into knots as the memories flood through me.

"Son of a bitch, Cami," she breathes, coming around the counter and tugging me into an inescapable hug. "I'm glad you're okay."

I pull back. "Thanks. I know I got lucky. If Xander hadn't been there..." I trail off, shaking my head as I force the thoughts away.

"Cami—"

"I accused him of working with my parents," I cut in, dragging a hand down my face. I am so not awake enough for this conversation.

She props her black legging-clad hip against the counter. "Why would you think that?"

I offer her a dry look in response.

"You seriously think it was an exercise to get you back into training?"

"The thought crossed my mind."

Harper frowns. "As much as your parents want that for you, I really don't think they'd use department resources in a ploy to convince you to train again. Plus, we both know the hunters have no way of controlling demons. Unleashing one in downtown Seattle would contradict the oath we take to protect everyone. Rachel and Scott wouldn't do that."

Pursing my lips in consideration, I let loose a heavy breath as my only response. She makes a valid point, but there's still an uncomfortable tingle at the back of my neck that feeds my suspicion. I'm not entirely convinced they didn't have anything to do with it. They've done some pretty messed-up things in the past to rope me back in. The odds of them coordinating the attack are low, but not impossible. Especially with having Xander there to step in and keep me from becoming demon food. I can't rule it out.

That said, the same reason I have for not wanting to train is exactly why my parents want me to. Danielle. They never knew the only reason I agreed to enroll at the academy was because I wanted to be like my sister. After she died, it didn't feel right to explain that. They would only be disappointed in me.

Harper shuffles toward the toaster to retrieve her breakfast. "I suppose you're off to campus?"

"Yeah," I say, peeling open the banana and taking a bite. Swallowing, I add, "I'll be home this afternoon."

She pauses, buttering her toast and looks at me over her shoulder. "I have training this morning and then class at two. We'll catch up tonight."

I nod, momentarily considering asking her to see if she can find out anything about last night's attack—about the hunter who saved me. I open my mouth, but her phone rings before I can get the words out.

She grabs it off the counter. "Shit, sorry. I have to take this." Hurrying toward her bedroom, Harper throws a quick "Have a good day!" at me before closing her door.

Leaving our apartment, I head toward campus, electing to walk so I can enjoy one of the last warm days before the temperature drops.

Halfway there, my phone buzzes in my pocket. I pull it out and my stomach swoops as I read the new message

Good morning. I wanted to make sure you were doing okay.

The butterflies in my stomach flutter to life, and I press my lips together at the sensation I have very little experience with. I chalk it up to the fact this guy saved my life and is undeniably attractive. But that's it.

I keep walking, glancing up every few seconds as I type a response.

Well, I'm alive thanks to you, so I guess that falls under "okay."

How convincing.

Have you talked to anyone about what happened? Your parents?

I haven't told them anything, but I talked to my friend Harper. She's in hunter training, and if I had to bet, she'll probably tell my mom.

Through no fault of her own, my friend has an inherent need to impress her superiors in the organization. It likely has to do with losing both her parents to demons and dedicating her life to hunting them, but that's really not my thing to explore.

Are you okay with that?

At this point, it doesn't really matter.

Even if they didn't orchestrate the attack, there's a good possibility they'll still use it to put pressure on me to enroll again.

I can tell you're super into this line of conversation.

My lips curl into a faint grin at the underlying sarcasm, but before I can type out a reply, another message comes through.

Can I see you today?

Cutting across the student parking lot, I approach the double doors to the university building, chewing my bottom lip as I go back and forth on how to respond. Do I want to see Xander again? The rational part of me says it's a bad idea. He's a demon hunter, and I've stayed as far away from that world as possible. Living with Harper is the only exception. She's my best friend and has been there for me for as long as I can remember. I can't imagine my life without her. But Xander...I don't know. The thrum of my pulse is making it difficult to deny wanting to see him again. Can I separate his job from the urge to spend more time with him? I'm not entirely sure why I even want to consider it, but there's something in my gut nudging me toward giving it a shot.

> I'm heading into class now. Busy until this afternoon.

It's not an answer to his question, which I'm still figuring out how to address. There's a voice in the back of my head, wondering why he wants to see me again. I'm sure I'm not the first person he's saved during a demon attack. Still, the notion that he wants to spend more time with me makes the swarm of butterflies in my stomach flutter wildly.

> Okay, no problem.

I tap my finger against the side of my phone as I linger in the quiet hallway outside the lecture hall. Harper's always encouraging me to put myself out there. Maybe Xander waltzing into my life last night—regardless of how it happened—was exactly what I needed.

I type another message and hit send before I can talk myself out of it.

> I'm done around 3 p.m. We could meet then?

> Sounds good. Meet me at Storyville?

The name is vaguely familiar. I don't recall ever going, but I've heard it mentioned more than once. I think it's located inside Pike Place Market, but I check with him to be sure.

> That's the one in the market, right?

> Yeah. It's become one of my favorite cafés in the city. Besides Hallowed Grounds, of course. To be fair, I've only been there once and was served day-old coffee.

Heat fills my cheeks, and I press my lips together against a smile.

> Funny. I'll see you later.

> Looking forward to it.

Pocketing my phone, I walk into class and drop into the seat next to my friend, Phoebe.

"Morning," she offers in a singsong voice. She, unlike me, is very much a morning person. Having a nine o'clock lecture doesn't stop her from curling her golden blond hair into loose waves or putting on a full face of makeup. She's also rocking some sandaled heels with a floral blouse and high-waisted black dress pants.

The fact that I'm out of bed this early is miracle enough. I grabbed the first pair of black joggers in my dresser and threw them on with a plain maroon T-shirt and running shoes. I also tugged a brush through my hair and threw it into a messy bun, so I feel as if I fit the student persona perfectly.

"Hey, Pheebs." I pull out my laptop and textbook, setting them up on the table in front of me. "How's it going?"

"Same old, same old," she says, turning toward me, sending a faint whiff of her perfume my way. It smells like the beach, all warmth and coconut. "You?"

"Me, too," I answer, which isn't entirely true if last night's events are any indication. But Phoebe has no involvement with the hunters or any idea demons exist. Which, if I'm honest, is part of the reason I enjoy hanging out with her. She also has the best personality of anyone I know. Phoebe is the human embodiment of sunshine, and being near her never fails to make me happier.

"Working tonight?" she asks, drinking from the to-go cup in her hand. She runs on caffeine.

The lecture hall quickly fills with students as it gets close to nine, and I shake my head. "I'm actually hanging out with...a new friend."

She wiggles her perfectly shaped brows. "A new *guy* friend?"

I nearly snort. "Yes. He is a guy."

"Oh my god, Cami," she squeals, her green eyes glittering. "This is so exciting. You have a date!"

I shush her, glancing around in anticipation of people near us eavesdropping. But everyone is either not awake enough or too occupied with their own conversations to care. I refocus on Phoebe. "I don't think—I mean, I don't know if it is."

She sets her coffee down, clicking her acrylic nails against the table. "Do you want it to be?"

I haven't given much thought to dating in the past. No one in high school interested me, and when I started college, my focus was on getting my degree and then a job that would take me away from Seattle.

"Relax, Cami. You don't have to decide right now. Just have fun." She shoots me a reassuring grin just as Professor Roth starts her lecture.

Halfway through, my phone buzzes. My stomach sinks when I see it's a message from my mom.

> I heard about the attack at Hallowed Grounds last night. It goes without saying that you should have reported it.

And yet, you said it anyway.

I flip my phone over as a pit forms in my stomach. I don't think me not reporting it matters now, considering the demon from last night is dead, not terrorizing other humans. My mom texting me has nothing to do with checking on *me*. She only cares about reprimanding me for not considering a protocol that, as someone who isn't a demon hunter, I have zero obligation to follow.

> I'm okay. Thanks for asking.

I should've just ignored the message. It didn't require a response, but I couldn't stop myself. Maybe it's childish, but part of me longs for her to recognize her text is missing what one would expect from a mother. A shred of evidence that she's relieved the demon didn't rip me to pieces would be better than what I got. I *know* she cares, but I'd like to *see* it during times like this.

I've had a strained relationship with my parents since we lost Danielle. I think there's a level of blame toward them left in my heart that I haven't been able to let go of. It doesn't help that at every turn, they're still trying to recruit me. My mom more than my dad, but that could be in part because he lives in New York. Not that I see her often, either, despite us living in the same city.

"You okay?" Phoebe asks quietly.

"Hmm?" I shake my head to clear it. "Sorry. Yeah, I'm just tired." It's not a complete lie. After the nightmares, I really didn't get much rest, and I'm feeling it now.

For the rest of class, I tune in and out, replaying both last night's events and my mother's subsequent reprimand on a loop until my temples are throbbing.

Phoebe and I walk out of the lecture hall together, and the fresh air feels like heaven on my skin.

"Are you sure everything's okay, Cami?" she asks.

I force a nod and attempt to pair it with a believable smile.

Her heels echo off the pavement as we walk across the student parking lot toward her car. "Okay, well I want to hear everything about your maybe-date with..."

Right. I hadn't mentioned his name before. "Xander."

"Oooh, that's a hot name. He's hot, right?"

My thoughts take a dive back to the kitchen at Hallowed Grounds. The way Xander took over and cleaned up my injuries when I was too freaked out to get my hands to stop shaking. The memory of his fingers brushing my skin makes me shiver. I certainly wasn't in a place to appreciate his looks mid-panic attack last night, but thinking about him now—

"You are *blushing*," Phoebe gushes, reaching over and squeezing my shoulders—just short of hugging me.

An awkward laugh slips past my lips, and I fight the urge to cover my face. "Yeah, he's hot."

She grins, fishing her keys out of her bag. "I knew it!" After a quick hug, she gets in and starts her car, rolling down the passenger window. "Text me later! Unless, of course, you're busy—in which case, you have my full support to turn off your phone and get some!"

I shake my head, laughing as she backs out of the parking spot and drives away. It takes me a full minute to realize the pit in my stomach all but vanished while I was consumed with thoughts of Xander.

I might be in trouble.

Four
Xander

Arriving at Storyville shortly before three, I grab a seat on the leather couch in the corner near the front entrance so I can spot Camille when she comes in. The space is rather busy for the middle of the week, making it too warm to have the wood-burning fireplace lit. Still, the café has a welcoming atmosphere, with hardwood floors and exposed light-bulbs hanging from the ceiling. Soft music, the smell of coffee and baked goods, and the hum of multiple conversations from people standing in line and sitting around the café fill the air.

I stand when Camille enters, waving to grab her attention.

Her eyes meet mine, and recognition shines in their soft brown depths as she approaches.

"Camille," I say in greeting. "It's good to see you again." She looks beautiful in a white long sleeve shirt tucked into black jeans and paired with ankle boots—casual but stunning. I can't look away, especially when pink blossoms on her cheeks under my gaze. She clearly likes the atten-tion, but isn't sure what to do with it.

Her lips curve into a faint smile. "Under better circumstances this time." She cringes, shaking her head, as if she wants to take back her words. "I mean, it's good to see you, too." After we sit on the couch, her eyes flit around the room, taking it in as she runs her fingers through her loose brown curls. "I can't believe I've never been here before," she com-ments before looking back at me.

I angle myself toward her, wanting to move closer but careful to not make her uncomfortable. The faint scent of her floral perfume reaches me, and I inhale slowly, finding myself wanting to savor it. "I'm sure everything is delicious, but I have to admit I've only ever ordered the chocolate croissant. Once I find something I enjoy, I tend to stick

Her eyes stay locked on mine as she nods. "That sounds good."

"What can I get you to drink?"

"Day-old coffee?" she says without missing a beat, amusement flickering in her gaze.

My lips twitch. "Look who's funny now."

Her lashes lower as she catches her bottom lip between her teeth for a moment before asking, "What are you having?"

"Americano."

She wrinkles her nose, then exhales a short laugh. "Sorry. I'm not much of a coffee drinker."

"Says the girl who works at a coffee shop," I tease, bumping her knee with mine.

"I know, I know." She turns her gaze toward the coffee bar. "Hmm, I'll probably just get a chai latte." When she reaches for the purse at her hip, I wave her away.

"I've got it."

She pauses. "Are you sure?"

"It's my treat," I assure her, standing. "Be right back." Joining the line to order, I pull out my phone and scowl at the message from Blake. He's my oldest, closest friend, but also the biggest pain in my ass—and today is no exception.

We've known each other for over a decade. Ever since my mother showed a sliver of decency and took him in when his parents abandoned him in a murder-suicide when we were both thirteen. To this day, neither of us know much about what happened. Just that Blake's mother stabbed his father in the heart with an obsidian blade before turning it on herself. We still don't know why.

It didn't take long for my mother to start his training with the most talented, high-level demons to make him my personal guard. In formal terms, that's what he is now, but he's always been more like my brother. Blake would die for me—I just hope he never has to.

How's your little project going?

Fuck off.

No need to be mean. I'm just messing with you.

I don't bother responding before slipping my phone back into my pocket. A few minutes later, I return to Camille with our drinks and a plate with two chocolate croissants. I set the plate down on the glass table in front of the couch, then hand Camille her chai latte, a faint sweetness and spice wafting from it.

"Thank you," she says. "Next time is on me."

I can't stop the smile that tugs at my lips as I sit. "Next time, huh?"

When the steaming mug is halfway to her lips, Camille realizes what she said. "Oh," she rushes to say, "I just mean that—"

"Hey," I interject, "don't try to take it back now. I'm going to hold you to it."

She lowers her drink, staring into it with a small smile and quietly replies, "Okay."

I take a drink of my Americano, giving Camille a moment to actually try her latte. "How is it?"

"Mmm, it's perfect," she says. "It always tastes so much better when someone else makes it."

I chuckle. "Fair enough." Shifting the conversation, I say, "You mentioned you were in class this morning. What are you studying?"

She sets her mug on the coffee table and leans against the back of the couch, tucking one leg under her. Some of the tension in my shoulders eases as she makes herself more comfortable before saying, "Political science. I'm going to rule the world someday."

Something in the deepest, darkest depths of me awakens at that, clinging to the weight of those words. She has no idea how dangerous they are. The sparkle in her eyes tells me she's joking, but the monster in me doesn't care. It's practically purring with delight.

"What about you?" she asks.

I cock my head to the side, letting my gaze roam over her face. "Am I going to rule the world someday?"

She scoffs halfheartedly as she tries not to smile, then shakes her head. "Smart-ass. Are you in school?"

On paper.

I nod. "I'm studying philosophy."

Her eyes widen a bit, and she nods. "That's heavy."

I reach for the plate of croissants, offering the first one to her. "And poli-sci is all rainbows and puppies, I'm sure."

Camille takes the buttery pastry, shooting me an amused look. "A lot of it is boring as hell, to be honest, but I have this naive idea that I could truly make a change for the good one day. I want to help people, and there are so many ways to do that."

"I wouldn't call that naive, Camille. It's admirable." I tear off a piece of my croissant and bite into it, enjoying the flaky sweetness as it melts on my tongue.

"Thanks," she says softly, taking a bite of hers before setting it back on the plate between us. "Do you know what you'll use your degree for?"

"Not a clue," I answer honestly.

She offers me a thoughtful smile. "Well, you still have time to figure out what you want to do with your future."

If I had any say in my future, it'd be an encouraging notion. I shove down the bitterness that brings up, burying it deep. Camille has no idea—and she can never know—that my future isn't my own. It never will be.

"I could say the same to you."

Camille tears off another piece of her croissant, popping it into her mouth and chewing for a moment. "Yeah." Her tone is light. Optimistic. "The opportunities are overwhelming but exciting." She glances around briefly, lowering her voice. "There was a time when I thought my life would be owned by the hunters. I don't think you can fully appreciate freedom until it's taken away from you."

I nod, understanding more than she can know. "You'd never consider going back?"

"Never."

I don't push it. The adamant tone of her voice is quite telling, and the last thing I want to do is have her pull back this early.

"How far are you into your degree?" she asks.

I chuckle. "Is that your way of trying to determine how old I am?"

Camille shrugs, and I find myself enjoying how at ease she appears. Any nerves from the start of our conversation have vanished. "Maybe. And the answer is?"

"Thirty-seven."

She shoots me a dry look, her eyes narrowed slightly. "Funny."

Grinning at her, I say, "I'm twenty-five and in my third year." I take another drink of my Americano, waiting for her to share information I already know—that she's twenty-two and in her second year.

Instead, she nods, fidgeting with the delicate gold chain around her neck. "Have you been at UW since freshman year?"

I shake my head, curious why she wants to focus on me. "I transferred this year."

"Oh? Where were you before?"

"I studied abroad for a year in London. A friend of mine lived there and convinced me to stay with him."

"Wow, that sounds like a really cool opportunity." Curiosity glimmers in her eyes as she hangs onto my every word.

"It was. I'd like to go back one day and see more of the UK as well."

"Did you grow up in Seattle?" she asks, taking another sip of her latte.

The back of my neck tingles, and I reach to scratch it, wetting my lips before I offer the answer I'd prepared in case it came up. "No. I spent most of my life in Michigan. Started college there, then moved to the UK, and now I'm here." Before she can ask anything else, I put the question back on her. "How about you?"

Camille nods, leaning toward me slightly.

I'm not sure she even realizes she's doing it.

"Seattle born and raised," she says. "The goal is to move away once I finish my degree."

My brows lift as I rest my arm along the back of the couch. "Any idea where you'll go?"

She purses her lips in thought. "I think I've narrowed it down to Chicago or Denver."

I chuckle. "You don't want to escape the cold weather?"

"Are you kidding? Fall is my favorite season. Give me sweater weather all year, and I'd be the happiest person on earth."

"To each their own," I offer lightly. "I prefer the warmer months."

She smiles, then asks, "Do you think you'll stay here after you graduate next year?"

I shrug. "Not sure yet."

Camille lowers her gaze. "I guess you have to go wherever the organization needs you, right?"

"To some extent, yes, but the more experience you have, the more sway you have with where you're posted."

"And you're in a position to decide where you want to go?"

I pause. *Where is she going with this?* Instead of answering, I say, "I thought you didn't want to talk about the organization." I force a teasing tone, pairing it with a smirk.

Her eyes meet mine again. "You're right," she says. "Let's talk about something else."

I lose track of time as we chat about refreshingly mundane things like books we've enjoyed and places we've traveled. When we reach the point in the conversation where it feels natural, I ask a question I already know the answer to. "Do you have any siblings?"

Any remnant of a smile vanishes from her lips. "I, um, no. I did...a sister. A demon killed her five years ago."

I lean forward, lowering my voice as I rest my hand on her knee. "I'm sorry to hear that."

She swallows visibly, and her eyes drift to where my fingers are still touching her. "I'm surprised you didn't know. It's fairly well known in the American hunter community."

"I haven't been back in the States long," I lie without a second thought.

Camille nods and takes another drink. "Do you have any siblings?"

I pull my hand back. "I don't, though I always wanted them. Being an only child comes with the weight of some heavy expectations."

"I think I understand that weight."

"I have no doubt that you do." The expectations Camille and I face couldn't be more different, but we share the fact they exist.

As the café gets busier with the afternoon rush of tourists and locals alike, we finish our drinks and croissants before heading for the door.

"I'm glad you suggested this place," Camille says as we walk through the crowded market, brushing shoulders every few steps.

I glance sideways at her. "You know what that means, right?"

"Uh, that you have good taste?" she guesses with little conviction.

The corner of my mouth kicks up. "Undoubtedly. But that's not what I meant. It's up to you to pick where we go for our next date."

Her lips twist into a smile that mirrors mine. "So, this was a date?"

"If you want it to be," I say. "I certainly do."

Her cheeks flush as we near the end of a row of shop stands and shift to the side so the hordes of people can still move around us. "Yeah, I do, too."

"Good." The scent of fresh flowers wafts through the air as we pass a florist stand, and I stop, selecting a small bundle of fuchsia orchids. I pay the shop owner before turning to Camille and holding it out to her. "Since we've established this was a date," I offer, chuckling at her surprised expression.

She takes the arrangement from me, the shock in her features morphing into a brilliant smile. Her eyes glitter as she lifts the flowers to her nose to smell them. "They're beautiful," she murmurs, glancing up to meet my gaze. "Thank you."

"The pleasure is all mine," I say as we keep walking until we reach one of the market entrances. I shift to stand in front of her. "Can I drive you home?"

"That's okay. I'm parked a few streets over, but thanks." Her eyes drop to my mouth, and anxious energy pours off her in waves.

I can't quite tell if she's worried I'll kiss her or worried I won't.

Before she can spiral any deeper, I step in, wrapping my hand around her upper arm, and dip my face to kiss her cheek. Her breath catches when my lips brush her skin, and it takes every ounce of control I have not to steal her mouth with mine. Today went well. I don't want to come on too strong and scare her off. More than that, I don't *want* to rush this. I want to take my time with her.

"It was good to see you, Camille." I step back, letting my arm fall to my side. "Text me when you get home safe."

Her heart is a heavy drumbeat as she nods. "You, too."

Once she's gone, I walk down the cobblestone street to where I parked my Camaro. I pull my phone out and find a series of texts from Blake.

> Are you coming home soon?

> You better tell me if you're bringing her here.

> You also better bring me one of those chocolate croissants.

> Get me a croissant.

> Are you getting my messages, X?

> Please confirm you have my croissant.

Something between an annoyed sigh and a growl passes my lips, and I pocket my phone without responding. Something tells me the bastard takes pride in annoying me.

I get behind the wheel and start the engine just before a call comes through on the bluetooth. "I didn't get you a fucking croissant, jackass."

"I certainly hope you didn't speak to the hunters' daughter like that." Lucia's voice fills my car.

I grit my teeth as my stomach plummets. I close my eyes and drop my head back against the headrest, gripping the steering wheel until my knuckles go white.

Swallowing a curse, I force a level tone. "Hello, Mother."

FIVE
CAMILLE

I can't stop thinking about Xander. I can't get the feel of his lips on my cheek out of my head. Will he kiss me for real next time? A shiver skates up my spine at the thought, filling my stomach with a warmth that travels lower as I get lost in the idea of his hands on me.

It's good the café is quiet tonight, because my thoughts are elsewhere—mainly, wondering when I'll get to see him again. I've only been on a handful of first dates, but that one was easily the best. Despite the mess of nerves in my chest from overthinking if it even *was* a date, I enjoyed myself. Being with him is exciting.

"Helloooooo?"

I blink quickly, snapping back to reality as my cheeks flush hotly. "Sorry!" Relief floods through me when I recognize the next customer. "Hey, Pheebs."

"You were totally daydreaming." She grins, her eyes twinkling orbs of green. "Sorry to interrupt."

I exhale a laugh as my pulse returns to normal, then look past her to Grayson and Adrianna. "What can I get you guys?"

He steps forward, dropping his arm around Phoebe's shoulders, and smiles. He dresses as if he's a trust fund kid whose family owns a country club—neither of which is true—and he'd give anyone the clothes off his back. Today, his pale blue polo brings out his eyes, which, on any given day, look either gray or blue. He and Phoebe met at a party in freshman year and have been dating ever since. "I'll take a cappuccino with extra foam. Thanks, Cami."

Adrianna purses her dark red lips as she studies the menu above my head. "Give me the largest size of your strongest blend. Harper and I have this stupid project due tomorrow, so I'll be pulling an all-nighter to finish my part."

I wince. "That's rough." I punch their drinks into the system at the register. "Do you want a snack to go with your bucket of coffee?"

"Hmm, yeah. Good call." She pulls her wallet from the pocket of her navy U Wash hoodie before checking out the display case of desserts. Adrianna fits the typical college student persona, wearing a sweater and yoga pants with a pair of slip-on sandals and socks. Her black hair is twisted into a messy bun, but behind her glasses, her eyes are fully done with eyeliner and lash extensions. I guess she looks more like a model for a college admissions pamphlet. "How about a blueberry muffin and a chocolate chip cookie?"

"You got it," I say before turning to Phoebe. "Anything for you?"

"I'm good, thanks. These two were desperate for caffeine. I just tagged along for the visit."

"Well, sit anywhere." I gesture around the empty café.

"Where is everyone?" Grayson asks, raking his fingers through his mop of brownish copper curls and looking around.

I shrug. "A Starbucks opened a few blocks down last week. Their prices are probably lower."

Phoebe shrugs off her jean jacket, draping it over the back of a chair before dropping into it. "Yeah, but Starbucks doesn't have *you*."

I send a grin her way while the others sit around the table. I make their drinks, bring them over with Adrianna's snacks, then lean against the counter so I can sneak back quickly if anyone comes in.

"I'm hosting a getaway at my parents' lake house in a few weeks," Adrianna says. "I'm telling you now so you can make sure you're not working then."

"Sounds fun. I'll let the owner know I need that weekend off." I can't see it being a problem, considering they've been cutting my shifts for the last couple of weeks. It's almost bad enough that I'll have to look for another job to pay next semester's tuition. Instead of dwelling on that right now, I ask, "Is Harper coming?"

Adrianna takes a drink of her coffee and sighs. "She said she'll try, but work is being hard on people asking for time off. So, I guess we'll see."

I make an effort to keep a neutral expression as I nod, but I have to fight the urge to roll my eyes. Work-life balance means nothing to the organization, even for those in training, who still have some semblance of a life outside hunting demons.

"How was your maybe-date with Xander?" Phoebe asks, nearly beaming. "I'm dying to hear all about it."

"Date?" Adrianna chimes in. "Cami had a *date*?"

I laugh. "You don't have to sound so surprised."

"Are you going to keep us in suspense, or are you going to spill?"

My lips curl into a smile as my thoughts drift back to yesterday with Xander. "It was really nice."

"*Nice?*" Grayson asks, arching a brow at me. "That's it?"

I blow out a breath, shrugging. "I don't know how to adequately express what it was. And before you roll your eyes at me, I realize how lame that sounds, but it's true. I haven't dated much, and I've never really enjoyed the ones I have been on."

"But this was different," Phoebe offers, her gaze filled with delight.

"It...Yeah. I was nervous until I got there, but I relaxed almost immediately. It was exciting but easy to be around him. I don't know how else to explain it."

"So you're going to see him again, right?" Adrianna asks, taking a drink from her massive cup of coffee.

I bite the inside of my cheek, my stomach fluttering with warmth. "I hope so. I haven't talked to him today." I cringe at my next words. "I didn't want to come off too eager, or whatever."

"Screw that," Phoebe says, leaning back and resting her feet against Grayson's chair. "Follow your gut. Don't be afraid to go after what you want, Cami. If that freaks him out, which I very much doubt it will, then he isn't right for you."

"True," Adrianna adds. "And it's better to know now than to waste your time."

She's not wrong.

I groan, raking my fingers through my hair as I redo the bun at the crown of my head. "Okay, okay. I'll text him when I'm done work."

Phoebe shoots me a wink. "Attagirl."

Not much later, they take off so Adrianna can finish her project, and I start my cleaning. There's still an hour left until I can lock the door, but I don't foresee many more customers.

Instead of waiting until I get home, I pull my phone out and send Xander a text before I can overthink it.

Thanks again for yesterday. I had a really great time.

I chew my thumbnail, staring at my screen as I wait for the message to change from delivered to read. The three dots appear when he starts typing a response, and my stomach flips.

> I should be thanking you for the same reason. I hope we can do it again soon.

I'm grinning like an idiot as I read his message.

> I'd like that.

> What are you doing now?

> Just finishing up work. I'm stuck on the closing shift again tonight.

> I was going to make a joke about watching out for demons, but it's probably a bit soon for that, huh?

I roll my eyes, but my lips still twitch.

> You're hilarious.

> Do you want me to come keep you company?

My teeth sink into my bottom lip as excitement zips through me like a current of electricity.

> Worried about me? 😉

I have no idea where the teasing response came from, but I can't stop smiling. I make quick work of counting the money in the register and recording it in the accounting log for the morning shift.

> Honest answer? It's an excuse to see you.

I press my hand over my heart as it beats faster. There's no question that I want to see him. But I'd rather it not be here, in an apron with my hair thrown up messily and my makeup probably half melted off my face by this point. As much as I'd like to think I don't care about superficial stuff like that, part of me does. It shouldn't matter. He saw me looking a lot worse the night we met.

After going back and forth on how to respond, I type what I hope sounds okay and hit send.

> Let's not have our second date where I work. I get to pick the place, remember? And this certainly wouldn't be my first choice.

> No? Where would your first choice be?

> Guess you'll have to wait and see. Goodnight, Xander.

A giddy sensation bubbles in my chest as I slip my phone into my pocket, and I spend the rest of my shift in a daze, thinking about when I'll get to see him again. Things with him are fun and exciting, and despite the way we met, I find myself more and more glad we did.

The next morning, Harper barges into my room at an ungodly hour. It's my only day off from class during the week, and I typically sleep in before working on any assignments or readings. As badly as I want to roll over and wrap myself in the blanket burrito, Harper successfully lures me out of bed with the promise of a mountain-sized stack of pancakes.

I've loved Mecca Café since the day we stumbled upon it in freshman year. The decor is loud and bright, with fire truck red walls and checkered ceilings, along with padded booths along one wall and bar seating along the other. The air is heavy with the smell of coffee and the bacon sizzling on the grill in the kitchen, mixed with the chatter of conversations around us and cutlery against dishes. The place is packed like usual at this time of day—we're lucky we got in. Mecca Café isn't much bigger than our living room, but I think that adds to its charm. And the delicious food certainly helps.

We sit in a booth, perusing the menu as if we don't already know what we're ordering. Just *in case* something new catches the interest of our taste buds. It hasn't happened in the two years we've been coming here, but it *could.*

Harper nurses a cup of coffee, tapping her fingernails against the dull green table. Once we've ordered, she sits back with a heavy sigh, and I raise a brow at her.

"Do I want to ask?"

"Probably not," she says, and I know what that means.

"What's going on?" I ask anyway, pouring a bit of sugar from the glass container onto my finger and stick it in my mouth, licking it off.

Harper shakes her head at me. "I'm just sick of the shitty assignments, that's all," she grumbles. "I've proven myself time and time again. I just don't get it."

I frown and set the sugar aside. "I'm sorry. I wish there was something I could do. Have you tried talking to anybody at HQ about it?"

She snorts. "Yeah. I made the mistake of trying to talk to Noah."

"Well, yeah, that was a mistake. What'd he say?" I remember him from my training days at the academy. He's a few years older than us and is one of the top hunters in the organization—and he certainly knows it. The fact he's ridiculously good looking is only more annoying. Did I still have an enormous crush on him? Absolutely. But I've done a damn good job scrubbing that from my memory.

"He gave me some bullshit response about utilizing my assets in the assignments that I'm given. I think it was meant to be some kind of backhanded compliment. I don't know. I don't even *care*. I've been working my ass off, taking extra patrols and volunteering at the academy whenever I have a spare second. I'm hoping they'll give me a better position come graduation."

I bite my tongue. A part of me wants to offer to speak to my parents about it, but I know that might put Harper in a worse position. God knows they would use that as yet another opportunity to shame me for dropping out and not completing my training alongside Harper. "How are things going otherwise?" I note the hesitation that flickers across Harper's face, and she lowers her eyes to the mug in front of her.

When she meets my gaze again, her expression is grim, her jaw tight and her forehead creased with tension.

"What's that face for?" I ask.

"I know I'm not supposed to share information with people outside the organization, but you're hunter-adjacent, so I'm going to tell you, anyway. Because this shit...it's bad, Cami."

I straighten against the back of the booth. "Uh, right. I'm not sure I want to know."

"I think it's important that you do." She glances around the room, making sure no one will overhear, then says, "The number of demon attacks in large city centers is rapidly increasing. Places like here and Chicago and New York. And we're not graduating hunters fast enough to keep up."

My brows knit, and I fight the urge to cross my arms as irritation prickles across my skin. "Is that why you're taking on all this extra crap?"

A horn blares on the street outside, but it doesn't distract us.

She blows out of breath, nodding. "We're all putting in more hours, and they're treating trainees who are within a year of graduating as if they already have. They don't have much of a choice. The fact of the matter is...we don't have enough hunters for the number of demons attacking."

My chest tightens, and I reach across the table, placing my hand on hers. "You need to be careful, Harper," I say in a firm voice. "You keep this up, and it won't matter how good you are. You can't spread yourself this thin—between training and school and going on missions—without faltering at some point."

Harper pulls her hand back, sitting up straighter. "I can handle it."

I frown. "I'm not doubting you. This is me expressing concern, because I promise the superiors you're trying to impress don't care about you as a person. You are an asset to the organization. That is it."

Her face falls. "Right." She takes a sip of her coffee, glancing around the restaurant again before returning her gaze to me. "I know what you're saying is true, but I dedicated my life to this, so I'm going to do what it takes—what's expected of me, and I'm not going to complain about it. To anyone besides you, of course," she adds with a forced smile.

"I get it," I tell her. "I really do. And I won't tell you to stop. But I will say that you need to take care of yourself, because if you don't, something's going to go wrong. You could end up hurt or worse, and I...I can't lose you, too."

She grabs my hands, holding them tightly between hers. "I will do everything in my power to make sure that doesn't happen."

I swallow past the lump in my throat, clearing it as the waitress approaches with our massive stacks of pancakes—mine blueberry with banana slices on top, and Harper's peanut butter chocolate chip. She sets them on the table and smiles before walking away, leaving us to devour our feast.

I want to bring up Xander, to tell Harper all about him, but it feels...I don't know, shallow when we were just talking about the danger of her career choice. So, instead, I keep my mouth full of delicious, syrup-drenched goodness. Besides, I'd rather bring it up in the privacy of our apartment. I'm confident Harper's response is going to be animated, and it wouldn't be fair to force a room full of strangers to endure that.

We spend the rest of breakfast chatting about school. Harper's telling me about the English project she and Adrianna have due today when her phone buzzes on the table. She swipes it up and curses under her breath. "I have to go."

My eyes widen, and I shake my head. "Wait. What's going on?"

"Cami, you know I can't. I already told you more than I should have."

Before I can protest, she grabs her bag, scoots out of the booth, and slaps her credit card down on the table. "Breakfast is my treat. I'll see you at home." Her combat boots thud against the floor as she hurries toward the front door.

I frown while the pit in my stomach grows, and the stack of pancakes suddenly feels like cement hardening in my gut as I watch her leave.

SIX
CAMILLE

Saturday morning brings a surprisingly busy shift at Hallowed Grounds. Arriving back at my apartment mid-afternoon, I hop in the shower and get ready—put on sweats, sans bra—to spend the rest of the day on the couch with a giant bowl of popcorn and a true crime docuseries I've had in my Watch Later for nearly a month.

My phone chimes from the coffee table, and I lean forward to grab it. My stomach swoops when I spot Xander's name on the screen. I swipe it open and read his message, my lips curling into a grin of their own volition. We've been back and forth a few times since the other night, but he's been wrapped up in schoolwork and hunting, much like Harper.

She hasn't told me what snatched her away from our breakfast date yesterday, so I'm left to assume it's related to the increased number of attacks she warned me about. I haven't seen her since then, but she texts every few hours, so I know she's okay. It still doesn't make me feel great about her out there hunting demons, but it's better than radio silence.

I read his message again, trying to focus on the giddy lightness in my stomach instead of the worry in my chest.

> I want to see you tonight. Dinner at my place?

I pull my bottom lip between my teeth, still grinning as I type out a response, the nerves already starting to swirl in my belly. Hanging with Xander in public feels far more casual than having dinner with him at home. It feels like a step toward something more serious between us, and as scary as it is, my gut tells me to take the leap—it feels right, and I want to explore it. He makes me feel good in ways I haven't experienced before. Talking to him is easy, and his effortless ability to make me laugh and feel wanted is definitely something I could get used to.

> I'd like that. What time should I be there?

His response comes a minute later.

7 p.m.?

He drops the pin with his address, and I quickly reply.

See you then.

It's nearly four in the afternoon, so I still have a few hours to obsess over my outfit and do something with my hair. I made the mistake of letting it air dry, and now it's a tangled mess.

By the time I'm ready to leave, my hair is straight and I've changed into a deep red blouse and black skinny jeans with simple flats. I went light on the makeup, not wanting to look like I was trying too hard. I shake my head at how ridiculous that sounds. After grabbing my wallet and keys, I jot down a quick note to Harper on the dry erase board we keep stuck to the fridge, letting her know I'll be out tonight. As far as I know, she's in a training session, or otherwise occupied with hunter stuff for the rest of the day.

Fifteen minutes later, I arrive at the address Xander sent me and have to circle the block a few times to snag a parking spot on the street. Approaching his building, I'm immediately impressed by the stunning architecture. It looks modern but classic in a way that is difficult to achieve. It has a black brick exterior with a revolving door at the front that I step through into an ornate lobby with white marble floors and gold light fixtures. Crisp white walls decorated with simplistic yet abstract art makes the space feel clean and open, and I admire it as I make my way to the doorman manning the front desk. My flats echo softly as I approach, and I tell the gentleman who I'm here to see.

He nods, his tone professional and polite when he says, "Mr. Kane is expecting you. Take the elevator on your left to the tenth floor. His suite is the last one on your right."

"Thank you." I smile at him, crossing the lobby to the bank of elevators close by. My stomach is a jumble of nerves as I get in the elevator and watch the numbers tick higher along with my pulse. I try to tell myself this is a casual dinner, but I can't stop thinking about what could happen *after* we eat.

Standing in front of Xander's suite, I lift my hand to knock and cringe at how my fingers are shaking. I clench them into a fist and blow out a slow breath as I knock.

A minute later, footsteps sound on the other side of the door before it swings open. The sight of Xander in a black T-shirt and jeans, looking so casually stunning, threatens to steal the air from my lungs. His hair is stylishly tousled and his lips are curled into a warm smile.

"Camille," he says in greeting, his voice deep and smooth. "Come in."

He steps aside, and I cross the threshold, taking in his apartment.

The entryway has dark gray walls and a small rectangular table with a round mirror hung above it and a small dish for keys. I toe off my flats, leaving them off to the side, then follow Xander into the open concept space that makes up his kitchen and living room. High ceilings with massive windows add to the room's spaciousness, and the dark leather furniture and exposed brick wall in the kitchen give it a masculine touch. Jazz music plays softly from somewhere deeper in the apartment.

It smells fresh and clean, like like fabric softener. Like *him*.

"This place is stunning," I comment, my gaze sliding toward the kitchen area and admiring the matte black cupboards and slate countertops. Exposed bulbs add warm light to the space, and the island acts as a dining space with ample room to host at least four people without feeling crowded.

"Thanks. I wish I could take credit for the design, but it came furnished. It's a good thing I don't mind the whole industrial look." He walks around the island into the kitchen and gestures to a fully stocked glass bar cart against the wall under one of the many floor to ceiling windows. "Can I get you something to drink?"

"Please," I say, sliding onto a swivel stool at the island counter. "A whiskey sour would be great."

Xander gets to work making my cocktail, first by adding bourbon and simple syrup to a copper shaker.

I take that opportunity to scope out the rest of the space, at least what I can see from my seat. The living room is a fair size, taken up mostly by an L-shaped couch and square, black wooden coffee table. The focal point is a huge flat-screen TV, and the rest of that wall is lined with black bookshelves that stretch from the hardwood floor to the concrete ceiling.

"I was thinking Italian for dinner," Xander says, pouring freshly squeezed lemon juice into the shaker, filling the space between us with the faint scent of citrus.

"I never say no to carbs," I tell him with a smile, watching as he separates an egg to add in a bit of the white next.

He sends me a grin, then focuses back on finishing the drink, giving it a quick dry shake before adding ice and shaking again. He strains it into two cocktail glasses filled with ice before walking around the counter to hand one to me.

"Thank you," I murmur, my skin tingling as our fingers brush.

"Cheers."

We clink our glasses, and I take a sip. The velvety citrus flavor bursts along my tastebuds, and I lick my lips. "This is amazing."

He takes a sip of his own, keeping his eyes on me. "I'm glad you like it." Walking back around the island into the kitchen, he fills a large pot with water and ignites one of the gas stove burners.

"Can I help with anything?"

Xander turns back to me after adding salt to the water. "You can tell me more about you."

I swallow another drink, pressing my lips together as the butterflies in my stomach give a healthy flutter. "What do you want to know?"

His responding smile makes my heart beat faster. "Everything."

A short laugh escapes me as I set my drink down. "Well, you already know about my...*unusual* family situation, so we can skip that part. And we covered school last time..."

"What do you enjoy doing outside of school?"

I consider it for a moment. "I used to love painting, but I haven't done it in a while with how busy school and work have kept me."

Xander leans against the counter, folding his arms over his chest, and I make a good effort to keep my eyes from dropping to admire them. "Do you miss it?"

I have his complete attention, and it makes it rather difficult to sit still. In the same beat, there's a part of me that seems to blossom from it. I feel more confident—wanted for who I am instead of who others want me to be. And what a dangerous feeling that is—an addiction in the making. I nod. "It's easy to ignore the complications of reality when you're so engrossed in a project that nothing else matters. I guess I miss the escape."

"I understand," he says in a deep voice, and I wholeheartedly believe he does.

Once he finishes cooking a deliciously fragrant penne pasta in vodka sauce, pairing it with a fresh and colorful garden salad, he joins me at the island counter. We eat in silence for a few minutes, and Xander angles his knees slightly toward me.

"What do you think?"

I swallow a mouthful, humming my approval. "There's a very good chance this is the most phenomenal pasta I've ever tasted."

He laughs, a deep sound that brings heat to my cheeks as my gaze collides with his. "I should have said this the moment I opened the door earlier. You look beautiful."

My mouth goes dry, and I fight the knee-jerk urge to look away. "Thank you," I force out in a low voice. I'm way out of my element here, and it's clear Xander has the upper hand when it comes to experience in this arena. I'm not sure how it's possible, but I'm equally comforted and intimidated by it.

After dinner, he carries our dishes to the sink before walking back to me. My breath catches in my throat when he holds out his hand, but I'm reaching for it before I can even consider resisting. He turns the stool I'm sitting on until I'm facing him, and his thumb brushes over the back of my hand.

"Camille," he murmurs, and his voice feels like a warm, gentle caress. The urge to close my eyes and lean into him grips me, and it's definitely not unwelcome.

Anticipation crackles through me like a sparkler as his gaze drops to my mouth. "Uh-huh," I say and immediately want to kick myself.

His responding chuckle stirs the hair at my temple, making me realize just how close he's standing. He lifts his free hand, and his thumb traces the edge of my bottom lip, making my skin tingle and my heart rate pick up. "I want to kiss you," he says, dipping his face closer.

I can't make my voice work, so I nod instead.

Xander closes the distance between us, and his lips touch mine, soft and exploratory, as his fingers sink into my hair.

My eyes slip shut and my lips move with his as I lean into him and grip the front of his shirt.

He lets go and slides his hand up my thigh, sending my pulse racing as heat blossoms in my chest and spreads lower. Gripping my hip, he makes a low sound at the back of his throat that nearly makes me melt into a puddle of desire before him. His tongue darts out, light and coaxing, until I part my lips to let him in.

A moan catches in my throat when his tongue grazes mine, flicking against the roof of my mouth as he tips my head back and deepens the kiss. My thoughts scatter and nothing else exists but the feel of his kiss and his touch.

When Xander breaks the kiss, I suck in a breath, my heart pounding and my head spinning as I refill my lungs with air.

His chest rises and falls quickly, and he rests his forehead against mine while we catch our breaths.

An unfamiliar need pulses through me, centering on the apex of my thighs. While my body is practically screaming at me to push things further, my senses are entirely overwhelmed with new sensations. I need a minute.

Xander must realize that, because he leans back enough to meet my gaze, tucking a stray bit of hair away from my face, and asks, "Are you up for a movie?"

My lips curl into a smile, still tingling from our kiss. "A movie sounds good," I say a little breathlessly.

A few minutes later, we've settled on the couch with fresh drinks. Xander pulls a blanket over our laps before pressing play on *Cruel Intentions*.

Halfway through my drink, I'm feeling brave enough to set my glass on the coffee table and lean into him. It's oddly natural, and my stomach flips when he shifts to wrap his arm around me and guide me closer.

He drops his chin to the top of my head and murmurs, "Is this okay?"

"Yeah."

He brushes his thumb back and forth over the top of my shoulder, and even as I try to focus on the movie, tingles ripple through me, feeding the subtle throbbing between my legs. I sink my teeth into my bottom lip, inhaling slowly in an attempt to slow my pulse. I manage to get my breathing to a normal pace as the movie gets going, and by the time it's an hour in, I've completely relaxed in Xander's arms.

Before now, I've dated two guys, though only one got to the point of this level of closeness, and it was after several months of seeing each other. Being with Xander now, I feel as if I've known him forever. There's an innate part of me that trusts him—maybe it has to do with the whole life-saving thing last week—and he waltzed right past my defenses, I think, without me even realizing it.

Each time I blink, my eyes stay shut a bit longer, the TV getting harder to focus on. I'm drifting off before I have a chance to feel any sort of way about being at Xander's apartment, pressed against him, with his arm securely wrapped around me.

Before I open my eyes, there are about five seconds of warm, ignorant bliss before I remember where I am.

Oh no. No, no, no—

I throw the blanket off as I sit up in a flash and get to my feet, wobbling slightly. Whipping around, my stomach drops when I find Xander in the kitchen making coffee in a French press. My cheeks flood with heat when his eyes lift to meet mine and his lips quickly form a smile.

"Good morning," he says in a light tone.

I round the couch and walk toward the kitchen. "Xander, I am so sorry. I—"

"Don't be," he cuts in smoothly. "Coffee?"

I stop mid-stride, my pulse in my throat as I take in his casual appearance, a light gray T-shirt and black sweatpants that he likely slept in. "I... Um, sure. Thanks."

"Did you sleep okay?" he asks, retrieving two mugs from the cupboard behind him. He sets them on the island counter that separates us.

"Yeah." I consider it for a moment. Despite the mortification I felt upon discovering I'd fallen asleep during our date and inadvertently spent the night, I am well-rested. "I really didn't intend to crash on your couch." Sliding onto the barstool I occupied at dinner last night, I tap my fingers against my thighs.

Xander chuckles, raking a hand through his sleep-tousled hair. "It's not a problem, Camille. You're welcome anytime. I would have carried you to the bedroom to sleep more comfortably, but I didn't want to upset you."

The idea of spending the night in his bed renders me speechless and immediately fills my thoughts, and I can't shake it out. I finally find my voice and say, "I appreciate the consideration."

He nods. "I was going to make breakfast, if you want to stay."

My chest quickly tightens, my throat going dry. When I inhale, it's uneven, and each breath is harder to take. Breakfast after spending the night makes this entire thing feel too real. Like we skipped a bunch of steps, and it's setting something off inside me.

"Camille—"

"Maybe another time." I slip off the stool, grabbing my phone and purse from the counter. "I actually have to get to work, but, um, thanks for a nice night."

He frowns, and dammit, even that looks attractive. "Are you—Have I upset you?"

"No, no," I say quickly, inching toward the door as my throat constricts. "I just...I'm sorry. I have to go." I spin on my heel and hurry toward the door, shoving my feet into my shoes as I open it, then speed walk to the elevator. The pressure in my chest doesn't dissipate until I'm in my car, driving away from Xander's apartment. I feel ridiculous over my reaction. Last night was amazing, and it's clear he wasn't put off by what happened, but I can't seem to shake the tendrils of anxiety winding through my rib cage like barbed wire.

At home, I flop onto the couch and groan to the empty apartment. Fishing my phone out of my purse, I send Phoebe a text to meet up. I need a distraction so I don't spend the entirety of my Sunday dwelling over something that likely isn't as big of a deal as I'm making it.

An hour later, after a change of clothes, I meet her at the Starbucks near her place to go over next week's class materials. We order blueberry muffins and drinks—an iced chai latte for me and a matcha for her—then find a quiet spot in the corner of the busy café.

"How's your weekend been?" I ask after taking a sip of my latte.

"Boring," Phoebe says around a mouthful of muffin. "Grayson went to Vancouver to visit his brother, so I spent yesterday cleaning my apartment and online shopping. Well, I added about five hundred dollars' worth of smutty romance books to my cart and then closed the tab, because money." She sighs, her disappointment evident in the heaviness of it. "How about you?"

I hesitate, not sure how to go about telling her about my date with Xander, worrying that bringing it up will make the struggle to breathe return. I take a slow inhale, then let it out and spill my guts about the whole night.

"Oh, girl," she says with a laugh. "First off, I promise he doesn't care nearly as much as you do. It's not a big deal. So, you fell asleep on his couch. He probably loved it. Second, I need to know everything about this guy who is making you blush like the cutest little smitten kitten."

THE DEVIL'S WALTZ

I press my lips together against a smile, the weight on my chest easing more with each breath.

SEVEN
XANDER

My apartment feels colder since Camille fled an hour ago. It's utterly ridiculous. Pathetic, even. I attempt to forget it by turning on the water to scalding and stepping under the rainfall shower head. I stay there, scrubbing my fingers through my hair, then over my skin until it's nearly raw.

After I get dressed in the first pair of jeans and T-shirt I grab from my dresser, I return to the kitchen to make a fresh cup of coffee. Leaning against the counter, I stare at where my phone sits on the island, torn between checking on Camille and giving her space. I don't believe for a second she rushed away to get to work. More likely, she panicked over spending the night on our second date. I said what I could think to re-assure her, but there was no getting through her panic at that moment.

Needless to say, I have my work cut out for me.

This morning aside, I'm off to a decent start. But the setup of our first meeting didn't help in the trust department like I'd planned for it to. I hadn't expected her to believe her parents had sent me, though I suppose that was a better alternative than her seeing through my disguise.

I'm still not convinced she's the answer to the never-ending power struggle between demons and hunters, though my mother seems to be confident in her plan to utilize the hunters' daughter against them. To leverage the upper hand and make demands, either by corrupting Ca-mille's loyalty to her family or by using her life as a bargaining chip.

Lucia Kane is the most power hungry demon I've ever known. Since before I was born twenty-five years ago, she's had my future mapped out—including exactly how she was going to use me to seize control of the human world.

There's an obnoxious pounding at my door, and I immediately know who's on the other side. I cross the apartment and open the door. "Since

His tall, broad form takes up most of the doorway and his vibrant green eyes sparkle with amusement. "Well, hello to you too, fucker," he greets in a smooth voice. He picked up a British accent during our time in the UK and hung onto it when we came to Seattle. It's been so long, I don't remember what his voice used to sound like. He makes a scene of bowing at the waist, knowing full well that if anyone else spoke to me that way, they'd lose their heart. "I lost my key."

I roll my eyes, walking back to the kitchen as Blake follows, closing the door behind him.

"You sure enjoy reaffirming my doubts about you."

"Dick," he mutters without heat, dropping onto a barstool. "Oh, good. You made coffee."

I snatch up my mug before he can swipe it for himself. "What are you doing here?"

"A demon can't check in on his best half-demon pal?" Besides pushing boundaries, Blake also loves to remind me I'm not a pure-blooded demon like him.

My father, whoever he was, was human. A plaything of Lucia's, I'm sure, and someone I'll never know, because he fled after one night with my mother. *Fair enough.*

For the first fifteen years of my life, I lived in hell with her until she decided I needed to be socialized with humans. She views my humanity as my greatest weakness, but also something she won't hesitate to use to her advantage.

For over a decade, I've hated the monster who gave birth to me.

I've never had a mother. Only a queen. And thanks to the twisted bond all demons share with our monarch, the desire to serve her that exists inside me is nearly impossible to fight.

That said, when Lucia advised me of the plan to target Camille, I quickly decided that I'd comply one last time and then I'd disappear. Of course, I can never truly escape my queen—she'd find me anywhere I went—but I have this pathetic feeling, something akin to hope, that she'll let me go. There is no shortage of demons whose loyalty she's never had to force. My position at her side is replaceable. At least, that's what I keep telling myself.

"Blake," I bite out, my tone a warning for him to get to the fucking point already.

He huffs out a dramatic sigh, raking his fingers through his spiky pink hair. He's been on a colored hair kick lately. Last month it was green. Both colors pop with his dark, thick eyebrows and tan, olive skin tone. "How are things going with the hunters' daughter?"

I swallow the rest of my coffee, barely tasting it, and turn to put my mug in the sink. "I don't want to talk about it."

"Because it's going well or because it's not?" he pushes, flicking a non-existent piece of lint off his black jean jacket. He's wearing it over a Sex Pistols T-shirt paired with black skinny jeans and Doc Marten boots.

"It's going fine," I say carefully, a muscle feathering along my jaw.

He notices and holds up his hands in mock surrender. "Don't bite my head off. I'm just making sure things are still on track. I'm here to help you."

Exhaling a heavy breath, I lean against the counter and cross my arms over my chest. "Things between Camille and I are progressing steadily. Since the attack almost a week ago, we've gone out twice. She stayed here last night—"

Blake lets out a whistle, shooting me a devious smirk.

I blink at him, straight-faced. "She fell asleep while we were watching a movie, jackass. Nothing happened." That said, I would've been more than happy to oblige had she wanted something to happen. The thought crossed my mind more than once while she was here.

"Oh. *Boringgg.*" He drags out the word in a singsong voice that makes me grind my molars.

"She took off this morning in a panic over it, but aside from that, I believe it's going well."

"In terms of a timeline...?" Blake trails off, waiting for me to answer.

"I don't fucking know. However long it takes. I can't force her to trust me—that would defeat the purpose of this entire charade."

"Right, but you know Lucia—"

"I know what she wants," I snap, my stomach clenching as my temples throb with pressure. Part of me bristles at serving her, following her every depraved demand. On the flip side, there's another part—a darker, twisted part—that craves it. It feeds the monster I try desperately to keep buried deep. Most of the time.

Blake seems to get the message, because he backs off. "When all of this shit is over, we need to get away for a while. You have that fae buddy with a hotel in Canada, right? Let's go visit the North."

"Toronto is south of Seattle."

He rolls his eyes. "Whatever."

"Besides, I'm sure he wouldn't really appreciate me bringing problems to his doorstep."

"You are so fucking stubborn, you know that? Why is the idea of your friends being there for you so hard to grasp?"

"He has his own questionable royalty to deal with, Blake. I'm not saying we can't go, just don't start packing a suitcase thinking we're leaving tomorrow."

Blake exhales, and the sound is deeply exasperated, as if I'm testing his patience. The thought makes my lips twitch.

"I can't believe I let you drag me out," I grumble as we join the back of the line outside the bar. Why it's so busy for a Sunday night, I have no idea. The building vibrates from the music blasting inside, and I focus on that rather than the chatter of the people around us.

Blake laughs deeply. "I've always been skilled at persuasion. I have this natural charm and—"

I smack the back of his head to shut him up.

He snarls at me, but I'm able to tell the difference between when he's being friendly versus sadistic and menacing. He steps in closer to ensure we aren't overheard. "My reason for bringing you here is twofold, my friend." He holds up a finger. "First, I feel like you need a night out away from all that tension you're holding in your shoulders." I shoot him a death glare that clearly doesn't faze him, because he holds up another finger and continues, "And second, because I'm pretty sure you're not feeding enough. I'm here to make sure you do." His tone is more pointed by the end of his sentence. Serious Blake doesn't materialize often, so I'm always a bit thrown when he does.

The pit in my gut turns to ice, and I grit my teeth. "You're meant to be my guard, not my babysitter."

He throws his arm around my shoulders, digging his fingers into my skin. "My role solely depends on your behavior, Kane."

I shove him away, scowling. "I didn't realize how far up my mother's ass you were."

He rolls his eyes. "This has nothing to do with Lucia. Believe it or not, this is because *I* give a shit about you. Shocking, I know. You don't always make it easy. But your response to me telling you the plan for tonight just solidifies what I figured." He meets my gaze. "You need this."

I wish I could refute his statement, but the monster in me is clawing at the bars of its cage, salivating at the thought of hunting tonight.

I haven't fed since before I met Camille, and realistically, I know it's smart to keep the monster satisfied. I'd be lying if I said I hadn't thought about feeding on her, especially when she fell asleep on my couch. It would have been so easy...I exhale a harsh breath. "Fine."

The line moves, and we're inside the bar within a few minutes.

With the stench of body odor and alcohol and smoke mingling together, it's a sickening aroma that burns my nostrils. I rub the back of my neck, wishing I didn't have heightened senses in this particular environment. The bass vibrates the walls and floor, and I scan the room in search of the bar.

If I'm going to endure this, I'm going to need a drink.

Blake follows me, easily catching the attention of the bartender—a petite woman with bright blue eyes and red corkscrew curls. My friend orders his drink of choice, a bourbon on the rocks, and before I can speak up to ask for a scotch, he orders that as well. I can't deny that he knows me, even on days I wish he didn't.

The bartender disappears for a minute to pour our drinks, then comes back, sets them on napkins, and slides them across the bar. "Do you boys want to open a tab?"

Blake says, "Please," at the same moment I say, "No," and drop some money in front of her. "Keep the change." I down the scotch, leave the empty glass behind, and turn away from the bar to prowl through the crowd. I want to get this over with as soon as possible.

He's at my side in a matter of seconds, speaking low over the music, knowing only I'll hear him clearly over the music. "You're ruining the fun of the hunt."

I cast him a sideways glance. "You know I've never been into this like you are."

"It's really too bad." He *tuts*. "It's that pesky humanity of yours."

I roll my eyes, raking my fingers through my hair. Some days, I can't help but agree with him. A lot of things would be much easier if my father had been a demon as well. If I wasn't part human. Hell, even if I could turn my humanity off.

I shove those pointless thoughts away. I can typically keep them buried deep, but they tend to crawl their way to the surface when I haven't fed in a while.

Blake scans the room, sipping his drink and moving his hips to the music. He swallows a mouthful of bourbon, his lips curling into a smirk. He's found his target.

I follow his line of sight and find a tall woman with long black hair, wearing a dress that clings to her like a second skin. She's with a group of friends, but it's clear that Blake has caught her attention as much as she's caught his.

"Are you good without me for a few minutes?"

"Go," I tell him. "Don't kill this one."

"I make no promises," he calls back as he saunters away.

I shake my head and watch him work. In less than a minute, he has her laughing, his arm draped around her shoulders as he murmurs into her ear, and the two of them walk off down a crowded hallway.

The odds of finding someone with fear palpable enough to feed on without having to create it are next to none. Something tells me Blake did that intentionally. He *wants* me to use my ability to bring the fear out of someone.

I close my eyes and allow myself to drown in my surroundings. The pulsing beat of the music and the thick, warm air. It's not exactly paradise, but it's enough to ground me for a fleeting moment before I let the monster take control. Exhaling a sigh, I walk toward the back exit, following people who are going out to smoke. All I need to do is pick someone and get them away from the crowd.

There's a small group of girls who look too young to be here, passing around a joint and laughing. I could interject and pull one of them away—it would be painfully easy. The darkest, most depraved part of me enjoys a challenge, but tonight, I just want to get this over with as quickly as possible.

I pause mid-stride, picking up the sound of a muffled female whimper and a sharp male exhale. My eyes narrow, and I'm moving past the group of easy targets and toward the other end of the back parking lot.

Fear is like a siren call, pulling me into the narrow space between two buildings. It's not wide enough to be considered an alley, making it the perfect spot for seclusion. It's far enough away from the smoking area that unless someone screamed, no one would hear a thing. Which begs the question, why isn't this girl screaming? The answer comes a moment later when I step into the dark, damp space and find her pressed against the building as a middle-aged guy holds a pocket knife to her throat.

Tendrils of fear pour off the girl. She can't be much older than twenty. Her cheeks are stained with tears and her pulse is jack-hammering, especially the arterial vein in her neck.

I wouldn't have to do anything to feed off her, save for knocking her attacker aside.

She turns her wide-eyed gaze to me and sucks in a breath.

My legs start moving on their own, and the guy turns to follow her gaze, his bloodshot eyes landing on me and narrowing.

"Get the fuck out of here," he grumbles, his breath rank with alcohol.

I arch a brow at him. "Or what?"

He blinks at me, perturbed at my lack of concern toward the weapon he's now pointing at me. Considering it's not made of obsidian, I don't have anything to worry about. Especially when I could easily pluck it from his hand faster than he could blink—which is exactly what I do.

The girl chokes on a sob, and the fear oozing from her makes me grit my teeth. The monster growls deep in my chest.

Take her. Take her. Take her.

I grab her arm, shoving her toward the end of the buildings, and bark, "Get out of here."

She flees without looking back, the sound of her crying growing quieter the farther she gets.

I can't take the chance of being caught out here if she reports what happened. I fold the knife shut and slip it into my back pocket, then turn to the guy whose heart is beating faster now that we're alone.

He shuffles back a step. "What the fuck is your problem?"

I shrug, picking a piece of lint off my jacket. "How long do you have?"

"Look, I don't want any trouble."

This is painfully cliché.

I laugh harshly. "I think that's exactly what you wanted."

"Is that chick your girlfriend or something? Fuck, she was all over me in the bar. She wanted—"

"Stop talking," I cut him off sharply. "And here's a tip—if she's crying and you have to threaten her with a knife to keep her quiet, she *doesn't* want anything to do with you." I shoot forward at a speed too fast for him to track, grabbing his throat and slamming him against the brick wall. His eyes widen at my all-black gaze and his lips part in a silent scream as I dig my fingers into his throat.

I'm not sure what he sees when he looks into my eyes. Everyone's worst nightmare is different. I could see it if I wanted to, but I'd rather get it over with than see what has tears streaming down his stubble-covered cheeks.

Fear ripples off him in black, silky ribbons. They wind around my arm, settling into my skin and making it tingle with electricity. I inhale slowly as energy fills me. My veins sing with power, and my grip on his neck tightens almost to the point of cutting off his oxygen.

His complexion turns paler by the second, his eyes bulging out of his face and his heart pounding in his chest. If it gets much faster, he'll likely have a heart attack.

I should let him die. It'd be a public service to wipe this scum off the earth for good. But it'd also be hypocritical after I told Blake not to kill anyone tonight.

The monster relishes in the vitality flooding through me as I step back, letting the man go.

He sinks to the ground, his shoulders shaking with quiet sobs. The front of his jeans is dark from wetting himself.

I don't look back as I walk away and pull my phone out of my pocket, texting Blake to hurry up. I'm ready to get the fuck out of here.

EIGHT
CAMILLE

I sit in my car in the university's student parking lot as heavy rain pours from the overcast sky and thunder rumbles through the air every couple of minutes. The storm has made the temperature drop and the atmosphere dull and gray.

I hate today.

Every year, I think I'll be able to have a normal day. To go to class or work or do *anything*. And every year, I end up spending hours staring out the windshield, trying to convince myself to get out of the car. To live my life as Danielle always wanted me to.

Two hours later, the rain has slowed to a drizzle as I start my car and drive out of the lot, heading back to my apartment with tears in my eyes.

Maybe next year.

I drop my book bag on the bench near the door and wipe my cheeks as I walk into the kitchen. There's a pint of chocolate chip cookie dough ice cream with my name on it. I intentionally saved it for today.

Harper is sitting at the counter that separates the kitchen from the living room, gulping down a bright pink smoothie. "Hey, Cami. There's some smoothie left, if you want it." She points to the blender on the counter across the kitchen. "It's strawberry-banana."

"No thanks," I say as I walk to the freezer and grab my sweet treat and a spoon. "Are you going to tell me what had you running out from breakfast the other day?"

She hesitates before sighing. "There was an attack. They called everyone in."

Everyone? My chest tightens as my brows knit. "That must've been a big attack."

"Don't stress about it, babe. It was fine. I think they're just being more cautious and on-guard these days."

I frown, my eyes flicking between hers. She isn't anywhere near as tense as I am, so I decide not to push it. She's not supposed to tell me anything regarding the organization, anyway.

"I saw your dad at headquarters this morning," Harper says next. "Did you know he was coming in from New York?"

"Yeah." I turn and lean against the counter, popping off the lid of the ice cream and digging in. "I'm having dinner with him and my mom later." All three of us get together only twice a year—for Danielle's birthday in April and today, the anniversary of her death.

Harper pauses, the mason jar with her smoothie halfway to her mouth as realization fills her expression. "Shit," she says on an exhale. "How are you doing?"

I shrug, shoveling a scoop of sugary goodness into my mouth.

Her brows pull together. "Cami—"

"I'm fine," I say automatically.

"Can I do anything? Do you want me to come to dinner?"

I manage a small smile. "No, thank you. It'll be fine—or it won't be, and I'll come home to drink about it."

She frowns. "When was the last time you saw your dad?"

I dig the spoon into the ice cream again. "We had lunch last month when he was here for a seminar." It was a quick visit. One that, by some stroke of luck, didn't revolve around me training again. Dad and I have a better relationship when my mom isn't involved, which is messed up, but I've somehow gotten used to it. Which only makes me dread tonight's dinner more.

A few hours later, my parents are already seated in a booth at The Pink Door when I arrive. It's where we always meet and, more times than not, we sit in the same booth near the back corner of the dining room. The space glows with chandeliers hanging from the ceiling and candles burning on each table. A wall of windows showcases the night-covered waterfront and the lit up Seattle Great Wheel. The menu here is a bit fancier than I typically enjoy, but this was Danielle's favorite place, so this is where we come to remember her.

Dad slides out of the booth as I approach, wrapping his arms around me tightly and pressing a kiss to the side of my head. His familiar sandalwood scent fills me, and I let myself exist in this moment, closing my eyes for a moment as we hug. "Good to see you, kiddo," he says as we pull away.

"You too, Dad." I pat his cheek. "You let your scruff grow. It looks good on you."

It matches his sandy blond hair, which is combed back and styled neatly. Scott Morgan is definitely rocking the professor look. With a navy cashmere sweater and black slacks, he appears younger than his forty-seven years. He always has. It likely has to do with the necessity of keeping in such good health as a hunter, because my mother is the same. She also spends an obscene amount of money on skin care products, but to each their own.

He smiles. "Your mother disagrees." His tone is light.

Mom scoffs halfheartedly.

I turn my attention to her. She makes no move to get out of the booth, so I drop into the chair across from her. "Hey, Mom."

"Hi, honey." She smiles, reaching across the table to squeeze my hand. "How are you?"

"I'm good."

"School is going well?" Dad asks, bumping my shoulder with his.

I nod, flipping open the menu on the table in front of me. I get some kind of pasta every time we eat here. Tonight is lasagna simply because my mouth watered when I read the description. "The semester is ramping up quickly, so it's keeping me busy."

"And you're still working at the coffee place?"

"Not as many hours lately, but yeah."

They both nod, and I wait for one of them—my first guess is Mom—to bring up the demon attack from last week. My posture is uncomfortably straight, as if my body knows I'm going to have to defend myself, but when neither brings it up, I let myself relax a little.

Considering we're here to remember the person we all lost during a demon attack, it's the decent thing to do. To not make the conversation about my run-in with one and inevitably use it as a point to persuade—manipulate—me into training again.

There's a brief moment when the waitress comes over to take our orders where I glance around the restaurant at the other tables—at the couples on dates, the families smiling and laughing, enjoying each other's company. I suppose our table must look like that, too. A family spending time together, making conversation over a meal. That said, it feels like the farthest thing from it. I'm only here to honor Danielle's memory. Otherwise, I don't spend much time with my parents. It doesn't help that Dad moved to New York City to run Ballard, the most elite demon hunter academy in the United States, when he and mom divorced fifteen years ago.

I usually visit once or twice a year. I have no doubt he still wants me to return, but he's nowhere near as persistent about it as she is.

I'm also certain Danielle would be happy I got out of the life our parents had planned for us both, just like I promised her I would.

"The life of a demon hunter is not one's own." She'd said that one night after coming back from an especially grueling training session. Her eyes had been tired, the dark circles beneath them making her appear older. "You should get out while you can, Cami. Do something more with your life. Do something you want."

It takes me a second to realize the waitress walked away while I was stuck in the memory of my sister. I swallow hard, reaching for my water glass and taking a long drink, then ask my dad, "How long are you staying in Seattle?"

"A few days. Your mom and I have back-to-back meetings with some executives at HQ tomorrow. And there are a few training facilities around here I'd like to visit before heading home."

I nod along, but I'm slipping away from the conversation, going back to that night, sitting on my bed with Danielle in one of the last moments I had with her. I cling to the memory, using it to harden my resolve to fight for the life I want, and remind myself there's absolutely nothing wrong with that.

Whatever happens, whatever my parents say to try to lure me back, I will never return to that life. I will never be a demon hunter.

"You're welcome to join me," he offers. "Some of the facilities are pretty high-tech. It could be interesting. Plus, we haven't spent much time together this year. I'd love to see you more while I'm here."

My stomach drops, and I exhale slowly. "Thanks for the offer, but I have class throughout the week. And then I'm at the café most evenings and weekends."

"I thought you said you weren't working as many hours there," Mom interjects, sipping from her glass of merlot.

I sit straighter, struggling to leash the attitude fighting to surface and make me snap at her. "I did, but I'm still working there. And when I'm not, I'm studying or working on assignments for school."

She says nothing to that, just sets her wineglass down and presses her lips together.

"It's okay, kiddo," Dad says in a soft voice. "We'll plan for something else soon. Maybe you can visit me in New York over winter break. I'm sure Noah would be happy to show you around the city while your old man is stuck at work."

I force a laugh, not sure I want to explore Dad's motivation for the latter suggestion. "I don't need a tour guide." Especially not *Noah Daniels*. "But I'd love to visit you. I'll look at my exam schedule when I get home and send you some dates."

He nods with a smile. "That sounds great."

I'm grateful Dad doesn't push me on spending time with Noah. *Does he remember the crush I had on him years ago?* I suppose it doesn't really matter, and I'm certainly not going to ask. Dad has always liked Noah, probably because of his skills as a hunter, but he's never trained with that cocky, emotionless brick of muscle and arrogance.

The rest of dinner is relatively quiet. I keep my gaze trained on my place, pushing around the layers of noodles and forcing myself to swallow a small piece here and there.

My parents chat about the renovations Mom is doing at the house she kept in the divorce—the place I grew up. Dad offers to stop by and check things out while he's around.

I tune them out, letting my thoughts drift back to the weekend, to unintentionally spending the night at Xander's on our second date. I try to focus on what Phoebe said yesterday, about how it's not a big deal. Theoretically, I *know* I'm blowing it out of proportion, but that doesn't allow me to stop thinking about it.

He hasn't reached out since I ran from his apartment as if it was on fire yesterday morning. I can't say I blame him.

I've almost texted him at least five times now. Every time, I type out the message but I can't bring myself to hit send. It's ridiculous, and I've never been so annoyed at myself or the anxiety that fills my chest every time my thoughts go back to it. I refuse to let my own messy thoughts sabotage whatever I might be doing with Xander. So I'll give myself the rest of the day, and if I still haven't heard from him by tomorrow, I'll *finally* text him.

Because finding a balance between comfort and enjoying new experiences is about compromising—often, as I've come to learn, with myself.

NINE
XANDER

I haven't heard from Camille since she left my apartment on Sunday morning. Yesterday was the anniversary of her sister's death, which didn't feel like the right time to reach out. I planned to send her a text this morning after my post-run shower, and was pleasantly surprised to find two messages from her waiting for me.

Hey, sorry I freaked out the other day. Thanks for being cooler about it than I was.

My friends Phoebe and Grayson invited us out for dinner and drinks tonight, but I know it's last minute, so no worries if you're busy.

Hmm. A double date. I'd much rather spend my time with Camille alone, but if this is what she needs to get back to that, then that's what we'll do. Plus, it's probably a good idea to get to know the people in her life she's close with. Especially her non-hunter friends. I suspect the roommate, Harper, will be something of an obstacle at some point, but I can't concern myself with that at the moment.

No apology necessary. Dinner sounds fun. Can I pick you up?

Pheebs made a reservation at The Cheesecake Factory for 6 p.m. Does that work for you?

Absolutely. I'll pick you up at 5:30?

The text bubbles appear and disappear a few times before her reply comes through.

Great! I'll see you then.

Her next message is a map link to her address.

Looking forward to it.

Pocketing my phone, I walk out of the bedroom and into the kitchen to make avocado toast with a fried egg for breakfast. It's nearly eleven, which is typically later than I start my day, but I slept through my alarm this morning. I'm inclined to blame it on feeding last night. It got rid of the lingering exhaustion that was clinging to me like a transparent film, but replaced it with a heaviness in my chest I can't shake. Ergo, staying unconscious as long as I could.

Feeding to appease my demon side has been something I've battled with for some time. I've gotten used to the lethargy that creeps in when I go for extended periods without it, much to my mother's dismay. She'd be far more satisfied if I embraced the monster she created within me. I've come close on a number of occasions, but have never fully committed. In a lot of ways, it would be so much easier than fighting with my humanity on a daily basis. But, as ironic as it sounds, the idea breeds a razor-sharp fear in me as much as it entices me.

Thanks to the human DNA that makes up part of me, I could get away with feeding a couple times a week to maintain my strength. Before last night, I hadn't fed in...fuck, probably a month. No wonder the recharge knocked me out when I got home last night.

My phone buzzes as I'm cracking a second egg into the pan, and I toss the shell in the trash, wiping my hands on my pants before pulling my phone out. "What's up, Blake?"

"Remind me to teach you some proper greetings, because yours are getting quite lackluster, my friend."

I roll my eyes despite him not being able to see me and debate hanging up without another word.

"Okay, okay," he cuts in before I can end the call. "I'm just checking in before I take off for a few days."

"Where are you going?" I grab a knife and the ripest avocado from the produce bowl on the island.

"Lucia has me escorting some high-level demon friend of hers to a summit in Vegas. I don't know what it's for and I truly don't care."

I slice the avocado before scooping it into a bowl and mashing it. "Great," I mutter dryly, adding a splash of lemon juice, salt, and pepper. "Who's she sticking me with while you're gone?"

Blake hesitates, and I curse under my breath.

That means I'll be forced to endure Francesca while he's away.

There was a time I wouldn't mind her company. Hell, there were many nights she warmed my bed, and I thoroughly enjoyed her particular set of skills. But that was before she tried to force my hand into a bonding ceremony that would give her status in our world. I don't trust her and I don't believe for one fucking minute that her standing in for Blake is a coincidence. She's been so far up my mother's ass—even after I told her where to go—that I'd bet Fran suggested Blake be the one to escort whoever to Vegas. Probably in the same breath she insisted she be the one to guard me in his absence.

"I'm sorry, mate."

"It's fine." I slice off a couple pieces of sourdough from the loaf I grabbed at the bakery down the street, dropping them into the toaster none too gently before slamming the lever down. I exhale a sharp breath, clenching my jaw at the situation—yet another one I'm completely powerless in.

"Believe me, I tried to get out of this trip. Your mother's friends are all fucking insane—and not in a hot way."

A shudder rolls through me as my stomach clenches painfully. The smell of the eggs cooking suddenly makes me feel sick. I've spent time with many of my mother's friends. It was never by choice and is something I would quite literally give anything to forget.

"Don't worry about it," I say as the toast pops up. I toss it onto a plate and smear the avocado over it before drizzling the top with olive oil. After I add the fried egg to each slice, I shake some red pepper flakes on top. It looks appetizing, but my stomach is so twisted in knots, I'll have to force myself to eat at this point.

"Should I ask how things are going on your end?"

I pull out my French press from the cupboard and set it up to make coffee. "I'm going out with Camille and her friends tonight. It sounds casual, which doesn't surprise me after her hurried exit a couple days ago."

"I hope things progress from here. Let me know if you need anything before I take off. I'll be around until tomorrow morning."

"I don't need anything," I say in a level voice, pulling out my favorite roast and a mug.

"Hmm. I trust you'll keep yourself fed while I'm gone and I won't have to drag you out again when I return?"

I close my eyes as a muscle ticks in my jaw. "Blake—"

"Don't," he cuts in, using a sharp voice typically reserved for people he doesn't enjoy speaking to. Even with his accent, it sounds cold. "If you don't eat food like humans need to, you will *die*. If you don't feed like demons need to, you will *also* die. I know you know that, so smarten the fuck up. Respectfully."

Lately, I've come to resent the part of me that requires hunting humans to survive. Demons are not immortal—half breeds even less so—however, they can for live centuries. If they feed regularly.

Many relish in the manipulation, in making humans experience their worst fears.

"I'll take care of it," I say in a voice that doesn't invite argument, then add, "Thanks for your concern."

Blake snorts. "Right."

My eyes narrow slightly, irritation prickling along my spine. "Was there anything else?"

There's a stretch of silence before he says, "You're in a mood today. Better turn on the charm before your date."

I bite back a sharp reply, though he's not wrong. There's a mix of unfamiliar sensations swirling around in my chest that I can't seem to shake. It's uncomfortable and impossible to ignore, and the more I try, the worse it seems to get.

"Alrighty then," he says, realizing I'm not going to respond. "I have to get going. See you in a few days."

I end the call and exhale a long sigh, setting my phone on the counter next to my untouched breakfast.

My mood lightens by the end of the day as I'm getting ready for dinner with Camille and her friends. I pick a black dress shirt and dark jeans, pairing it with black combat boots and my favorite leather jacket. Standing in front of my bathroom mirror, I run my hands through my hair, messing with the dark brown waves until they're tousled enough to set with gel. After a light spray of cologne, I grab my wallet and keys off the dresser and head for the elevator.

Pulling up outside her apartment a few minutes early, I cut the engine and stride across the sidewalk and into the entryway. There's a screen adjacent to another door in the main lobby, and I find her name on the resident list.

Tapping the call button, I wait as it rings a few times before an out-of-breath voice says, "I'll be right down."

"Take your time," I say, my lips curling into a faint smile, as if she's already standing in front of me. The simplest thing—the sound of her voice—melted away some of the unease in my gut from earlier, and the power of that is certainly not lost on me.

Five minutes later, the elevator slides open. Camille steps off looking downright angelic in a navy long sleeve blouse and black high-waisted pants. Her shoes have a small heel, putting her a bit closer to my height, and her hair falls in long waves. There's a tinge of pink in her cheeks when she glides closer, smiling at me.

"Hi."

"Hi," I say back, matching her grin, and step closer to kiss her cheek, catching the slight hitch in her breath. There's a part of me that enjoys, probably too much, how I affect her. "How are you?" I ask as we leave the building.

"I'm good. How was your day?"

I bite my tongue as I open the passenger door for her. "I spent it looking forward to this," I say, in lieu of a real answer.

She pauses at the curb, tipping her head back to meet my gaze. "Me, too. After how I left your place the other day, I wasn't sure you'd want to." Her eyes flick between mine. "I'm glad you're here."

I tilt my head to the side, keeping my voice gentle as I say, "Try as hard as you can..." The corner of my mouth kicks up, and I dip my face so my lips are level with her ear, the monster in me vibrating at her quickening pulse, the hint of fear hiding beneath the surface. "You won't scare me away, Camille."

There's a beat of silence before she turns her head and plants her mouth on mine.

Without hesitation, my hands drop to her hips, and I pull her against me, deepening the kiss as a soft growl of satisfaction rumbles in my throat.

Camille's heart pounds in her chest as she grabs the front of my shirt, leaning into me as we lose ourselves in the feeling of each other.

"We're going to be late," I murmur against her lips.

Her grip on my shirt tightens. "Don't care."

I chuckle, sliding my hand up her arm, and cup the side of her neck, running my thumb along her jaw. My tongue darts out to flick along her lips until she parts them to let me in with a quiet moan that tears through me, drowning me in the desire to take her at this exact moment. The tension sparking between us is as powerful as a magnet, pulling us closer with each thundering heartbeat. I can't get enough of her. I want *more*. My tongue slides along hers, reveling in the sweet taste of her, and our kiss turns into something more frantic.

I'm thoroughly aware of the lack of romance in having my way with her against the side of a car outside her apartment. I shove that primal urge away with a noticeable amount of effort.

Still, I force myself to pull back and rest my forehead against hers while we catch our breaths. "We should get going. I'd hate to make a bad first impression by keeping your friends waiting." I lower my voice. "Besides, all the things I'd like to do to you shouldn't be rushed."

Camille sucks in a breath, her heart racing. There's a flicker of surprise in her expression that I can't help but smirk at. She's so responsive...It's so fucking temping.

"Right," she says, then clears her throat and steps back, letting go of my shirt.

I have half a mind to stare at the wrinkles her ironclad grip left behind. Instead, I close the passenger door after she gets in, then walk around the front of my Camaro, getting behind the wheel and starting the car. "All set?" I ask, glancing over to make sure she's buckled.

She nods. "I'm excited for you to meet my friends. Phoebe is a literal angel, and Grayson is the funniest person I know."

I pull away from the curb, shooting her a smile. "I'm sure we'll get along great." So long as this friend of Camille's isn't *actually* a celestial. Then things would get a lot more complicated—very fucking fast.

The restaurant is buzzing with dozens of lively conversations and dishes clattering. I can see food being prepared in the kitchen behind a mostly glass wall at the back of the vast dining space. The lighting is dim, giving the room an atmosphere of warmth and comfort.

A middle-aged hostess guides us toward where Camille's friends are waiting in a booth near the back.

Phoebe's eyes light up the moment she sees us, and she immediately starts nudging Grayson to get out of the booth, nearly bouncing with excitement. She follows him out and wraps her arms around Camille in a tight hug, whispering in her ear, "You were right. He is smokin' hot. Well done, Cami." Her voice has a teasing lilt, and she laughs softly as she steps back.

My lips twitch, and I smoothly turn to Grayson, sticking out my hand. "Xander," I offer as we shake hands, getting a subtle whiff of his crisp smelling cologne. I figure he's around my age, considering he goes to school with Camille.

"Grayson," he replies in a friendly voice, pairing it with a polite smile. His blue-gray eyes allude to sincerity when he adds, "It's good to meet you, man."

"Likewise."

The girls break apart, and Camille goes to hug Grayson, ruffling his coppery brown curls, while Phoebe eyes me up for a moment before stepping closer. My posture stiffens briefly when she throws her arms around my neck and hugs me, overwhelming my senses with the warm scent of vanilla and coconut.

"If you hurt her, I swear I will *obliterate* you in ways you can't even fathom." Her tone is soft and sweet, which only serves to make her words more severe.

Literal angel, huh?

I nod and speak so only she can hear me. "Understood."

"Amazing." She steps back, smiling at me before she and Grayson take their seats again.

Camille slides into the other side of the booth across from Phoebe, leaving me on the end across from Grayson. I'd much rather be looking at my date, but having her next to me is almost as enjoyable. Especially since I can slide my hand up her thigh under the table, and when I do, I'm rewarded with a subtle hitch in her breath.

When the waiter stops by our table with water and bread, we order a round of drinks before taking in the small novel that is the menu. I lean closer to Camille as she glances it over.

"There are too many options," she says with a halfhearted sigh.

"You can never go wrong with pasta," I point out, giving her knee a gentle squeeze.

She chuckles, her cheeks tinged pink. "*Hmm.* That is very true."

A few minutes later, our waiter returns, and we place our orders. Once he walks away, Grayson stretches out, leaning against the back of the booth and draping his arm over Phoebe's shoulders. "You're coming to the lake house in a couple of weeks, right?" he asks Camille.

She nods around a mouthful of bread.

"Adrianna hasn't stopped talking about it." She shares a laugh with Phoebe. "At this point, I don't think we have the option to not go." Her voice is light and paired with a fond smile.

Adrianna, from what I've been able to gather, is another of Camille's non-hunter friends.

"Xander, you should come, too," Phoebe chimes in cheerfully, making Camille's pulse jump.

I can't decipher if she's excited or scared by the invitation, though I don't feel dark ripples of fear coming from her. Perhaps it's something to discuss when her friends aren't around. Maybe she didn't want to invite me, in which case, I have more work to do than I thought.

I offer a polite smile. "Sounds fun."

"Oh, it will be," Phoebe assures me, resting her elbows on the table and her chin atop her hands. "So, tell us about yourself, Xander."

I was prepared for this, so I smile easier, relaxing into the booth. "What would you like to know?"

Her eyes flick to Camille, then back to me. "Let's do a little rapid fire."

I chuckle. "Sure."

"Is that really necessary?" Camille asks, her cheeks pink.

Phoebe nods. "Absolutely. He has to pass the friend test if he wants to spend more time with you."

My date groans, and I pat her knee. "It's okay. I'm happy to let your friends learn about me. Just like I want to learn about them."

"Good answer," Phoebe says with a grin.

Grayson offers me a sympathetic look and slides his fingers into the back of his girlfriend's hair. As she gears up to start her interrogation, he turns his attention to her, his expression affectionate.

The first question is simple. "Age?"

"Twenty-five."

"Are you in school?"

"I am."

"What are you studying?"

"Philosophy."

"What year?"

"Third."

She purses her lips as she considers what to ask next. "How'd you meet Cami?"

I feel Camille stiffen next to me, and brush my thumb back and forth over her knee in an attempt to calm her. "We met at Hallowed Grounds." It's not a lie, and considering these friends don't know about demons, omitting that part of how we met feels natural.

"A little coffee shop meet-cute?" Grayson says in a teasing voice as he glances over at Camille.

She laughs softly. "Yeah, kinda."

Phoebe sits back, seemingly satisfied with my answers. "Okay…I guess you can stay." She finally cracks a smile at me.

Camille noticeably relaxes.

She genuinely cares what her friends think of me, and her response makes me think she hasn't introduced many guys to them, if any.

Perhaps I've made good progress with her after all.

I attempt to show the same interest by asking the same questions of the couple, learning that they're both sophomores, like Camille. Phoebe is also in political science, while Grayson is studying business.

Halfway through the meal, as I continue getting to know Camille's friends, I come to understand why she cares for them so deeply. Phoebe has a soft aura of warmth about her, and Grayson exudes a calming energy that seems to spread to those around him.

As laughable as it is, I find myself comparing them to Blake. His aura is the opposite of sunshine most days, and his energy can really only be summed up as chaotic. That said, I can't help being curious about what would happen if the three of them met. Mostly how Blake would respond to them. I press my lips together at the thought, hiding my smile by taking a drink as the conversation continues around our table.

After dinner, we part ways from her friends and head down the street toward the parking lot where we left my car. There weren't any spots on the crowded street left when we arrived, so we're several blocks from the restaurant. The wind has picked up, making the air cooler, so I wrap my jacket around Camille's shoulders and tuck her against my side as we stroll down the sidewalk.

She laughs. "Thanks."

I give her a gentle squeeze. "Anytime."

We approach the Camaro, and I unlock it, reaching for the passenger side door handle to open it for her.

The demon comes out of nowhere.

She grabs me from behind, pulling me away from Camille and shoving me against a brick storefront, snarling in my face with pitch-black eyes. Her growl is nearly loud enough to drown out the sound of Camille shouting, her voice a mix of fear and surprise. The demon's brows tug together, and she recoils as I reach for the obsidian dagger I conveniently kept in my jacket pocket...which is still wrapped around my date.

"Xander!" Camille's voice cracks, and the demon in front of me gasps, those endlessly black eyes widening.

"Camille—" I'm about to shout at her for the dagger, but it's already in her hand, her grip ironclad and her expression grim as she moves with lethal grace.

I'm briefly stunned by her actions. This is nothing like her response to the demon the night we met, when she froze instead of fighting back. Her heart is pounding in her chest, but she isn't backing down this time.

The demon whirls on her, barking out a laugh when she spots the weapon Camille is wielding.

I move without warning, grabbing the demon from behind, much like how she grabbed me a moment ago, and restrain her. Holding her arms behind her back, I grit my teeth, breathing hard, as if I'm exerting every ounce of strength I have to keep this demon trapped. I open my mouth, but before I have a chance to direct Camille to move, she strikes, slamming the dagger into the demon's chest.

The demon stiffens in my grip, hissing and crying out in pain as Camille plunges the obsidian blade straight through her heart. The demon's eyes bulge out of her face, and her mouth opens in a silent scream. Then she turns to ash, littering the pavement with the only remaining evidence of her existence.

My stomach twists with nausea at the sight. I didn't know the demon, but part of me and *my* existence felt connected to her.

She was a means to an end, I remind myself, shifting my gaze to where Camille is standing frozen, staring at the remnants of the demon.

"You can't tell anyone about this," she whispers unevenly, wiping her hands against her thighs as she backs toward the car.

I offer her a look that I hope resembles understanding and nod for extra measure. "For someone who's been out of the game for years, that was impressive," I tell her, collecting the dagger and tucking it into the back of my pants.

Camille's face is pale, her brows furrowed. "I...don't know what happened. I feel like I blacked out for a minute and—"

"Saved my ass," I offer, stepping into her. "Thank you."

Confusion still clouds her expression. "That demon seemed like she knew you."

My muscles tense briefly, but I manage to keep my expression neutral as I nod. "I was part of the team that raided one of the popular demon spots in Spokane last week. She and I fought, but she got away before I could finish her." When Camille doesn't say anything more, I touch her shoulder gently. "Come on. I should get you home."

"They're being more conspicuous these days," she comments in a detached voice, sharp with fear. "Since when do they attack so openly? They used to be more secretive about it. Harper said the number of attacks is increasing and—"

"Breathe," I urge in a soft voice. "The demon is dead. I'm okay." I step in front of her, placing my hands on her shoulders. "You're okay." Her gaze is hazy as she continues blinking rapidly. "Camille, look at me."

She sucks in a breath, as if coming back to herself. Her eyes are still glassy when they meet mine. She swallows hard, her pulse still ticking unusually fast. "I...Sorry. I'm fine."

"That's right." I give her an encouraging nod. "Take a deep breath with me." I inhale with her, then exhale slowly. "Good. Another one." We stand there for a couple more minutes, breathing together until her heart rate returns to normal before getting into the car.

Camille is quiet on the drive to her apartment, and when we pull up outside, I walk her to the door. She hands me back my jacket, and I step closer, tucking her hair behind her ear. "Tonight probably didn't go the way you expected it to, and I'm sorry." I lean in, lowering my voice. "I'll make it up to you this weekend, if you'll let me."

Her lips curve into a faint smile. "Yeah. That sounds nice."

My gaze drops to her mouth, and her pulse ticks faster as I hook my finger under her chin. "Good night," I murmur, my lips brushing hers in the whisper of a kiss.

Her breath hitches, and she leans into me, her hands tentatively sliding up my chest.

I should step back. Turn and walk away. Instead, I slant my mouth over hers, kissing her slowly, softly.

When I pull back, Camille presses a quick kiss to the corner of my mouth and murmurs, "Good night, Xander."

Once she's inside, I walk back to my car with an unfamiliar pressure in my chest and a thumping in my rib cage. I have a hunch Camille is going to challenge everything I know, and I'll be wholly unprepared for what's to come.

TEN
CAMILLE

In the days following the second demon attack I've experienced in a week, the pit in my stomach doesn't show any signs of dissipating.

I killed a demon.

During my years of training before I left the hunter organization, I didn't have any kills. Missions potentially featuring *real* action are reserved for senior trainees.

I never made it that far.

Needless to say, Xander and I got lucky. I'm not naive enough to believe my very minimal training would've been enough to keep us alive. That demon must've been weakened or caught off guard facing off with the same hunter she escaped previously. There's no way I would have stood a chance against a high-level demon.

That said, something in me clicked the moment I needed most. I acted on instinct, using Xander's dagger to turn the demon attacking him to ash. Looking back on it, it feels like a distant, dreamlike memory—as if I blacked out or acted without conscious thought. The more I think about it, the more conflicted I feel, which is likely the reason for my chronically upset stomach.

The few times I've seen Harper this week—in between classes and her training sessions—I kept what happened to myself. I'm still trying to figure out how I feel about it, and I don't want to give Harper false hope there's a chance I'll return to the academy. More than that, I'm worried she'll relay what happened to my mom, and that's definitely not a conversation I'm ready to have.

Besides, Xander must have reported it, so there's really no need to involve more hunters. He was understanding when I asked him to leave my involvement out of whatever account he'd make, but there's still a part of me that's waiting for a call from my mom.

THE DEVIL'S WALTZ

By Saturday I haven't heard from her, so I try my best to let that worry go, and focus on my studies. I spend the morning at work, then stay at the café a few hours longer, taking over one of the tables near the front window to make progress on an assignment I have due next week.

Making good on his promise of a better date, Xander texts me with plans to take me to dinner tonight. I head home with just enough time to shower and blow dry my hair, then tug on a knee-length, strapless black dress and heels before applying a bit of makeup. I'm swiping on a thin layer of lip balm when the buzzer sounds, and I rush over, pressing the intercom to let him into the building.

The air gets caught in my lungs when I open the door and my gaze lands on Xander standing there. He's in a black dress shirt and pants, with his hair stylishly tousled and a faint grin on his lips. Then my eyes drop to the bouquet of deep red roses.

"Hey," I murmur, my heart beating faster as I step back so he can come inside.

"You look stunning," he says in greeting, closing the distance between us and dipping his face to gently kiss my cheek before handing me the flowers.

The scent of his cologne paired with his proximity makes me stutter out a quiet thank you as I take the bouquet and walk into the kitchen to put it in a vase with water.

Xander follows, leaning against the island counter and watching me. His attention has my nerve endings tingling.

There's a newly familiar part of me that wants to blow off our dinner reservations. To explore the sensations rippling through me as Xander moves closer, smoothly taking the vase from me and sliding the bouquet into the water.

He sets it on the counter and turns to face me. "Ready for dinner? I made a reservation at Lowell's."

My stomach grumbles, reminding me I haven't eaten since my break at work hours ago. I swallow past the dryness in my throat and nod. "That sounds good."

There's a glint of humor in his eyes, and for half a second, panic spikes in my chest, thinking he can sense the warring feelings in me. But then he steps back and offers me his arm. I accept it, grabbing my clutch off the island, and we walk out of my apartment.

The restaurant is packed when we arrive. The hostess takes us to our table and sets the menus down before hurrying back to serve the people who came in behind us. We're seated on the third floor by a large window overlooking the bay. The view is stunning, especially with the sun setting at the perfect spot, so it isn't blinding through the window. The muted pinks and blues in the sky are blended together beautifully.

After we've ordered our drinks and food, the waiter leaves us alone.

Xander reaches across the table toward me until his fingers graze mine. "Do you want to talk about what happened the other night?" he asks, turning his hand up to offer me his palm.

I slide my fingers into his, and he brushes his thumb back and forth over the top of my hand.

"Are you asking as a hunter or my—" I stop myself before the word can leave my lips. Heat floods my cheeks, and I drop my gaze to the table.

Xander squeezes my hand. "Would it change your answer if I asked as your boyfriend?"

My gaze jumps back up to meet his, and I find him grinning softly. I shake my head, struggling to string together words to answer him. Instead, I ask, "Do you want to be my boyfriend?" The word tastes odd on my tongue. It doesn't feel significant enough for the emotions fluttering in my belly, and that alone is terrifying.

He doesn't miss a beat. "I would very much like that—if you'll have me, Camille."

I open my mouth, my heart beating so hard I feel it in my throat. When no words form, I reserve myself to pressing my lips together and nodding. His gaze is locked on me, and I have no doubt I'm wearing everything I'm feeling on my face, which means he's seeing it all.

Xander licks his lips as if he's about to speak, but catches something behind me, causing him to snap his jaw shut.

"What—"

"I thought that was you." An unfamiliar accented—British, I think—voice fills the space between us.

My eyes lift as a tall, built guy with spiky pink hair waltzes up to our table, staring at Xander with a wide grin. I can't help the way my eyes widen at his appearance. I didn't know a leopard print button-up could actually look good on someone, but paired with black jeans, combat boots, and a distressed leather jacket, he's pulling it off. It helps that he exudes confidence, making me think no matter what he wore, it would work for him.

A muscle ticks in Xander's jaw, and I get the impression this guy isn't exactly a welcome guest. "Blake," Xander says in greeting, but his voice is laced with annoyance.

The newcomer—Blake, apparently—shifts his gaze from Xander to me and smirks. "Well, well, well. Who is this pretty little thing?"

My brows lift. "Pardon?"

"Ignore him," Xander cuts in. "Blake—"

"Easy, Kane. I'm just saying hello." Blake keeps his eyes on me. "What's your name?"

"Oddly enough, *not* 'pretty little thing.'"

Our third wheel laughs deeply, seemingly not concerned about being so loud. He's probably disturbing the people having dinner in the booth across from us. He tosses a quick look at Xander as he says, "She's a funny one."

"I'm sorry," I interrupt. "Who are you?"

His expression turns serious, but the playful light in his emerald eyes remains. "My apologies, love. I'm Blake."

"Blake...?"

"Just Blake," he says without missing a beat.

I blink at him. "Right..." I draw out the word, disbelief clear in my voice. "How do you know Xander?"

"Xander is my brother from another mother. Thank god." He shoots my date a wink before returning his attention to me. "And how do you know my man?"

He saved my life from a demon.

"We met at the café where I work."

"Ah. How...quaint."

"Sure," I say, feeling like Blake's presence is really putting a damper on an otherwise great night. "Do you need something, or...?"

"I'm here with some pals and saw you lovebirds over here having a merry old time."

"So you wanted to ruin it?" I toss out.

He smirks. "You're rather fiery."

"Would you mind letting us get back to our date?" Xander chimes in. "I'll catch up with you later."

His eyes shift to Xander. "As you wish," he mutters in a mockingly formal tone, clapping him on the back. "Have fun, kiddos."

Once Blake is gone, Xander frowns. "Sorry about that."

I wave him off. "No apology necessary. He seems—"

"Like a total pain in my ass? Yeah."

I nod, lowering my voice before asking, "Is Blake a hunter too?"

Xander exhales a short laugh, shaking his head. "The hunter lifestyle of rigid rules isn't exactly Blake's vibe."

"I mean, fair enough. I certainly don't blame him for that."

He nods thoughtfully, and we chat about school for a few minutes until our food arrives. After dinner, we head toward the pier, my stomach fluttering with nerves as Xander slips his fingers through mine. The breeze coming off the water helps cool my heated cheeks.

"I have an idea," he says, breaking the comfortable silence as we walk along the pier.

I cast him a sideways glance. "Oh?"

"How do you feel about heights?"

My stomach dips, and I cringe inwardly. "It depends. Are we talking flying in an airplane or...?"

"How about taking a ride on The Great Wheel?" he offers, squeezing my hand. "I've never been. Have you?"

Nervously pulling my bottom lip between my teeth, I hum softly and shake my head.

"Do you want to?"

"Sure," I answer automatically. I'm not prepared to tell Xander my pulse is pounding beneath my skin or that my heart is attempting to break free of my rib cage. I'm not scared of heights. But getting *stuck* somewhere I can't control...that's another thing entirely.

We stand in line, and I shove my hands in my pockets so Xander can't see the way they're shaking.

"Are you sure you're okay with this?" he asks, watching me with a raised brow as he shrugs off his jacket and wraps it around my shoulders.

I swallow hard and plaster a smile on my lips. "Yeah, I'm fine."

Xander frowns. "Camille—"

"All good," I say in a confident tone, though my voice wavers slightly.

Once it's our turn to get on, Xander gestures for me to go first, so I stick one foot in front of the other until I'm inside the cart. I drop onto the seat and stare ahead as Xander gets in. The ride operator closes the door. And a minute later, the wheel starts moving.

Everything glimmers in the dark. Lights along the pier and the entire Space Needle glow, and the bright moon reflects off the Puget Sound. If I wasn't so worried about being stuck in here, I might be able to appreciate the stunning city views on one side and the water on the other.

"You can see most of the city from up here," Xander muses, a faint smile on his lips as he takes in the sights.

"Yeah." My voice comes out breathy as I press my hands flat against my thighs and try to focus on filling my lungs steadily, knowing the ride will be over in a matter of minutes.

Just when I think I'll be able to manage this without losing control of my nerves, the wheel jerks to a stop with us at the very top, and my stomach drops.

No, no, no. Oh, god. I can't do this.

Xander moves into my view, his brows drawn together. "Camille?"

I look away—right out the side of the cart, which sends my pulse racing faster, to the point my head spins. "I can't..." My voice cuts off, the dryness in my throat making it impossible to speak. The thundering of my heart vibrates my chest, and I close my eyes. It doesn't help. Control is slipping through my fingers like water and my throat is so tight I can't pull in a breath.

"Camille." His deep voice breaks through the wall of anxiety that's currently laying heavy bricks of overwhelm on my chest. In the space of a heartbeat, he moves across the cart, pulling me into his lap with one arm while his other hand sinks into my hair and cradles my neck. I suck in a startled breath in the second before his mouth steals mine.

I've been kissed a few times before, even by him, but I've never experienced *this*. This all-consuming parallel dimension where nothing else exists but us. His tongue sweeps along my bottom lip, and I forget how to breathe. It might be embarrassing, if I could bring myself to care about anything besides the feel of his chest pressed against mine or the thundering in my chest. Xander's presence is grounding, pulling me back from the waves of fear threatening to pull me under.

I fist the front of his shirt as he tips my head back, deepening the kiss and wringing a soft moan from my lips. Heat fills my cheeks, and I gasp against his mouth when he slides one hand along my thigh.

He pulls back just enough to trace the shell of my ear with his lips, making me shiver. "Keep your eyes closed," he purrs.

"You're trying to distract me," I offer in a breathy voice.

His chuckle tickles the nape of my neck, and my skin tingles in response. "Is it working?" He moves his hand higher up my thigh, reaching dangerously close to an almost foreign pulsing between my legs.

"Hmm," I hum, keeping my eyes shut as I lean into his touch.

"If I'm taking things too far—"

"You're not," I say instantly, my anxiety momentarily caught on him stopping the only thing keeping me from a full-on panic attack.

Xander's fingers stay curled around the side of my neck, while his other hand glides over the bare skin of my inner thigh for a moment before he pulls his jacket from around my shoulders and drapes it over my lap. Reaching underneath, he gently nudges my legs apart, and I bite my lip to keep from moaning aloud as he traces his finger over my panties.

Holding me open to him, he dips his face and presses his lips to the pulse at my throat. "Okay?" he checks.

There is no hesitation when I nod in response.

"Use your words," he teases in a deeper voice, pausing his delicate ministrations.

I swallow hard. "Y-yes."

Xander kisses my jaw, pressing his thumb against the bundle of nerves at the apex of my thighs.

I suck in a breath, my head spinning with lust. I can't think straight. The only thing that exists is the pleasure elicited by his touch.

He takes his time, teasing me through the scrap of lace, the only barrier between his fingers and my molten skin.

Too soon, the light brushes of his fingers aren't enough.

I need more.

"Xander," I breathe, wrapping my fingers around his wrist, urging him to give me what I crave.

He curses under his breath, pulls my panties to the side, and slides his fingers over my heated—and now bared—skin. I bury my face between his neck and shoulder, my breathing quickening as his deft fingers press firmly to the heat between my legs, stroking expertly.

I tense a little as he pushes a finger inside me, and he pauses.

"Talk to me," he murmurs.

I blow out an unsteady breath, loosening my grip on his wrist. "Keep going." The words are barely a whisper.

He hesitates before continuing. It takes a few more strokes of his finger inside me and his thumb circling my clit to adjust to the invasion.

We settle into a rhythm as the ride starts moving again, though I barely notice it as Xander brings me to new heights of pleasure. There's no question he knows what he's doing, and I lose myself in him, giving myself over to the sensations flooding through me.

I clamp my jaw shut as sparks of electricity shoot through me, my muscles tightening as I race toward the edge and am eventually launched right over it.

Xander pulls his hand back, pressing his lips to mine in a whisper of a kiss. "You can open your eyes now."

His words caress the softest parts of my mind, and I blink a few times, squinting at him as I swallow past the dryness in my throat.

Xander's eyes are dark, hooded with lust and something I can't quite place that has my pulse jack-hammering beneath my flushed skin. I finally turn my gaze away and realize we're back on the ground.

He slides his hand through mine, entwining our fingers, and guides me out of the cart.

"Thank you," I murmur once we're away from the crowd.

Xander casts me a sideways glance and offers a faint smile, his gaze shimmering with understanding.

My chest swells at the sight moments before boldness grips me, and I blurt, "Harper is at training tonight." This is entirely new territory for me, but there's no doubt in my mind about what I want right now.

The corner of his mouth kicks up. "Oh?"

I nod slowly, chewing my lower lip for a moment before asking, "Take me home?"

ELEVEN
XANDER

The monster in me wants her almost as much as I do.

The risk of losing control with her, to being exposed when I can't keep my demon side caged, should give me pause. Instead, I snake an arm around Camille's waist the moment we step off the elevator, pulling her against my side as we walk toward her apartment.

She laughs softly as she fishes out her keys.

I don't let go as she unlocks the door, and as soon as we're inside with it shut, I cage her in between my arms.

She pulls in a sharp breath, her eyes flitting across my face as her heart pounds like a steady drumbeat. Her eyes are wide, unsure, but her body tells me she wants exactly what I do.

Her pulse thrums and the heat between her thighs has me biting back a growl as my nostrils flare at her sweet scent. It's a delicate mix of arousal and fear—I'd enjoy nothing more than to drown in it.

I drop my hands to her hips, tilting my face to speak low in her ear. "We should take this slow." I'm mindful of the fact that being with a new partner can be overwhelming. As much as part of me wants to take her against the door, I'm going to move at a pace she's comfortable with.

Camille reaches up, draping her arms over my shoulders, and turns her face to press a soft kiss against my cheek. "What if I don't want slow?"

Well, I'll be damned.

I pull back to look in her eyes, tucking a bit of hair behind her ear. "Whatever you want, it's yours."

She cups my cheeks in her hands and seals her mouth over mine, kissing me hard as she presses herself against me. Her fingers slide into my hair, and I close my eyes, reveling in the feel of her body flush with mine.

My own pulse kicks up as my body fills with warmth. I tip her head back to claim her mouth, nipping her bottom lip, then tease it with my tongue.

She makes a soft sound at the back of her throat, and my grip on her tightens instinctively as we move toward her bedroom.

I kick the door shut behind us, guiding Camille closer to the bed with my hands on her hips.

In seconds, we're lost in each other's touch.

The darkest parts of me light up for her.

For a tragically fleeting moment, I allow myself to set aside the reason I'm here. To pretend we're different people than we are. To forget I won't ultimately hurt her.

When she pulls back to catch her breath, I dip my face to pepper kisses along her jaw until my lips reach her ear, and I murmur, "Still with me?"

"I'm here," she breathes, fisting the front of my shirt, as if to steady herself while keeping me close.

I'm about to kiss her again when a flash of something akin to panic in her gaze makes me pause. Fear flies off her in dark red sparks, and a muscle feathers along her jaw.

"Maybe we should press pause?" I suggest, despite it being the last thing I want. I won't push her if she doesn't want this. I may be a monster, but there are lines I will not cross. I have my father to thank for that shred of humanity.

"What?" She shakes her head. "No, I just—Sorry, I'm a bit out of my element here."

I nod. "Being with someone new is usually nerve-racking."

Her cheeks flush a deeper shade of pink and her gaze drops to her feet. "Right. Well, I think it's probably more intense the first time."

There's a stretch of silence before I say, "You've never been with anyone?" My voice is gruff and filled with disbelief.

She presses her lips together, shaking her head, her cheeks tinged pink. "I, um...I understand if that changes things for you."

Fucking hell. I'm the last person on earth who deserves to be her first.

If I was a better man, I'd walk away.

But I'm not.

I grip her chin between my fingers, holding her gaze. "That changes nothing for me," I assure her in a gentle voice. "I want you, Camille."

Her breath hitches, and she nods. "I want you, too."

We reach for each other at the same moment, falling back into a frenzy of kissing and touching and laughing as we fumble through taking off each other's clothes. Once we're standing face-to-face in nothing but underwear, I take the lead and step into her.

I reverently glide my fingers up her arms and smile at the way her skin breaks out in goosebumps at my touch. "You are so beautiful, *mo shíorghrá*," I murmur.

Her eyes widen momentarily before her lashes lower, as if she can't stand to hold my gaze at that moment.

Before she can question the term, I kiss her deeply, not prepared to share its meaning. I shouldn't have said it—it will never be true and to even pretend otherwise is ridiculous.

Shoving the thought away, I take my time exploring the curves of her body as my fingers wander lower. I savor each moment, every caress, the anticipation of what's to come palpable in the air between us.

Camille traces the hard lines of muscle in my stomach as her fingers make their way upward to my chest, and I fight the urge to guide her hand to my groin.

I hook my fingers under the strap of her bra, pulling it down her shoulder before doing the same to the other side.

She leans forward, inviting me to reach behind her and unclasp it.

I drop it on the floor next to the bed, keeping my eyes on her face to gauge her response.

Her eyes are glazed over, her pupils dilated with lust, and her cheeks are flushed a lovely shade of pink. I'd like nothing more than to commit this moment to memory, to ingrain the way she's looking at me right now to the forefront of my subconscious.

Between one moment and the next, Camille reaches for me, pressing her bare chest to mine as she captures my lips in a feverish kiss that has my heart beating faster, in time with hers.

Backing her up until she reaches the bed, I guide her to sit on the end and kneel before her, my hands on her knees as I spread them open. Her breathing quickens and my cock hardens as I lower my gaze to the light blue panties that match her discarded bra. Leaning in, I brush my lips against her bare thigh, my mouth curling into a grin when a shiver ripples through her and she exhales a breathy sigh. I make quick work of pulling her panties down her legs, dropping them onto the floor.

At the first pass of my tongue between her thighs, her hips jerk off the bed.

I grip them, pushing down with a soft chuckle, and band my arm across her hips to keep her in place. Circling the bundle of nerves at her core with my tongue, I alternate speed and pressure as her pulse pounds harder.

"Xander," she pants.

I look up and rest my chin below her navel. "Talk to me. Tell me what you want."

Camille swallows hard. "Just...keep going."

My lips twist into a smirk as my eyes flit across her face. And then I lower my mouth back to her core. The monster in me purrs with delight, relishing in the taste of Camille on my tongue as I thoroughly devour her.

She grips the sheets with one hand and my hair with the other. Her breathing quickly turns shallow as her thighs tighten around me, and I fight back a growl.

I adore how responsive she is, and knowing that I'm in control of her pleasure gives the demon part of me a dangerously bloated sense of ego.

Seconds later, Camille clenches around my tongue, filling the room with a desperate moan as she comes hard.

I flick my tongue lazily against her center as she shudders, and when I can't hold back any longer, I pull back to look at her again. I stand slowly, leaning over her as I skate my fingers upward along her sides. "Do you have—"

"Shit," she cuts in, shaking her head as a hint of disappointment fills her gaze briefly. "Wait. Harper might have some in the bathroom." She moves to sit up, but I stop her with a gentle hand on her collarbone.

"I'll go."

She bites her lip. "It's the door across the hall."

I press a soft kiss to her lips before sliding off the bed and walking to the bathroom, where I find what I'm looking for. Returning to the bedroom with the foil package between my fingers, I approach her. I stop at the foot of the bed to tug my boxers down, leaving them on the floor as I crawl over her. I tear the wrapper open with my teeth, rolling the condom on before I settle between her thighs.

"Are you sure?" I ask her.

"Yes," she replies in a steady voice, despite the thundering beat of her heart.

"If you want me to stop at any time, you just need to tell me, okay?"

"Okay," she confirms, nodding for extra measure.

"Take a deep breath," I say softly, holding my tip at her entrance. It takes every ounce of willpower I have not to slam into her, but as badly as the monster in me desires to claim her, I want her to enjoy this.

Camille inhales slowly, her chest rising as her heart pounds. She licks her lips, keeping her eyes locked on mine as I slide one hand from her stomach up her chest, then cradle the side of her neck. I push inside her an inch, and she grips me like a vise, hissing out a shaky breath. Her brows knit in concentration, her cheeks flushing a deep pink.

"Exhale now," I murmur, stroking her jaw with my thumb as I push in a bit more. "Keep breathing slowly and try to relax."

She nods.

The determination in her expression makes my lips curl into a faint grin as I bury another inch of myself between her thighs, reveling in how tightly she grips me. Once I'm fully sheathed inside her, I dip my face toward her and capture her lips with mine, kissing her deeply. When I pull away from her mouth, I kiss each of her cheeks, her forehead, then lastly, the tip of her nose.

She laughs softly and finally begins to relax around me.

I give her a few minutes to adjust, kissing her until her eyes flutter shut. The kiss turns feverish, and when her hips start making little circular movements beneath me, I pull back, splaying my fingers across her cheek.

"I'm going to move now," I tell her.

She blinks her eyes open, meeting my gaze, and dreamily offers a soft, "Okay."

I pull out almost completely before carefully pushing back in.

She clenches around me, making a quiet sound at the back of her throat, a mix between pleasure and pain.

It spurs me to repeat the action a few more times until sweat dots her brow and her cheeks and chest are flushed.

"How does that feel?"

Camille licks her lips before she says, "It's a lot, but I think I like it."

I chuckle softly, stirring the hair at her temple. "You *think*? Perhaps I'm not doing a good enough job." I thrust harder, reaching a deeper spot that makes her lips part in a silent gasp.

"Do that again," she pants.

My lips twist into a grin, and I happily oblige once, twice, three more times until she's writhing under me and breathing hard. I pick up speed and angle my hips to reach another new depth, gripping her hips to hold her in place.

She tightens around me, trying to muffle the sound of her moans by pressing her lips together as I reach between us to strum her clit with deft fingers.

"I want to hear you," I purr in a smooth voice, encouraging her not to hold back.

Her heart lurches and her lips part as she stops fighting her own pleasure. She sucks in a sharp breath, clinging to me as another orgasm slams into her, making her cry out.

I roll my hips, pushing into her at a faster pace as the muscles in my stomach coil tighter. Her soft mewls of pleasure ricochet around my head, and I barrel toward my own climax, grunting deeply at its powerful arrival.

Holding still inside her as she continues pulsing, I close my eyes and try to commit this feeling of bliss to memory. Then I slowly pull out, enjoying the way she shivers in the delight of orgasmic aftershocks, then drop onto the bed beside her. Our heavy breathing the only sound in the room as we stare at the ceiling.

Pressure pours into my chest and my jaw hardens with tension as I grit my teeth against the unfamiliar and sharply overwhelming sensations flooding through me. When Camille slides her fingers through mine, my next breath gets caught halfway up my throat.

"Was that okay?" she asks in a small voice.

The tightness in my chest squeezes painfully, and I turn my face toward her, biting my tongue until I taste blood. How do I say *that was everything* to the person I'm going to destroy?

TWELVE
CAMILLE

Xander is gone when I open my eyes the next morning. My stomach sinks when I reach for him and my fingers only find cold sheets.

He left?

I move to sit up and press my lips together at the dull ache between my legs. A pulsing reminder of what we did last night. It was intense and overwhelming and amazing, all at once. I don't think I had expectations for that experience—if anything, they'd be that my anxiety would rear its ugly head. But I managed to keep it at bay, too consumed by Xander's touch and the pleasure it brought that nothing else had the chance to infiltrate my thoughts.

He'd held me after we came down from the high of being together, nuzzling and kissing my neck as I drifted to sleep with a satiated smile on my lips.

So why isn't he here this morning?

Did he leave as soon as I fell asleep?

Was it not good for him?

Does he regret it?

I blow out an agitated breath, shaking my head at myself. This isn't me—I don't want to be the person who spirals after having sex for the first time, over-analyzing every moment. I want more control over myself than that.

The bedroom door opens, and Xander slips inside, wearing yesterday's clothes. He's carrying a takeout tray with to-go cups in one hand and a paper bag in the other.

My brows lift, my pulse ticking faster as a mix of relief and excitement tangle together in my chest, making my stomach flutter.

"I was hoping to get back before you woke up," he says in a hushed voice, approaching the bed. He sets the drinks and bag on the nightstand.

I stare at him for a moment that goes on too long before I find my voice and say, "Hi."

"Hi," he echoes with a faint grin, leaning down to kiss me softly. His lips brush mine, his fingers sliding along my jaw to tip my head back. "Did you sleep okay?" he asks after pulling back and perching on the side of the bed.

I nod, pulling absently at a loose thread on the duvet. "I can't remember the last time I slept through the night. That was incredible."

"I agree with that sentiment," he says, reaching toward me and tucking my hair behind my ear, his knuckles grazing my cheek. "Are you hungry? I grabbed lattes and chocolate croissants from the café down the street."

"Mmm," I hum, "that sounds amazing." I scoot over to make room for him, and we sit with our backs against the headboard. I tuck my legs under me and face him, taking the to-go cup he hands me. "Thank you."

"Of course." He sets the paper bag between us. "How are you feeling after last night?"

I pause, the cup halfway to my lips. "A little sore, but good." My gaze drops to my lap as I contemplate my next words. "I, um... When I woke up and you weren't here, I thought you left sometime last night. Then I found myself questioning the whole thing," I admit reluctantly. "I don't want to assume anything and I can only speak to my experience, so..." I trail off, not sure what else to say.

Xander's expression is thoughtful, and he grips my knee, giving it a gentle squeeze. "There is absolutely nothing about what happened last night, from my perspective, that you need to question." His thumb glides back and forth across my skin, and I become hyper-focused on how it makes my stomach coil with a newly familiar tingling sensation. "I'm here," he continues, "and I will be so long as you want me to be."

My heart lurches, and I can't stop the grin forming on my lips. "I'm glad to hear that."

Xander shoots me a playful smirk. "Good. Now that we've established we're on the same page, let's eat."

I dive into the bag and pull out a croissant, handing it to him before grabbing another for myself. Taking a giant bite, I moan at the sweet, chocolaty flavor, and my cheeks heat when I catch the hunger in Xander's gaze. My mind immediately goes to last night, and while I'm not sure I'm physically prepared for another round so soon, parts of me definitely disagree.

He takes a bite of his croissant, keeping his eyes on me, and my pulse kicks up. "You're thinking about it, too, aren't you?" he says in a low voice.

I pull my bottom lip between my teeth, forcing a nonchalant shrug.

The corner of his mouth tugs upward. "Keep looking at me like that, and the ache between your thighs is going to be much more pronounced, *mo shíorghrá.*"

Holy shit.

His words steal the breath from my lungs, and all I can think about was how he took care of me, making sure I was okay with everything we were doing, going at my pace. As far as first times go, I have to think I was dealt a pretty damn good one.

"About last night..." I find myself saying.

He takes a drink of his latte then sets the cup on the nightstand. "Yes?"

"You know that was the first time I was ever with someone like that, but I'm thinking it wasn't yours?"

There's a split second of pain that crosses his features, but it's gone so quick, I wonder if I even saw what I thought I did. "I wish it had been," he murmurs.

I reach for him, and he meets me halfway, kissing me slowly, as if he wants nothing more than to take his time memorizing the taste of my lips. He tastes like coffee and the promise of pleasure as his mouth moves firmly against mine, making the butterflies in my stomach flutter to life.

The sound of my phone chiming from the other room breaks us apart. I groan, not wanting to get up. "I should check that. It could be work needing me to come in." I slide out of bed and pad through the apartment. I retrieve my phone from my purse on the bench near the front door where I left it when we got back last night, opening the new text.

> I spoke with your father and would like to see you to discuss something. I have time at 2 p.m. today. Can you come to HQ?

I sigh at her request, wanting to immediately deny it...or ignore her altogether, but that has never worked in my favor in the past.

> Okay, but I have work at 3 p.m. so I can't be long.

That's a lie, but I need an out that she can't argue with if I'm going to force myself to go there. It's probably going to be a lecture about not reporting the demon attack over a week ago, and I can only tolerate so much of what I'm sure will be a colorful tirade from my mother.

When I return to the bedroom, Xander is exactly where I left him, and the sight of him in my bed makes the dark cloud of dread over going to hunter headquarters a little less heavy.

"Everything okay?" he asks.

I exhale a deep breath, shrugging. "I've been summoned to HQ," I tell him, checking the time on my phone. It's a little after eleven, so I still have a few hours to overthink the meeting. *Great.* "I'm kind of surprised it took my mom this long to question me about the attack, considering it happened outside my work."

"I'm sorry." His brows tug closer, and he frowns. "I know that puts you in a difficult position with her. I'll take you there, if you want?"

A small smile blooms on my face, and I nod, plopping onto the end of the bed and reaching for another croissant. "Thank you."

We pull up out front of the commercial building downtown a few minutes before two.

Xander shifts his Camaro into park and turns toward me. "Do you want me to go in with you? I can explain what happened that night, and maybe that'll take the heat off you?"

My chest swells at his offer, and I wish there was a way I could express just how much it means to me. "I appreciate that—you have no idea how much—but I won't ask you to do that."

He reaches over and takes my hand. "You're not asking."

I exhale a soft laugh. "I think I need to do this on my own. But maybe we can hang out later and you can make me feel better about the shit show I'm undoubtedly walking into?"

Xander chuckles, lifting my hand to his lips and pressing a soft kiss across my knuckles. "It'll be my pleasure. Do you want me to wait here for you?"

I press my lips together against a smile and shake my head. He doesn't need to wait around for however long this meeting is going to take. "That's okay. Thank you, though."

"Are you sure?"

I squeeze his hand before letting him go. "I am."

"Okay," he says softly. "I'll see you soon."

I do my best to cling to the warmth his words elicit as I get out of the car and step onto the sidewalk.

After he pulls away, I stare up at the tall glass building with disdain. The memories associated with it still unsettle my stomach.

When I was in training, I was on track to become one of the most esteemed and skilled hunters affiliated with the organization. Nowadays, Harper has taken that spot and will graduate at the top of her class if she has her way—which she usually does.

I push through the revolving door and step into the marble-floored lobby. It's empty save for the middle-aged blond woman behind the mahogany reception desk.

She looks up, and when recognition passes over her features, her smile turns almost sad. Evidently, my black sheep reputation is still known around here. *Awesome.*

"Your mother is waiting for you in her office," she says softly. "I'll let her know you're on your way up."

"Thanks," I say with a nod.

"Camille," her voice stops me before I can walk away, and I turn to face her. "It's good to see you, hun."

My eyes widen slightly. "Thank you."

After walking to the bank of elevators, I get in and bite the inside of my cheek on the ride up until the skin is raw and stinging. It stops a few floors before the office, and my heart lurches when Noah enters.

His eyes snap to mine and fill with suspicion. "Didn't think I'd see you around here again."

"Nice to see you too, Noah," I remark dryly.

He narrows his blue-gray eyes, and I'm reminded of how often I found myself staring at him during training. "What are you doing here?"

"What are *you* doing here?" I cross my arms over my chest and lean against the mirrored wall. "Shouldn't you be at Ballard?"

Noah smirks. "Still keeping tabs on me, I see."

I roll my eyes. "Hardly. Harper told me you're teaching now."

"Hmm," he murmurs. "I had a meeting with Rach—your mom—and a few of the global directors this morning."

"Lucky you."

"I'm assuming you're here to see her?"

I level my gaze at him. "You know what they say about assuming things."

He all but glares at me. "Grow up, Cam." *Cam.* He's never called me by my full name since I've known him.

I used to find it endearing. It made me feel special. *Noticed.* Now it's just a reminder of the life I want left in the past.

"No, thanks. Not if 'growing up,'" I use air quotes, "means turning into someone like you."

He pulls the emergency stop before I even realize what he's doing and moves closer, towering over me by at least a foot. "What the hell is that supposed to mean?"

So dramatic.

I shrug, swallowing past the dryness in my throat at his proximity. "When was the last time you did something for fun? Or for yourself instead of for the organization? Hell, when was the last time you smiled?"

A lustful and smug smile plasters across his lips, and he lowers his voice. "Last night."

I scowl, shaking my head. "Gross." Glancing past him to the buttons on the elevator panel, I gesture to it. "Can you please turn the elevator back on now? I want to get in and out of here as fast as humanly possible."

It's his turn for the dry tone. "Of course, you do."

"What's it to you?" I snap. "Why does everyone have a stick up their ass over me not training anymore?"

He leans in close enough for me to count the freckles dusted across the bridge of his nose, slightly crooked from having been broken while on assignment. "Wasted potential," he says in a low voice.

"Screw you, Noah. I don't need this." I shove past him and slam my fist into the emergency stop button to reset it, making us continue the ascent. When the doors open on my floor, I step off without a word and don't look back.

Noah may be hot, but the guy is a complete ass. His status has seriously gone to his head. It's a shame, too, because so many hunters—in training and full-fledged—look up to him. When I was enrolled, *I* looked up to him.

His voice echoes in my mind, making the walk from the elevator to my mom's office seem far longer than it is.

Wasted potential.

I shove his words away as hard as I can and step into the office of Rachel Morgan.

She's on the phone when I walk in and close the door, so I take a seat on the couch overlooking the city until she's finished.

My eyes flit around the room. I haven't been here in years, but Mom's office is the same bright, open space, bland and not personalized whatsoever. Maybe that's how she prefers it, maybe she doesn't want any personality in her workspace. Knowing her, she probably thinks that would show weakness. God forbid her co-workers know anything about her life aside from her disappointment of a daughter quitting the team.

I can't stay much longer. The more time I spend here, the more cynical my thoughts become. It's almost like a reflex. Learned over time, I'm sure, but automatic, nonetheless.

"I saw Noah on my way up," I say when she sits beside me, because I'm not sure how else to start the conversation.

"It's been some time since you've seen him," she comments.

"Yeah," I mutter, "it was a real treat."

She frowns at the bite in my voice. "He's under a lot of pressure these days, Camille. A lot of responsibility falls on his shoulders around here and at Ballard."

I shrug, glancing around her fancy-pants office. "Good for him. He's still an asshole."

Mom sighs. "I'm sorry if he was rude to you."

"It's fine." *No, it's not.* I just want her to get to the point of why I'm here. "What's up, Mom?"

When she smiles at me, my stomach drops, and I can't help thinking there's something seriously wrong with that.

She reaches for an envelope sitting on the glass coffee table in front of the couch, holding it out to me.

I arch a brow at her, hesitantly taking it. I flip it over, but there's nothing on the outside. "What is this?"

"Open it," she instructs, trying to hide a smile.

I tear the end off, dropping it onto the coffee table, and pull out the paper that's inside. Correction—I pull out the *check* that's inside. My eyes scan it frantically, reading it over and over, certain that it's some sort of joke. The check is payable to...me—in the amount of ten thousand dollars.

"Cami—"

"What is this?" My voice cracks as my gaze flies to hers.

"It's for school."

I look back at the check. It's not one of her personal checks. In the top left corner, it has the company name the government uses to hide the hunter organization. My stomach twists into painful knots, and I'm somewhat worried I'm going to be sick. Part of me hopes I vomit all over her couch.

"This isn't your money," I say in a low voice, setting the check on the coffee table and folding my hands in my lap so she can't see how badly they're shaking.

"No," she says, pressing her lips together. "Consider it a signing bonus. With an additional check applied to your tuition each semester and reimbursement for the last two years of school as well."

Tears burn my eyes and the back of my throat goes dry. "Each semester I train," I say through my teeth.

"Camille, please. Just think—"

"Why are you doing this?" I demand, the tears gathering in my eyes making my vision blurry.

She frowns. "Because I truly believe you'll change your mind."

"Do you think I'll be happy about it if I do?" I shake my head. "Does that even matter?"

"If you accept our offer, the company will pay your full tuition. We are offering you the best of both worlds. Isn't that what you want?"

What I want.

All I want is for her and Dad to genuinely accept the life I'm building for myself and not keep trying to force me into one that is guaranteed to make me miserable.

I bite my tongue, stopping myself from sharing the last conversation I had with Danielle. The one where I promised her I'd get out of the life our mom is actively attempting to lure me back into. I'm not entirely sure what keeps me from telling her. Maybe I'm worried she won't believe me, or that she will and it'll tarnish the memory she has of Danielle. As much as I resent Mom for being so manipulative, I can't take that chance.

I lick the dryness from my lips and wipe my cheeks. "This is what you were talking to Dad about?"

She nods. "We're in agreement." Not surprising. They never had trouble getting along when it came to work. Just when it came to being in love with each other.

"In agreement about asking me to give up my life for what you want for me."

"Please try to understand, Camille. Your dad and I—" She sighs, seemingly rethinking her words. "Now, more than ever, it is so important for you to have the skills to protect yourself against the demons. This offer I've presented you with is a compromise. You'll have to put in more work to catch up, but once you graduate hunter training, you'll be scheduled part-time so you can still attend classes and get your degree. Once you work your way up the ranks and step into a position in the Senate—which we can help with as well—you'll work in association with the hunters."

My heart is pounding in my throat and my stomach is roiling. *They've mapped out my entire future.*

"What about the job I have now?" I point out. It's the least of my worries, considering my mom is giving me a near-irresistible offer—with a dozen strings attached. I need her to see how manipulative this is.

"You'd have to resign," she says simply. "Think of it this way, you won't need to be scraping together money to pay for school, so you won't need a job. We'll even provide a special training allowance for personal purchases." She sure knows how to wrap a bribe in pretty packaging.

My head is spinning so fast, there's a good chance I'd fall on my ass if I wasn't already sitting down.

"It's a lot to consider," Mom cuts in through my frantic, racing thoughts. "We're giving you one month to decide. After that, this offer will be rescinded."

I nearly scowl. Of course, she's putting a ticking clock on it. "Fine," I force out, standing on unsteady legs and hurry out of the office, leaving the envelope on the table. I speed walk to the elevator, pulling out my phone to call Xander as I do, hoping that he can come back and get me away from this place. *I should have asked him to stay.* I wish I had a getaway car right about now.

The sound of muffled but distinctly angry voices makes me pause outside a boardroom with frosted glass walls. I take a few more steps to stand near the clear glass door, and vaguely recognize a few of the higher-level hunters from my time with the organization.

Every seat around the long table is filled with hunters, including Noah, who has his back to me.

"We need to be proactive here," a middle-aged female hunter says in a firm voice.

"And we are," Noah assures her. "Scott is sending a team from New York, and more are coming from Chicago and Boston. We'll get him. I've sent around the profile, so you should all have a copy of it, including his photo. This is who we're hunting."

My brows draw closer, and just as I'm about to keep walking, someone minimizes the report on the screen to reveal a photo that makes my blood run cold.

THIRTEEN
CAMILLE

"Pick up, pick up, pick up," I chant into the phone as the line rings through to Harper's voicemail. After the beep, I say, "Call me back as soon as you get this, please. Fuck, Harper, things are really bad. I need you." I hang up and fumble with my keys to unlock our apartment. The second I'm inside with the door shut, I text her.

Call me ASAP.

SOS!

"Harper?" I call out, my voice breaking. I cross the apartment and knock on her door before poking my head inside in case she's home, but the room is empty. "Fuck," I breathe, my heart pounding in my chest. Maybe I should have gone back to my Mom's office after what I saw in that meeting instead of fleeing headquarters, but the whole thing happened so fast. It was like an out-of-body experience, and I still feel miles away.

Because in what world could Xander be a demon?

It doesn't make sense.

He *saved* me from a demon the night we met. And then another one attacked him the other night after dinner with my friends.

The pit in my stomach doubles in size, a painfully familiar pressure building in my chest as each breath becomes harder to take. Bile burns my throat as I pace the length of our living room, unshed tears stinging my eyes. A strangled sound escapes my lips when my phone starts ringing. I've never answered a call so fast.

"Cami—"

"Harper," I cry into the phone.

"Take a breath, babe. Where are you?"

"Home," I force out. "I'm at home."

"What's going on?"

"I think...oh god." I stop myself, shaking my head, as if that will make what I was about to say not true. I keep moving, walking into my bedroom and closing the door, falling back against it.

"Talk to me," she says in a calm voice.

I swallow the lump in my throat, squeezing my eyes shut, then whisper, "I think I'm falling for a demon."

The line is silent for several beats. "What are you talking about?" Her voice is low, laced with a gut-wrenching mix of concern and confusion.

Biting the inside of my cheek until I cringe at the coppery taste of blood, I let out a shaky exhale and blink my eyes open. "I'm in a relationship with Xander Kane." My gaze lifts from the floor, landing on my unmade bed...where we slept together last night. Dread coils tight in my stomach as tears pool in my eyes. *How could I be so stupid?*

"Isn't he the hunter who killed a demon outside Hallowed Grounds?"

"He's not a hunter," I force out in a low voice because I don't think I can bring myself to say, *Xander is a demon.* Nausea rolls over me like a dark wave, and I grit my teeth, willing it to recede so I don't vomit on the floor.

"Wait, what? Did *he* tell you he's a demon?"

"No," I rush to say. "I was leaving HQ after seeing my mom and stumbled upon a hunter meeting." I pull in another uneven breath. "I saw the report and his photo."

"I have so many questions."

You and me both.

"I don't have any answers." My voice is low, broken.

"Whatever report you saw hasn't been sent out yet, but I'm sure it's coming. What are you going to do?"

"I don't...Harper, I don't know. I feel like I can't breathe right now and I—" I choke on my next shaky inhale. "I've never been this scared before." I'm shaking uncontrollably, my entire body chilled to the marrow of my bones.

"Stay there. I'll be home in half an hour."

After we hang up, I leave my room and walk into the kitchen, turning on the kettle to make tea. I need to try to warm up and keep myself busy. I can't let my thoughts wander, otherwise I'm going to spiral out of control, and Harper will walk in to find me a mess on the floor.

I try to distract myself by doing the dishes but I'm fighting back tears the whole time, questioning every moment I've spent with Xander since we met two weeks ago.

It's only been two weeks.

A demon made me fall for him in two *fucking* weeks.

A painful mix of shame and embarrassment fills my face with heat, and I suddenly get the urge to throw the mug in my hand across the room.

My phone rings again, and I frown at Harper's name before I answer.

"I'm on my way, but traffic is a goddamn nightmare. I'll be there as soon as I can, but Cami, there's more you need to know. Noah just sent out the profile you saw to the entire organization. They've put out a seize and detain order on Xander."

I bite my bottom lip to stop it from trembling, but my chin continues to quiver. "Not a kill order?" I force out, gripping the edge of the counter until my knuckles are white. There are very rare instances where hunters are tasked with bringing in a particular demon instead of hunting them on sight.

"He's believed to have information on the queen."

I grit my teeth against the bile rising in my throat. "Why?"

"Because," she says in a grim tone, "Xander is her son."

I nearly drop the phone. "*What?*"

"She must've kept his existence hidden for some reason, because this is the first we're hearing of an heir to the throne. It's why we never learned about any royals aside from the queen in the first year of training. There wasn't any information about Xander until recently."

"Okay, but—" I suck in a sharp breath at the sound of knocking at the door. "Harper, someone's here."

She curses. "I forgot the maintenance guy was coming to look at the dryer exhaust. I told him to let himself in if we weren't home. Just tell him he'll have to come another time."

"Um, okay," I say, walking toward the door. "How close are you?"

"Fifteen minutes."

"Okay," I repeat, flipping the lock and opening the door.

When my eyes meet Xander's, the air is sucked from my lungs in a vicious *whoosh.*

The prince of hell is standing in my doorway, wearing the most angelic smile I've ever seen. The sight of it punches a hole through my chest.

"Cami?" Harper speaks in my ear.

"I have to call you back," I say in a monotone voice, ending the call without breaking eye contact with Xander.

"Hey," he says in a light tone as he leans against the doorframe. "I wanted to surprise you with an early dinner after your meeting. I thought we could eat, then talk about the meeting with your mom. If you want."

I open my mouth, but no sound comes out.

"Camille?" He tilts his head to the side. "Are you okay?"

"I..." My mouth is too dry to speak, but the pounding of my heart says it all. And fucking hell, *he can hear it.*

He exhales slowly and frowns. "You know."

Those two little words make my pulse spike. The panic in my chest surges when he takes a step toward me, and I reel back to slam the door shut, but his foot is there too fast, pushing it open.

Xander steps over the threshold, closing the door as I shift backward in an attempt to keep some distance between us. My back hits the wall separating the living space from the bedrooms and bathroom before I get very far, and my stomach tightens. *I need to get out of here.*

He's in front of me in the time it takes me to blink, his hands pressed against the wall on either side of me. His wrists brush my shoulders as alarm bells blare in my temples.

I swallow hard and force out, "Tell me it's not true."

Lie to me, I want to say. *Let's pretend you're not evil and go back to how things were before I knew you were a demon.*

He leans in close enough that his breath skates across my cheek, and I have to fight a shudder. "Really, Camille?" He sounds disappointed.

I shake my head, my jaw clenching until a dull ache pounds in my temples. "I don't...How is this even... *Why?*"

He wets his lips. "Why?" he echoes with a short, quiet laugh. "Does it really matter?"

Before I know what's happening, my palm cracks against his cheek, sending sharp pain through my hand.

Xander has the decency to look surprised, but he blinks it away in an instant. "Not bad," he comments, "but you'll have to do better than that."

Angry tears fill my eyes as I try to shove him back.

He doesn't budge.

"Get out," I growl.

"So that's a 'no' to dinner?" he checks, and I shoot him a dark look. "Hmm. That's too bad. I was hoping you and I could have a little chat."

"There's a team of hunters on their way here right now." *Every hunter in the organization is hunting you.* I have no idea what's keeping me from telling him that. Maybe he already knows. Either way, I can't make the words form.

His lips twitch, and he finally retreats a step. "Is that so?"

Not exactly. Harper is, but she'll most likely be alone. She's a damn good hunter, but I'm not sure even *she's* skilled enough to take on Xander by herself.

"You need to leave," I say in a low voice.

"I should take you with me. Those hunters are a dangerous bunch. I don't want you getting hurt." His voice is laced with amusement, giving me the itch to slap him again.

This whole thing is a game to him.

"Who are you?" I whisper before I can stop myself, because I can't help feeling as if I'm looking at a stranger.

He glances down briefly before closing the distance between us once more. With a sigh, he murmurs, "You need me to say it?" When I don't respond, his fingers catch my chin, and he tilts my face up to meet his gaze. "I'm Xander Kane, Prince of Hell." His eyes flash black, and I choke on the dryness in my throat.

Demons' eyes turn black for a few reasons. They're hungry, angry, or territorial. At this moment, I don't want to know which has Xander's eyes looking like pools of darkness.

Something in me snaps, and I tap into what little training I can remember from my time with the hunter organization. Ducking under Xander's arm, I put some distance between us so I can take a few breaths—and so I'm no longer trapped.

He turns around to follow my movement and takes in my stance with a sigh. His eyes return to the slate gray I'm used to, and there's a flicker of regret there. I almost miss it, it's gone so quickly. "I don't want to fight you, Camille."

"And I don't believe you." I advance with my fists raised and strike out, aiming for his jaw.

He deflects my attack with an infuriating amount of ease, sidestepping my blow. It pushes me to fight harder, and my muscles protest as I pivot swiftly, transitioning into a series of kicks and punches, aiming for any opening I can find.

But he has demonic strength and speed on his side. He anticipates every move I make, though that doesn't stop me from trying. His mouth is set in a tight line, his eyes focused on me, and the shimmer of sadness there catches me off guard a second too long. He moves faster than my eyes can track, and the next thing I know, he has me pressed against the wall again, my wrists secured in one of his hands and pinned above my head. "Please, Camille—"

The soft tone of his voice urges me to immediately fight his grip, using every ounce of strength I have, trying to break free. It's useless. There isn't a world where my extremely limited abilities are any match for a high-level demon.

It's painfully clear how my lack of continued hunter training is hurting me in this situation. And I hate how my mother's voice echoes in my head, reminding me of the hunters' offer to re-enroll.

The universe sure has a wicked sense of humor...

"Stop fighting me." Xander's voice is low in my ear, shooting a shiver down my spine.

My jaw clenches, and I continue tugging on my wrists, but he doesn't let go. "Get away from me," I seethe, venom dripping from each word.

"But you wanted me to explain myself, didn't you?" He leans back enough to meet my gaze and uses his free hand to tuck a rogue bit of hair behind my ear, his knuckles grazing my cheek as my chest rises and falls rapidly.

Before I can form a response, the door flies open, smacking against the wall as Harper charges inside and slams it shut.

Xander glances over his shoulder at my best friend, and frees me from his grasp, turning to face her. "Harper, I presume," he drawls. "It's nice to meet you."

"*You* don't talk," she snaps, wearing an expression sharp enough to cut glass aimed at him.

"Where's the rest of the cavalry?" He takes a step toward her, and I move without thinking, grabbing his wrist to pull him back, to keep him away from my friend.

He glances down at where my fingers are wrapped around his wrist, white at the knuckles, as if I'm holding on for dear life. I am—*Harper's.*

She'll attack him without blinking, without considering the consequences of doing so.

"Get away from her," she growls, inching closer.

His gaze shifts back to her. "Or what?" he taunts. "What are you going to do, little hunter?"

"Please. I'll kick your ass straight out that door." Her eyes narrow. "I'll enjoy it, too."

I move in front of Xander, putting my back to him. Just another thing to add to the list of stupid things I've done. "Harper, please," I urge her with wide eyes.

This situation needs to deescalate before someone snaps.

"Cami, you need to move. I have a direct order."

Xander laughs behind me, which doesn't help the murderous look on Harper's face.

"I'm asking you to stand down," I all but whisper.

She turns her anger on me. "Are you insane?"

"I don't want you to get hurt."

She barks out a laugh. "I've been training a long ass time for a moment like this."

"Yeah, and I'd rather it not be your last," I say through my teeth and tense when I feel the heat of Xander's body closer at my back.

"No one needs to get hurt," he says in a level tone.

"It's a little late for that," I mutter, blinking away the sting of tears in my eyes.

"Cami, I'm not going to ask again." Harper's voice is firm. She's not going to let up.

I step closer to her with my heart in my throat. "Whatever you have planned, it's not going to work." I lower my voice, and my bottom lip trembles. "He's the prince of hell. You're not going up against one of the most powerful demons in existence."

Her eyes are wide, still burning with rage. "I'm sure as shit not going to leave you *alone* with him."

I close my eyes, my hands balling into fists at my sides. "In the hall," I say before grabbing her hand and dragging her out the door, leaving Xander inside.

He makes no move to stop us, and everything in me is screaming to run. Run fast and far, but demons love nothing more than the chase.

We wouldn't get far, and I won't put Harper in danger.

He must know that. Otherwise, I doubt he would let us leave. I think. I don't know anything for sure—not anymore.

She barely waits for the door to close between us and him before jumping in. "Do you understand what's happening right now or are you in shock? Because—"

"I need answers."

"What if he lies? Are you expecting him to say something that'll make you feel better?"

"No," I answer honestly, "but I need to know why."

"I don't know for sure, but I have a pretty good idea why. And it starts and ends with your parents."

The color drains from my face.

Son of a bitch.

"He's using me to get to them," I breathe.

"That's all I can come up with."

I glance over my shoulder at the closed door. "I want to hear him say it." I turn back to her. "You can stay here—*right* here—but I'm going back in there."

He's already had plenty of time to kill me if that's what he wanted to do. But he obviously needs me for something. So long as that remains true, he'll keep me alive. The notion sours my stomach, but it gives me enough courage to face him again.

Harper opens her mouth as if she's about to protest, but then pauses. "Fine," she finally says, "but if I think for a second something's gone wrong, I'm coming in."

"Deal." Turning to open the door, I pause when Harper says my name.

"Be careful. Please."

Exhaling a heavy breath, I take a second before walking back inside, closing the door behind me.

Xander is leaning on the wall he held me against only minutes ago.

I rip the bandaid off. "What's your endgame here? Did you just want to screw with me because of who my parents are?"

He flicks his tongue over his bottom lip, and I hate that I track the movement. "Are you scared of me because of who my mother is?"

I cross my arms. "I'm not scared of you." My voice has taken on a defiant tone now, but it's nothing but false bravado.

The subtle twitch of his lips that used to make my stomach flip now makes me want to cry. "You want to try that again with a little more force? I don't quite believe it."

I swallow hard. "What do you want with me, Xander?"

He pushes away from the wall, closing the space between us, and my back stiffens. "It's not about what *I* want. It never was. Trust me, if it was, this situation would be very different."

My brows scrunch up, and a stupid flicker of hope ignites in my chest. "What does that mean?"

"You'd like to know why I'm here? Why that demon attacked you the night we met?"

His words snuff out any hope I was clinging to as bile rises in my throat. Everything is connected. *Of course, it is.* I shouldn't be surprised. But hearing him say it out loud...I'm not sure I can handle this.

"Part of your evil plan, I'm guessing?" I mutter, forcing myself to hold his gaze.

"To put it simply."

I shake my head and bite out, "Fine. You're evil. Good for you. I still don't understand why you pretended to show interest in me, to get close to me. What exactly did it accomplish?" My voice sharpens. "Was I just a means for entertainment? Is your life really that dull?" I want to switch off everything I've ever felt for him, forget every moment we've shared, so maybe this won't hurt so damn much.

He offers a bitter chuckle. "It truly has nothing to do with my entertainment." His eyes meet mine. "You have information she wants."

My pulse spikes as my stomach drops—it's a dizzying mix of responses that makes me clench my jaw. "What are you talking about?" I quickly deduce that the *she* he's referring to is the queen of hell, otherwise known as his mother, but everything else remains a giant, twisted question mark.

"Your parents are in charge of the organization that poses a risk to my kind."

"No," I interject, "*your* kind poses a risk to humans. You think creating nightmares and making people hallucinate their worst fears—just so you can *feed* on them—isn't heinous?"

Xander doesn't answer. He just stands there looking at me like I'm some kind of curiosity to him.

My breathing falters. "Did you ever feed on me?" I can't help but think of the night on the ferris wheel when I was having a panic attack, and he...he helped me through it.

He doesn't miss a beat. "No."

I stare at him for too long without speaking. The doubt in my gut feels like a brick, but I don't have much of a choice but to believe him. "Why not?" I push. What am I expecting him to say? *Because you mean something to me. Because I could never bring myself to hurt you like that.* Wishful thinking is an unforgiving bitch. Xander doesn't care about me—he probably never did.

Confusion passes over his face. "Because that's not what you're meant for."

Hurt slices through my chest like shards of glass, the burn of betrayal not far behind. "Then what, Xander?" I demand. "Tell me! What am I *'meant* for'?"

"You'll find out when Lucia wants you to know."

I shake my head. "That's not an answer."

He shrugs. "It is, just not the one you want."

"I'm not going to help her do whatever she thinks I am."

His expression remains impassive but there's a tinge of something I could almost mistake as disappointment when he says, "You will."

"Go to hell," I growl, unable to hide the tears swimming in my eyes.

He leans in before I can turn my face away and brushes his lips across my cheek. "Come with me," he murmurs.

I don't give myself a moment to consider what he could possibly even mean by that before I jerk away. When I come to the conclusion he isn't going to give me the answers I'm looking for, I say, "Leave."

He shifts back, giving me room to breathe. "Take some time. Think carefully about what I've said." Xander walks toward the door and reaches for the handle, then turns back at the last second. "I don't need to tell you if you or your hunter friend try anything, there will be consequences," he says in a level tone and then he walks out the door without looking back.

Seconds later, Harper flies through the door. "What the actual hell?"

I pause, letting out a breath. "Pretty much that."

A vicious scowl vibrates through her. "I swear to everything unholy, I'm going to—"

"Do nothing," I cut in, panic gripping my tone as I replay Xander's thinly veiled threat over and over in my head. "We can't do anything. Not right now. It's too dangerous, and I wouldn't be able to live with myself if you got hurt."

"I'm not going to get hurt," she insists. "We need to report this to HQ immediately. There's an organization-wide hunt for this son of a bitch. We're going to catch him, and he's going to pay—"

"Harper, *please*," I beg, my voice cracking as my eyes burn and panic clamps down on my chest, making it hard to breathe.

Harper opens her mouth but hesitates, then says, "Okay." She frowns, closing the door, and starts toward me. "I'm so sorry, Cami. Are you...?"

Pressing my lips together while tears fill my eyes, I shake my head.

I'm the farthest thing from okay.

She closes the distance between us and throws her arms around me as I shatter.

FOURTEEN
CAMILLE

I don't know how long Harper holds me, but eventually the tears stop falling long enough for her to guide me into the bathroom and turn on the shower. She waits right outside the door and wraps her arm around me when I come out in a bathrobe.

We sit on the end of my bed for a few minutes before Harper sighs softly. "I don't know where to start," she admits.

I nod, my eyes burning with exhaustion from crying. Swallowing, I clear my throat before I say, "He tricked me into thinking he was a hunter the night we met."

"And he killed one of his own to sell the story," she says in a grave tone, and my pulse kicks up.

My head is racing so fast, I drop my face into my hands, squeezing my eyes shut as I will the dizziness to pass. I have to consider the attack after dinner with Phoebe and Grayson was also orchestrated by Xander. But why would that demon sacrifice herself?

"I know you're worried about what's going to happen now, but I think that's even more reason to report everything that's happened since that night."

I press the heels of my palms against my eyes. "Harper, please. I'm not ready for the repercussions of that." I sit up and turn toward her. "I know everything will come to light eventually. It has to. But I can't talk about this yet. Not with my parents." The thought of them finding out that their daughter was seduced by the prince of hell...It fills my chest with dark, heavy tendrils of shame. I can already picture the look of disappointment I'm bound to get from my mother. And it brings a fresh batch of tears to my eyes when I can't decide how my dad is going to react.

Harper offers me a thoughtful look. "I understand. And I want to give you as much time as you need to figure this out, but there's so much at stake here, especially when we don't know what he and the queen are planning. I'll give you a week, but after that, you have to tell Rachel and Scott. And I'll go with you to HQ to make the report if you think that'll help. I'll do whatever I can to make this easier for you." She takes my hand and squeezes it, lowering her voice. "But if Xander is caught before then, I'll have to tell the organization what I know."

I nod, struggling to swallow past the lump in my throat. I understand I'm asking a lot of Harper—putting her in a difficult position to disregard protocols and orders. Even in this state, none of that is lost on me. "Thank you," I finally say.

She sighs, pulling me into a tight hug. "Try to get some sleep. We can talk more tomorrow."

After she leaves my room, I change into sweatpants and a hoodie, hoping to combat the chill in my bones. The shower helped some, but when I get under the blankets and curl onto my side, I can't stop shivering. So much so, my teeth are chattering. I try to slow my breathing, counting the seconds of each inhale and exhale, but I can't get to a level of relaxed enough to fall asleep.

Some time later, I roll onto my back and stare at the ceiling above my bed for what feels like an eternity. I finally drift off for maybe forty-five minutes before I open my eyes again and can't get back to sleep.

I'm emotionally and mentally exhausted, but physically I'm wired. My thoughts are too loud, too fast, too many, and I can't escape them as desperately as I want to.

I toss and turn for the next several hours until the sun rises outside the window and my alarm chirps from the other side of my room at seven. I grumble in response and haul myself up to turn it off.

There's no chance I'm going to class today.

I crawl back into bed, tugging the blankets up around me, and go back to staring at the ceiling.

Harper left for training around six, and I pretended to be asleep when she knocked on my door and poked her head in to check on me. Call it avoidance, but I didn't have the emotional capacity to talk any more about what happened last night.

I must doze off again, because it's almost noon when I blink my eyes open next and reach around to find my phone. I open my texts to find one from Phoebe wondering why I'm not in class.

I type out a short message back and hit send.

> I have the flu. Will probably be out all week.

Her reply comes a minute later.

> Oh no! I'm so sorry. Can I bring you anything?

I feel bad for lying, especially when her first response is to offer help, but the thought of seeing anyone right now makes my stomach churn.

> Thanks, Pheebs. I'm okay.

After I send that message, I type one to the owner of Hallowed Grounds, using the same excuse to call out of work. Without waiting for a response, I turn off my phone, closing it in the drawer of my nightstand before rolling over and curling into myself.

Over the next week, I barely leave my bed. I haven't heard from Xander since he left, but I haven't stopped thinking about him. Replaying our last encounter on a loop in my head until my eyes are burning with tears and my stomach is clenched so tightly it hurts.

If it weren't for Harper, I likely wouldn't eat or drink anything, either. She even dragged me out of the burrow of pillows and blankets to force me to shower. When she's not training, she's with me, going so far as to skip class herself to make sure I'm okay.

But when I woke up this morning, I didn't let myself even consider staying in bed any longer. I got up, took a shower, and dressed for work.

Standing in front of the bathroom mirror, I frown at my expression. I may not have had the flu, but I look pretty wrecked. After applying makeup, it's a little better. It doesn't really matter—I can't skip work anymore. I still need to make money to pay for school, and the *offer* from my mother isn't something I'm actually considering, so this is what I have to do. Pretend my life didn't just implode and serve people coffee all day.

I arrive for my shift a few minutes early and slip into the back office to hang up my jacket and bag. The owner is sitting behind the old desk, squinting at her computer screen.

"Hey, Marion. How are you?"

She looks up and smiles warmly. "Cami, sweetheart. I hope you're feeling better. Can I speak with you quickly before your shift starts?"

My pulse ticks faster as unease trickles in. "Uh, sure," I tell her, closing the door, then sit in the chair across from her.

"I let the rest of the staff know last week that I've decided to retire."

"Oh, wow. That's...um, congratulations." I'm not sure what else to say.

She smiles. "Thank you. I'm looking forward to spending time with my grandchildren."

I nod. "So are you selling the café?"

"I considered that, but after speaking with my children about it, we decided it was best to close. Business hasn't been doing very well for some time now and the process of selling a business isn't easy. Quite frankly, I'm too old to deal with all of that. Shutting things down is what I need to do."

"I understand," I say, trying to mask my disappointment. "When are you closing?"

"The end of the month. That said, I'm letting the majority of the staff go now, which unfortunately includes you after your shift today. I'm very sorry, Cami." She tries to offer me another smile, but it appears forced paired with the sadness in her eyes.

"I understand," I say automatically and stand to walk out for my shift.

As much as I needed the distraction of work to keep my mind off the situation with Xander, now that I'm officially unemployed, I can't stop my thoughts from drifting back to my last conversation with my mom. The last thing I want to do is consider re-enrolling at the academy. The life of a demon hunter is not what I want. But I hate how tempting the offer is feeling right now.

No. I'll start job searching when I get home and find something that works on my terms. This is a minor setback. I will figure things out. *I have to.* I won't let them win—not Xander and Lucia, or the organization.

At the end of my shift, I hang up my apron and shrug on my jacket before shouldering my bag, waving to the barista on my way out the front door. The weather has cooled down—given it's the first week of October, it's to be expected. I zip up my jacket, slide my hands into the pockets, and walk down the sidewalk toward the parking garage where I left my car. I cross the street, then stop abruptly when someone cuts into my path.

"You look like a woman on a mission," an accented male voice drawls, and I get a subtle whiff of warm cinnamon.

Immediately I step back, pulling my hands out of my pockets, and when my eyes meet vibrant green ones, they narrow. Because there isn't a chance Xander's pink-haired friend being here right now is a coincidence. Which brings me to the conclusion that Blake is likely a demon, too. Considering it's broad daylight and there are clusters of people around, I'm less concerned, but still uneasy when it comes to his motives.

He flashes a dazzling smile, cocking his head to the side as he regards me. Today he's wearing a lime green V-neck under a black leather jacket, paired with white jeans and black combat boots. "Hello, love."

"What do you want, Blake?" I ask in a careful tone, stepping to the side to let a few people pass us as I give him a once-over. I can't figure out this guy's style.

His smile widens. "You remember me. I'm touched." He rocks back on his heels, shoving his hands into his pockets.

"And I'm not going to stand here and talk to you."

Blake's smile morphs into a pout. "Mean. What did I ever do to you?"

I arch a brow, crossing my arms over my chest. "You're here, I'm going to say stalking me, so I think that's plenty to warrant my response."

He blinks at me, his lips twisting into a faint smirk. "Hmm. A bit presumptuous of you, don't you think?"

"Okay," I say, my heart still beating faster than normal, "please feel free to correct me, then. Better yet, turn and walk the other way, and we can both forget this interaction even happened."

"Tell me, if you hadn't found out Xander's a big, scary demon, would you still be so prickly toward me?"

My gaze whips around, checking our surroundings, which is something Blake is clearly not concerned about. *His arrogance knows no bounds.* "I guess that depends on if you're one as well." This whole conversation is making my temples ache, threatening a headache from the conversational ping pong. I'd like nothing more than to walk away from him. But something tells me Blake would follow, and the last thing I need is to get stuck in a parking garage alone with a demon.

He chuckles, his gaze glimmering with amusement before his eyes flash black.

I don't flinch, expecting the display of darkness this time.

Cocking his head to one side, he asks, "Are we pretending you don't already know?"

"No," I say in a level tone, ready to wrap up this encounter. "So, I'll ask again. What do you want, Blake?"

His expression turns serious, though his eyes return to normal. "Xander asked me to pay you a visit to let you know he wants to see you, but he's being forced to keep a low profile. You know, with your hunter friends paying him so much attention at the moment." His eyes narrow slightly, making me stand taller as he continues, "You likely won't hear from him for a while. At least until the hunters inevitably give up their pathetic little search. Our guy is rather popular right now." Despite his dark expression, his tone is light, humorous even, and it makes me grit my teeth.

Perhaps that has more to do with the conflicting emotions filling my chest, because I should be *relieved* at having space from Xander. And yet... "*Your* guy," I mutter cooly.

Blake whistles softly, his brows shooting up his forehead. "If you're breaking up with him, that is *not* a message I'm passing along. Xander is very much the type to kill the messenger." Then he adds with a wink, "Blame his demon side."

I bite the inside of my cheek, glaring at him as my stomach flips at his words. I can't even think about it right now, if I'm being honest, because that is a can of worms I'm not prepared to deal with. So, instead of addressing the status of my relationship with Xander, because that's not something I can talk about, I ask, "Aren't you his best friend?"

He shrugs, keeping his hands in his pockets. "Best friend, confidant, personal guard."

"Right. Because he has a bodyguard," I say almost to myself, shaking my head at how ridiculous it sounds as I let my arms fall back to my sides.

"Xander is the prince of hell—he's royalty in our world, love. Of course he has a guard." He says it so matter-of-factly, but the weight of his words settles heavily on my chest.

"So, that's what you want to do with your life? Risk it again and again to protect someone else?"

Blake steps closer, lowering his voice. "I wouldn't be alive if it wasn't for Xander. He saved my life years ago, took me in and gave me a home, and I will forever be in his debt. So, yes. Happily."

My eyes widen before I can get a grip on my composure, and my feet turn into blocks too heavy to move, cementing me in place. I open my mouth to respond, but nothing comes out, because what am I supposed to say to that?

He steps back, that easy smile fully in place once more. "He'll be in touch when he can."

"Okay." The word falls from my lips before I can clamp my mouth shut. Shame burns in my cheeks. I don't want him thinking I *want* to hear from Xander, especially if Blake is going to tell *him* that. I shouldn't want to see Xander, but there's still a part of me that feels a pull to him. It doesn't make a lick of sense—I recognize how messed up it is—but I can't seem to shake it no matter how hard I try.

"Is there something you'd like me to tell him?" Blake asks.

I shake my head, not trusting myself to speak.

He lifts his chin, his eyes dancing across my face as he studies my expression. "Are you sure about that?"

"Yes." *No.*

"Hmm, okay then. Follow up question, just for funsies. Did you know demons have exceptional hearing? That I can hear the uptick of your pulse when you lie?"

My eyes narrow, and I swallow past the dryness in my throat. "This conversation is over." I sidestep him and, by some miracle, he doesn't stop me from walking away.

FIFTEEN
XANDER

There are few places I'm able to feel a semblance of peace. My apartment *used* to be one of them. I mentally cross it off the list when I step out of my bedroom and find my mother sitting at my kitchen counter. The moment I opened my eyes, I knew she was here. I sensed it like a pit in my stomach before the smell of the coffee she's drinking even registered in my nose.

She has her back to me and doesn't acknowledge me yet.

I cross the living room toward the kitchen, but I pause at the violently graphic images that flash across my eyes. The largest, sharpest knife from the butcher block on my counter, slashed across her delicate, porcelain throat. Blood as black as her eyes spilling down the front of her deep purple blouse.

"Good morning, son." Her regal yet melodic voice snaps my focus back to reality as I keep moving.

"Is it?" I ask, stopping beside her to press a chaste kiss to her cheek before I move around the counter into the kitchen. Her smoky lavender scent fills my senses, and I clench my jaw, unable to escape it. A smell that should bring me comfort—coming from my mother and only parent—turns my stomach.

"Hmm. You seem to have gotten yourself into quite the predicament."

I cross my arms, leaning against the counter opposite the island where she's perched. "So that's why you're sitting in my kitchen, drinking my coffee?"

She clicks her black painted nails against the side of her mug. "I am here, Xander, because you and Blake have been neglecting your communications." She turns her head enough to glance toward the living room. "And where is he now?"

I shrug. "I don't keep a leash on him, mother. He comes and goes as he pleases, and I've told you before he doesn't live here."

She huffs out an indignant sigh as she faces me again. "That will not do. Your name is on the top of every hunter hit list in the state, if not the country. As heir to my throne, you must have protection."

A muscle ticks along my jaw, and I shove my thoughts toward the memory of Camille sitting in the spot my mother is currently occupying. That experience—cooking dinner for her, watching her fall asleep during the movie, simply being around her—was one of the best of my existence. Topped only by the night we shared in her bed.

"Mother—" I start.

"I will have Francesca take over if Blake cannot perform his duties."

I bite back a growl. There's not a chance she's stepping foot in my apartment. "Fine. I'll talk to him and let him know he needs to be here to wipe my ass."

"Enough," she snaps. "Do not forget who you are speaking to."

How fucking could I? I swallow the bile in my throat and meet her sharp blue gaze. I can't remember the last time she looked at me with even a hint of softness or care. Perhaps she never has. "My apologies," I force out.

She nods, taking a sip of her coffee. "Now, we must discuss what we are going to do about that pesky little human."

My eyes narrow a fraction as the hair on the back of my neck stands straight. "I'm doing what you want," I say carefully.

"Not fast enough. And now that she knows who you really are, things need to progress quickly. I am moving up the timeline."

I pinch the bridge of my nose, closing my eyes and exhaling a sigh. "How do you expect to do that when the last interaction I had with her, she had just found out about me and my relation to you?" I don't think I'll ever get the look on her face out of my head. The raw disbelief and hurt that she felt. It made me sick, but it also called to the darkness inside me, who ate up every second of Camille's misery like sweet candy.

Lucia offers an icy smile. "Figure it out, Xander. Use that charm of yours and do what needs to be done."

I nod stiffly, because even if I hate it in the marrow of my bones, I *will* do what's necessary. It's what I've told myself since the night Lucia shared her plan of using the hunters' daughter to infiltrate the organization. Camille has always been a means to an end—the end of me being tortured by the queen of hell simply for existing with a soul.

It doesn't matter that I'll be ruining Camille. Taking everything she gave me and pretending to care for her.

Pretending? The twisted, demonic part of me cackles with amusement at what it perceives as a weak, pathetic lie. And there's not a thing I can do to defend myself, because it's right. At some point, whatever I was doing with Camille wasn't an act anymore. At least, not all of it. But it doesn't matter. I'll see this plan through and then I'll escape my mother's clutches forever. I'll flee to the other side of the world if it means I'll be free of the monster who raised me.

Lucia stands, pinning me with one last look. "Go to her. You are running out of time, and my patience wears thin. You know the plan you agreed to."

"I'm well aware," I say firmly.

She looks as if she might say more, like hurl an insult my way or remind me of what a disappointment I am, but instead, she presses her lips together, inclining her head in a subtle nod. "Keep me apprised of all developments. I expect daily updates from here on out."

I rake my fingers through my hair, still a mess from sleep, and exhale a sigh. "Is that entirely necessary?"

"Are you questioning me?"

She'll leave faster if you're more agreeable.

"Of course not," I say in a forced but level tone.

"Good." Between one moment and the next, her form shifts, fading into black smoke. It's something only the oldest, most powerful demons can do. Lucia disappears from my sight in a matter of seconds, leaving me with a tightness in my chest and a storm of nausea in my stomach.

It takes all morning for those feelings to pass. Instead of going for a run along the pier, I settle for the privacy of my building's gym, where I'm less likely to run into a hunter. Considering only three people know where I live, and all of the real estate documentation for this place is under a different name, I'm relatively unconcerned about being tracked here. As angry and hurt as Camille is, it's been a week and my door hasn't been broken down by an army of hunters, so I think it's safe to say she hasn't told her parents about us.

I can't imagine the secrecy going over well with that hunter friend of hers. Harper Gilbert is an interesting complication I can't say I was entirely prepared for. Of course, I knew Camille lived with her, and her association with the hunter organization, but the connection I witnessed between them last week caught me off guard. Mostly by its similarity to what I have with Blake. I have no doubt those girls would kill and die for each other.

Turning up the speed on the treadmill, I sprint until my legs ache, begging for a break. And then I keep going. I don't decrease the speed until I'm panting and my chest feels as if it's about to explode from physical exertion. It's a pleasant change in the pain I've been feeling there as of late.

I gulp down half my water bottle as the TV on the wall catches my attention. The sound is muted, but it's a news broadcast about the increase in what the local police have told the media are "gang-related" attacks.

Demon attacks have never been this rampant in my lifetime. The hunters can't recruit trainees as fast as demons seem to be pouring into the streets, wreaking havoc for the hell of it. Most are coming out of hiding from remote places across the world, but some of the most dangerous are coming from the deepest, darkest pits of hell. Places I never ventured to during my time there growing up. Creatures even I wouldn't want to run into. A human wouldn't stand a chance against the high-level demons. It makes me believe Lucia's plan to take down the organization and hold power over the humans could work.

I turn away from the TV and cross the quiet room toward the rack of weights against a mirrored wall. Picking the bench at the far end of the row, I lift weights until my arms burn, my muscles trembling with the same exhaustion in my legs. I've been in the gym for close to two hours by the time I pull out my phone and notice the time.

There's also a series of texts from Blake. The first one addressing the message I sent him after Lucia left earlier.

> Geez. Queenie is getting a bit paranoid.

> What the fuck does she mean 'daily updates'? That's all you, mate. Your mother scares the shit out of me.

> Wait. If we live together, how am I supposed to bring home dates?

I roll my eyes, downing the rest of my water before typing a response.

> That would require you to go on dates, so it's really a non-issue.

Prick.

You set yourself up for that one.

I drag myself to the elevator and ride back up to my apartment, taking the longest shower I've had in a long time. When I get out and change into jeans and a T-shirt, there's another message.

I guess I'll pack my shit and bring it over later.

There's an extra key in the safe I keep at the bar. Don't lose it.

Fine, fine. What's the combo? 666?

Your humor is lackluster today.

Please. I'm fucking hilarious.

I don't plan to respond, but then Blake sends another text.

I paid a visit to your human, as requested.

The sudden unease in my gut makes my brows knit. It's too risky for me to go to Camille right now, but that hasn't stopped me from thinking about her.

How did it go?

I like her, mate. She's very fiery.

I roll my eyes.

What happened?

We had a quick chat. I let her know you'd be in touch when you can, and while she seemed like she wanted to say more, her response was 'okay.'

I only realize I've been clenching my jaw when my temples start throbbing. I type out another message, intending to end the conversation.

Thanks for the update. See you later.

A minute later, my phone buzzes with another message. I sigh.

I'm hanging with Fran and a few others. They want you to come out with us tonight, but I told them you were incognito until further notice.

Blake is the only one who calls Francesca that, and she hates him for it. Which begs the question of why they're hanging out, but I don't bother asking. The three of us grew up together in hell before Lucia decided I needed to spend time among humans. Her forcing me to come to earth and attend high school surrounded by them was its own form of hell.

Blake came too, and we didn't see Francesca for almost five years. When she joined us topside, she told me that my mother had picked her to be my wife.

The whole thing was utterly ridiculous.

Francesca's father has been part of Lucia's inner circle for many years. He's one of the few demons she trusts, and he earned it through decades of loyalty, which extended to his daughter—my betrothed, apparently.

I couldn't see myself falling in love with Francesca, not that something as trivial as human emotions mattered in that scenario. We were close enough at one point that we'd sleep together when either or both of us were lonely. But her entire attitude toward me shifted once she discovered the power she'd gain if we wed. I've been clear from the moment I learned of our supposed engagement that we would never marry, but she refuses to give up, still hoping I'll change my mind.

Perhaps she'd change her mind if she knew I wanted nothing to do with the throne she so badly craves to sit upon.

Perhaps she could take my place.

I drop onto the couch, shooting a quick response to Blake.

Have fun. Don't stay out too late.

His response comes in the form of a group selfie at his bar where, if I had to bet, they'll spend the afternoon drinking before they hit the streets to hunt tonight. While one side of me longs to join them, practically salivates at the thought, the other side is relieved I have an excuse to stay holed up in my apartment.

That said, part of me feels a bit like a prisoner as I lay on my couch, scrolling through my phone until I end up opening the last text conversation I had with Camille. I find myself wondering what she's doing now. Thinking about what she did when I left her apartment last week.

I groan to the empty room, tossing my phone on the coffee table and covering my eyes with my arm.

How the fuck am I supposed to convince her to betray everyone she loves? And for what?

But if she doesn't, there won't be enough hunters to protect her from Lucia's wrath.

The thought of losing Camille wasn't an outcome I expected to consider. It certainly wasn't something I was prepared to *feel* something over. But I can't escape the way it squeezes the air out of my lungs, making the walls of my apartment seem so much smaller.

This...*this* is what fear must feel like.

SIXTEEN
CAMILLE

I spend the entire morning conflicted about going to Adrianna's lake house. At the last minute, I throw clothes and toiletries into a duffle bag, walk out the door, and get into my car. She's been excited about having everyone at her family's lake house since the beginning of the semester, and I don't want to let her down. Plus it'll be a good distraction and a much needed break from the city.

I've been here before in years past, but it's been awhile, and I always seem to forget how stunning it is. Only a few hours outside of the city, it's hard to believe something so secluded and peaceful exists, and that it looks so modern. It's not one of those creepy cabins in the woods out of a horror movie. This place is a multilevel, borderline resort home, with a view of the lake from almost every window.

The front door opens, and Adrianna comes out and jogs over to me, the gravel crunching under her sandals. "Cami," she shouts with a wide grin, throwing her arms around me in a tight hug. "Phoebe told me you were sick, so I wasn't sure you were coming. I'm so happy you're here!"

"Me, too." I hug her back before we break apart. "This place is in-sane," I tell her, as if she can't see that herself.

She laughs. "You say that every time we're here."

I shoulder my duffle bag as we walk toward the house. "Yeah, and it's true every time." I shake my head at the height of this place now that we're standing at the base of it.

"Tell you what," she says, pushing the door open and stepping inside, "you can have the primary suite this weekend."

My eyes practically bug out of my face as I follow her into the foyer. "Are you serious?"

She shrugs. "Sure. I've never stayed in it and I'd rather sleep in my usual room, anyway. It's all yours."

"Wouldn't it make more sense to give it to Grayson and Phoebe?" I need to shut up. She's offering me the nicest room in this place, and I'm over here questioning it, basically trying to hand it to someone else.

She arches a brow at me, clearly thinking I'm insane. "Do you *want* me to give it to Grayson and Phoebe?"

"No way," I rush to say, and she snorts. "Thanks, Adrianna."

"Of course," she says with a grin. "Where's Xander? Phoebe thought he'd be driving with you."

My stomach sinks, and I shake my head, struggling to find my words all of a sudden. "He, uh, couldn't come," I finally manage to force out.

Adrianna frowns, leaning in the doorway between the hallway and family room. "That's too bad. We'll still have an epic weekend, though."

I force a smile and nod before I make my way up the winding staircase to the second level and pad down the hardwood hallway until I reach the set of double doors at the end. Feeling dramatic, I open both at the same time in a flourish and enter the room. My eyes go wide at how big it is. I've been here a dozen or so times, but I've never been inside this room before. I shut the doors behind me, and my eyes sweep the room. They go from the four-poster king bed to a sitting area complete with black leather couches, a glass coffee table, and a wood-burning fireplace. Leaving my things mostly unpacked, I walk toward the wall of windows and push the drapes open, sucking in a breath at the view of the water, the reflection of the sun making it sparkle.

"Holy crap," I mutter to the empty room. Walking over to the bed, I set my bag on the end of it and place my phone on the nightstand, which matches the table on the other side.

I grab my toiletry bag and step into the en suite bathroom. Everything is pristine, white marble and sparkling, especially the grand chandelier hanging from the ceiling. There's a pleasant lavender scent coming from...I don't even know where and a fully stocked cabinet beside the toilet with everything you could ever think to need, from lotions and soaps, to extra sanitary products.

I set my bag on one of two vanities and stare at my wide-eyed reflection in the mirror. My lips break into a grin as I spin around and spot the jacuzzi beside a rainfall shower. I desperately want to climb into the tub and stay there for an hour, but there isn't time before the rest of the people Adrianna invited arrive, so I opt for a quick shower instead.

Afterwards, I return to the bedroom and dump my bag out to find something to wear. I packed mostly comfy clothes—leggings and shirts, as well as hoodies and sweatpants for the cooler nights. Without much thought, I snag a pair of black leggings and an olive-colored long sleeve shirt and get dressed. I slip back into the bathroom and dry my hair.

Voices from downstairs are muffled through the floor, but it sounds like people are starting to arrive. I'm not entirely sure how many people to expect, but knowing Adrianna, the odds of this place being packed are pretty high.

Once my hair is dry, I don't bother applying a full face of makeup, but I do dab a bit of concealer under my eyes and over a few blemishes. I swipe on some mascara and lip gloss before walking out of the bathroom.

The voices downstairs are louder now, which either means more people have arrived or they've gotten into the liquor—or both. I follow the sounds, closing the bedroom door behind me so no one is likely to wander in, and head down the stairs.

"Cami!" someone squeals, and I turn in the direction of the cheery voice. Phoebe is already tipsy.

I shake my head, grinning at her. "Easy there," I tease her.

Grayson is standing beside her with a beer in his hand. He lifts his bottle to me in greeting, his other arm wrapped securely around Phoebe's waist.

I wave on my way to the kitchen to get myself a drink.

A group of people I don't recognize are gathered around the island in the middle of the kitchen, playing a game of beer pong.

I reach for a cup from the stack on the counter, but Adrianna swoops in before I can. "What—"

"We're doing shots in the other room." She loops her arm through mine before I can protest and pulls me out of the kitchen.

I'm not usually one for shots, but this weekend, I've decided, is about forgetting the shit show I left in the city. I'm going to do that whatever way possible, so shots it is.

Phoebe hands me a red SOLO cup with—I take a whiff—tequila, then nods toward the table they've set up in the middle of the room with lemon wedges and salt shakers. I lick the back of my hand before shaking salt on it, then grab a lemon wedge. We *cheers*, lick the salt, then take the shot, finishing with a bite of lemon.

"Woo!" Grayson cheers, grinning like a kid on Christmas morning.

Phoebe pours another round, and we take the shot as someone turns up the music—some popular rock song that everyone starts singing along too.

Three shots later, I slip out of the room to find an actual drink. There's a punch bowl filled with spiked lemonade, so I pour myself a tall glass and take a sip. It's perfectly sweet and tart, with a tiny bite of alcohol.

My cheeks are warm and my head is swimming with a pleasant haze as I return to the other room to dance with my friends. I lose myself in the music, singing and drinking until my cup is empty and we're all laughing at nothing. My belly aches, and I can't stop smiling—it's everything I needed this getaway to be.

I sneak away from our group to use the washroom and top up my drink, and when I return, Adrianna is dancing around someone new. My legs stop moving as I stare at his back. Even though I can't see his face, I know immediately and without a doubt who it is.

Adrianna notices my return and beams from where she stands with her arms wrapped around one of Xander's. "Cami! Look who showed up!"

Xander turns, and the moment our eyes meet, my heart lurches.

His expression is friendly and laid back, but there's a veil of darkness in his gaze that steals the air from my lungs.

I force my legs forward and convince my lips to form a smile. I have no idea what Xander is doing here, what he's planning. *If my friends are in danger.* I need to be careful, which means, as much as I want to throw him out, I have to pretend as if everything is fine. Like I'm happy he's here.

He meets me halfway, pulling me against him with an arm around my waist and dips his face to kiss me. It's over as quick as it happened, but I can't help the spike of my pulse as I move away from him.

"Xander, you're at least three drinks behind," Phoebe tells him with a warm smile before handing him a cup.

He takes it, grinning at her. "I'm sure I can catch up."

I try to inhale, but my breath gets lodged in my throat. Heat flashes through me from head to toe and the back of my neck tingles as I swallow at the sudden desert in my mouth. Between one moment and the next, the room starts to feel tiny, as if the walls are moving closer, and the music seems louder, the bass pounding in my ears. My limbs tense, and I feel as if my insides are quivering. I press my nails into my palms, desperately trying to ground myself, but everything is slipping out of my control, filling me with an inescapable sense of dread. Its tendrils weave through my ribs, circling my lungs until—

I can't breathe.

I flinch when Adrianna touches my arm, then turn my gaze to her. She must've said something because she's waiting for me to answer.

"Sorry," I croak. "I just—I need some air." I set my cup down and hurry out of the room, squeezing through the growing crowd in the kitchen to slip out the French doors to the back deck.

The cool air is an immediate reprieve from the stuffy warmth of the crowd in the house, but I don't stop moving once I'm outside.

Xander saw me flee the room. He might be giving me some space for a minute, but there's no chance he won't follow me. It doesn't make sense, but I both hope he will and dread it just as strongly.

I make my way down to the dock, and while I can still hear the music and people up at the house, it's much quieter. The sound of the water hitting the rocks along the shore is soothing enough I can almost tune out the rest of the noise.

Crossing my arms over my chest, I shiver from the breeze coming off the water. I should've grabbed a sweater before I came outside, and if I'd been in the proper headspace, I would have. Inhaling a deep breath, I hold it for a few seconds before letting it out slowly. After repeating the breathing exercise a handful of times, I feel marginally better. The tightness in my chest eases some, and I'm not as worried my legs are going to give up holding me upright.

"There you are."

My heart lurches at the sound of Xander's smooth, deep voice, but I refuse to turn around. The dock moves slightly as he walks closer, stopping at my back. I can feel the heat of his body against mine, and the urge to lean into him is so strong, I want to throw myself into the lake.

Dropping my arms to my sides, I swallow hard before I say in a low voice, "What are you doing here, Xander?" I clench my jaw when my teeth chatter over his name.

"I was invited."

"You..." I shake my head in disbelief. "I thought our last encounter would've made it clear you were *un*invited."

He exhales a soft breath. "I wanted to see you."

Before I can say anything in response, he drapes his jacket over my shoulders, flooding my senses with *him*. His warmth, his scent, everything. It makes my head spin, and I close my eyes against the dizzying sensation. My heart is hammering in my chest, and knowing he can hear it makes it next to impossible to slow down.

"Camille." His voice is a gentle caress against my senses.

I grit my teeth at the lump in my throat. I'm afraid to speak for fear my voice will break. One of the first things I learned in hunter training—something that stuck with me even after I left—is to never show a demon weakness. It only feeds their twisted enjoyment of playing with their prey. And I have to believe Xander is no different, even though I desperately wish that weren't true.

Opening my eyes, I stare out into the darkness. "Why are you here? What happened to you keeping a low profile? Last I checked, every hunter in the organization is looking for you."

"Right. Well, I suppose I should consider myself lucky that your friend has demons as friends instead of hunters."

I whirl around to face him, unable to keep the shock out of my voice when I say, "There are other demons here?"

He nods. "You might not believe me, but I'm here to keep you safe."

A strangled breath of laughter escapes my lips. It's harsh and void of humor, though the sincerity on his face fills my chest with a pressure I fight to ignore. "Safe from what? You're the one I should be afraid of."

He pauses, his eyes searching mine for a moment before he says, "Except you're not. Because there's a part of you that knows I won't hurt you, and that is true. But there are demons who would, given the chance. Demons who know how important you are."

"Important to your mother," I say bitterly, though I can't help but feel a tinge of *something* at him acknowledging he won't hurt me. I want to shove it away, because in a sense, he already has. Him being a demon hurts me.

Xander sighs. "Yes."

"What's her plan?"

He lowers his gaze, wetting his lips before he looks at me again. "Lucia is going to destroy the hunters' organization, and she plans to use you to help her do it."

Harper and I already guessed I was targeted by Xander because of the position my parents hold in the hunter organization, but having it confirmed makes my stomach coil with dread.

I shake my head, unable to form words. Without the hunters, demons would run rampant. Humans would have no defense against the monsters that feed on their fear—there would be mass chaos. It would be literal hell on earth.

"How—" My voice cracks, and I clear my throat. "How can you be okay with that?" It's a stupid question, one I fully expect him to dodge.

"I'm not." His words make my breath hitch. "At least, part of me isn't." He rakes a hand through his hair, exhaling heavily. Lowering his voice, he says, "My mother may be the queen of hell, Camille, but my father wasn't a demon. He was human."

I stare at him with wide eyes. "I—What...what does that mean?"

He chuckles humorlessly. "It means, as Blake loves to remind me, he is more demon than I am."

I shake my head, not following.

"It means," he continues, "I'm part demon—and part human."

Part human.

There's no stopping my thoughts from immediately going to what that means for us. It's selfish, considering he just told me his mother wants to essentially allow demons to take control, but I can't help it. Because if there's any world where I don't have to watch my best friend and family hunt the guy I have feelings for, I can't deny wanting that.

His hand reaches for mine. I should pull away, but I don't have the strength to resist when he entwines our fingers and guides me around to face the water again.

My back touches his chest, and I'm leaning into him before I can stop myself. When he does things like this, it's so easy to get caught up in the desire I feel for it to be real. Maybe in some ways it is. Except Xander is still a demon, still the prince of hell. A lump forms in my throat when he presses his lips against the side of my head, and I decide that I would give anything to stay in this moment forever.

But we can't.

After this weekend, we'll go back to Seattle. He'll still be the enemy.

"Is this what you want?" I murmur before I can think otherwise. There's humanity somewhere in him. I can't be sure how strong it is, but I'm going to test it. I'm going to find a way to get past his demon side and through to his human side. The part of him that clearly cares for me.

"Hmm?" His voice is right at my ear, sending a shiver down my spine.

I stare out at the glittering darkness, the moon reflected in the water. "Us," I whisper, then boldly add, "like this."

"I'm here, aren't I?" His voice is gentle but cool, building a wall between us.

It makes me want to take the words back and continue standing in silence. Pretending we can be more than this fleeting moment allows us. The thought that he could want it too fills me with a profound sadness, opening a chasm in my chest. It squeezes the air from my lungs, the sensation so painful it threatens to bring me to my knees. Because this is so much bigger than either of us. What we want is nothing compared to the stakes held by both sides.

Whoever said *knowledge is power* evidently never experienced the blissfulness of ignorance.

I hesitate before turning to face Xander. Lifting my eyes to meet his, my resolve almost crumbles at the vulnerable softness in his expression, but I grip it tightly. "Are you going to try to persuade me to help Lucia with her twisted plan to take down the hunters?"

He wets his lips, and my gaze drops to his mouth before I force it back up. "That's what she wants me to do," he finally answers.

I nod slowly. "And you?"

His eyes flick between mine. "What about me?"

"What do *you* want?"

"It's not about me," he says simply, as if he has no skin in this game, as if the outcome doesn't matter to him.

Irritation tugs at me, and I shake my head. "That's bullshit, and you—"

His lips crash against mine, sealing us together, and damning us all the same.

Our mouths dance, setting my body ablaze as I pull him closer, gripping the front of his shirt in my fist. He makes a sound at the back of his throat, as if I'm hurting him, but I don't stop. If I'm going down, I'm dragging him with me. We'll burn together.

Xander nips my lower lip, and I gasp into his mouth. His lips curve against mine as he deepens the kiss, flicking his tongue out to graze mine and sending my pulse racing.

My head spins and my stomach clenches in ways I've only ever felt with him.

Finally, I force myself to break the kiss. Resting my forehead against his, I press my lips to Xander's and then I whisper, "I'm not going to help you hurt people I care about."

He lifts his hand and cradles the side of my neck, holding me in place. "It would be so much easier if you did," he murmurs, his eyes flickering with the darkness of his demon side.

Fear digs sharp claws into my chest, planting me there. *What have I done?* Why did I let him kiss me? Why did I think we could ever be more than we are?

"I can't," I force out, swallowing and forcing the fear down. "I *won't*."

He sighs, and his fingers slip away from my neck. "She's not going to stop until she gets what she wants. It doesn't matter who gets hurt in the process, Camille." He lowers his voice, and the air of sadness is unmistakable when he says, "You won't win this."

I step back, forcing myself to stand straighter, to appear more confident than I feel. "You're so sure I'll lose. What's your plan, then?"

Xander rubs his jaw, his chest rising and falling slowly. "You—"

"What are you going to do?"

His brows inch closer. "Camille—"

I blink past the burning in my eyes, refusing to cry. "Are you going to kill me if I don't do what your mother wants?"

"*No,*" he practically growls, a muscle feathering along his jaw.

"Then what?" I snap, venom dripping from each word. "What are you going to do? What's. Your. Plan!"

"I don't fucking know!" His eyes fill with darkness, and I stumble back. He reaches for me, grabbing my shoulders to stop me from falling into the water.

My eyes widen, and I stumble over my next words, still reeling in surprise. "Y-you caught me."

"Always," he murmurs, his eyes returning to normal as he guides me further away from the end of the dock.

Silence stretches between us until I finally break it. "What are we doing, Xander?"

He tilts his head to the side, pressing his lips together briefly. "Exactly what you think we are." He drops his hands to my hips and leans in until his nose grazes mine. "We're pretending I'm not a monster. That you don't hate me. That we're both going to make it out of this alive."

I suck in a breath, my eyes burning, threatening tears of anger, sadness, *fear.* "I hate this," I admit before I can clamp my jaw shut.

"I know," he murmurs, his lips brushing mine. "So, let's pretend for as long as we can."

I wish more than anything I had the strength to walk away from Xander. But I don't. My hands rest against his chest, my eyes closing as his heart beats steadily against my palm. He slants his mouth over mine, sealing our lips together, and I can't help but feel he's sealing our fate in the same breath.

SEVENTEEN
CAMILLE

Xander and I walk back to the house, and I don't pull away when he laces his fingers through mine. At least here I can tell myself I'm allowing it to keep up appearances in front of my friends.

The party is still in full swing, and the rest of the night passes in a blur. I sip on the same cup of spiked lemonade, scanning the room with what feels like new eyes. Every person I look at, I can't help but wonder—*worry*—if they're a demon. Xander doesn't leave my side all night, so I'm less concerned about being targeted myself and wary of my friends' safety.

Except, what if...No. There's absolutely no way any of them are demons. Right?

That's what you thought about Xander.

My back stiffens, and I grip my cup tighter, frowning as liquid sloshes over the side.

"Camille," Xander murmurs in my ear. "No."

I lick the dryness from my lips, turning my head to look at him with furrowed brows.

He chuckles softly. "You're not exactly being subtle. It's not too difficult to read what you're thinking at the moment."

Nodding absently, I glance across the room where Adrianna, Phoebe, and Grayson are all dancing together, laughing over the music. "They're not..." I can't bring myself to say it.

"They're human," he confirms, taking the cup from me and setting it aside before grabbing a napkin from the side table near us and wiping my hand clean.

I snatch it back after far too long. "It's fine. You don't have to—"

"I enjoy it."

I exhale a heavy breath and mutter, "You're so confusing."

Xander tilts his head to the side, offering me a faint smile, which only makes things more confusing, especially when my cheeks heat and my stomach flutters. It's almost as if my body forgets what he is and why he's here when he's this close.

So stop letting him get this close, that pesky voice of reason scolds. It makes a good point, even if I don't want to hear it.

As the party winds down, a lot of the attendees trickle out, calling on their designated drivers and figuring out carpool configurations.

Grayson is chatting with Xander about the craft beer he's been drinking all night, and I take that opportunity to sneak upstairs to get changed. I need a minute alone, to clear my head and recenter myself. Tonight has been...*a lot*, to say the least, and I'm still not entirely sure how I feel about everything.

When I step out of the bathroom, my eyes immediately land on where Xander is leaning in the bedroom doorway.

I clear my throat, walking toward him. "What are you doing?"

He readjusts the duffle bag slung over his shoulder. "After that conversation with Grayson, I'm not sure I've ever been so exhausted."

I lift a brow at him. "You didn't answer my question."

The corner of his mouth quirks as he pushes away from the doorframe but remains in the hall. "It might raise suspicions if we don't share a room."

I open my mouth to tell him he can sleep outside for all I care—which is a lie he'd likely see right through—but knowing he's wasn't the only demon in attendance tonight stops me. Instead I say, "I'm not sharing a bed with you." There are some boundaries I'm going to enforce and this is definitely one of them. He doesn't get to lie to me over and over, and then crawl into my bed.

Xander nods, thrusting a hand through his hair. "I understand that, but it could make things weird with your friends in the morning if I sleep in the living room."

He's not wrong, and that's a possibility I'll have to risk, because this feels dangerous. The way he's looking at me with a mix of desire and something I could easily mistake as *hope*.

It makes me want to let him in. To surrender to my own desire. Because even after everything he's done, I can't stop wanting him, and I hate myself for it.

"Hmm." I nod, reaching for the door handle as I find the strength somewhere deep within myself to refuse him, to send him away. "Good night, Xander." I close the door in his face, flipping the lock over. I stare at it and take a deep breath.

Of course he could break it without any effort, but something tells me he won't.

A minute later, the sound of retreating footsteps echo down the hall.

Xander is gone when I wake up the next morning. He sent me a brief *I've missed you* text that sends me into a spiral the entire drive back to Seattle. He makes it too easy, at times, to forget why I'm supposed to hate him.

Arriving home, I'm more confused than ever. I can't stop replaying the moment with him on the dock until the pressure in my chest makes it near-impossible to take a breath.

When Harper walks through the door and finds me deep cleaning the kitchen, she immediately calls me out on what I'm distracting myself from.

I drop onto one of the barstools at the counter, wiping the sweat from my forehead. "If I tell you, you can't judge me."

She gives me a look. "*Please.* Who am I?"

I nod, licking my lips before I say, "Xander showed up at Adrianna's party last night."

Harper blinks at me, her mouth set in a tight line. "Is there more? Or can I start in on him now?"

I cringe inwardly. "He...kissed me."

Anger fills her gaze. "The *fuck*? How did that happen?"

Frowning, I run my hands along my thighs. "I don't really know. He showed up, I went outside to get some air when I felt a panic attack coming on, he followed me, and then we talked."

"You *talked*," she echoes, leaning against the counter next to me and crossing her arms over her chest. She's wearing all-black, skin-tight clothing and her hair is tied back neatly, so she must've come from training. "Talking led to kissing?"

I groan, raking my fingers through my sweat-dampened hair. "To put it simply."

She casts me a sideways glance. "What'd you talk about?"

I press my lips together for a moment while I go over the conversation in my head. "He told me his father was human."

I press my lips together for a moment while I go over the conversation in my head. "He told me his father was human."

She blinks in surprise, then says, "Was? So he's dead?"

I shrug. "I didn't ask. I was too hung up on him being part human."

Harper nods. "Fair enough. And you believe him?"

My mouth falls into a frown, and I shrug. "I...Yeah, I do." She didn't see him on that dock. The expression on his face, his rigid posture. It was like he was fighting a battle with himself.

"Please explain what's happening here, because I'm really struggling, Cami. You know I love you and will have your back no matter what, so help me out here."

I take a deep breath before saying, "I have to believe it, Harper. I can't let myself think that he's lying. Because the alternative is too messed up to consider. Because if I fell for someone who could truly never care about me, who could do what he's done without an ounce of remorse, what does that say about me?"

Her eyes narrow, and I can practically feel the anger radiating from her. "Fucking nothing. What that son of a bitch has done does not reflect on *you*. For the love of god, Cami, you are one of the kindest, most compassionate people I know."

"And look where it got me," I mumble, blinking quickly to alleviate the burning in my eyes.

Harper's voice is firm when she says, "Xander being a demon is not your fault."

"No, but letting myself fall for him is."

She sighs and pushes away from the counter, reaching over to squeeze my shoulder. "Are you ready to tell your parents?"

"I don't know."

She frowns. "You can't keep putting it off. I told you I'd give you a week, and it's been more than a week. I didn't push it right away because things have been quiet around HQ, but you need to tell them." Her voice softens. "If you want me to be there, you know I will," she says, repeating her offer. "It won't be easy, but I'm here for you—whatever you need."

Swallowing past the lump in my throat, I nod as I slide off the barstool. Before I do anything, the sweat rolling down my back reminds me I need to take a shower.

Harper drives my car, because there's a very good chance if I got behind the wheel, I wouldn't take us to hunter headquarters. It hasn't been somewhere I've been comfortable since losing Danielle, and even more now, considering our reason for coming.

"Deep breaths," Harper tells me as we pull into the parking garage below the building.

"Easy for you to say," I grumble, though I'm thankful she's here. As much as I wish I had the strength to do this on my own, her support—her being here to drag me into my mom's office if necessary—is probably the only thing keeping me together at this point.

After we walk through the concrete garage, Harper scans her access badge to let us inside.

"Did you let her know we were coming?" she asks as we walk through a quiet lobby. There are a few people sitting on the couches around a small coffee table, chatting in hushed voices, but aside from that, the room is empty. TV screens line one wall, a different news channel playing on each, with the volume muted.

"Yeah, I texted her." I kept it simple, just letting her know I was coming by without divulging why. She probably figures it has to do with the organization's offer, so she's in for quite the shock.

We're silent on the elevator ride up, and I wipe my palms on my thighs as we step off. A few hunters pass us, speaking soft greetings directed at Harper, and my pulse ticks faster the closer we get to my mom's office.

Harper reaches for me, squeezing my shoulder. "I can stay out here if you want to talk to her alone, or—"

"Don't go," I blurt unevenly as my anxiety crests, making it harder to breathe. If it keeps going, I won't even make it to starting this long-overdue and stressful conversation.

"I'm here," she assures me, holding my gaze and giving me a firm nod.

I don't know what I'd do without her.

Taking a deep breath, I knock on the frosted glass door, waiting to hear her muffled invitation before pushing it open and walking inside. Harper is right behind me.

Mom glances up, then between us before standing. She rounds her desk, pursing her lips as we meet her halfway.

"Hey, Mom," I say in a low voice.

"Camille." Her eyes shift to Harper. "What's going on?"

I take a deep breath, focusing on Harper's shoulder brushing mine, anchoring me. "I, um, need to talk to you. About Xander Kane."

Her eyes widen briefly as they cut back to me. "What do you know about the prince of hell?"

I know what he tastes like.

The blood drains from my face, making my head spin. "I...Maybe we should get Dad on the phone?" Having to repeat this conversation isn't something I'm going to want to do.

Concern etches into her features, but she nods, returning to her desk. Harper and I follow, sitting in the uncomfortable chairs on the other side, while she stands and hits a button on her phone.

"Scott Morgan," he answers before I even hear it ring.

"I have our daughter in my office," she says, keeping her eyes on me.

His voice is softer when he says, "Hey, kiddo."

"Hi, Dad," I force out. "Harper's here, too."

"What's going on, Rach?" he asks.

Mom sighs, her brows scrunching together. "I'm not entirely sure. Camille, would you like to explain?"

I grip the armrests until my knuckles are white. "The night I was attacked outside Hallowed Grounds, the hunter who stepped in and saved me was Xander Kane."

Mom's face pales. "What?"

"Please," I rush to say, "let me get everything on the table before you start reprimanding me."

Her eyes are wild, as if she's going to start yelling despite my plea, and Dad remains silent on the phone. Finally, she nods.

I let out a shaky breath. "We started seeing each other shortly after that. There was another demon attack one night after Xander and I were leaving dinner, and I—" My voice cracks, and I swallow twice before trying again. "I daggered her to save him."

"You killed a demon?" Dad asks, his tone laced with concern.

"Yeah. It all just happened so fast, and I didn't have time to think about it."

"Was this before or after we spoke about your future with the organization?" Mom chimes in.

I can feel Harper's eyes on me, because I hadn't had a chance to tell her about the offer my mom presented me that day. Honestly, I have no idea why it even matters, but I say, "It was before. But right after our conversation is when I discovered Xander's true identity."

She presses a hand to her lips, nodding slowly. "And what happened between then and now, Camille? That was over a week ago."

I exchange a look with Harper. "I was...figuring things out."

"We're going to need more than that, sweetheart," Dad says.

Harper puts her hand on my knee, giving it a gentle squeeze.

"Xander didn't come into my life by coincidence. His mother, the queen, had a plan for him to get close to me. To use me to infiltrate the organization with the intention of destroying it."

The anger on Mom's face makes me want to hightail it out of here, but I wrap my ankles around the legs of my chair.

"I'll kill him myself," she says in a dangerously quiet voice, and my throat dries up.

"Mom, no," I croak.

"You'd defend that monster?" she demands.

"He's not—" I stop myself.

"His father was human," Harper speaks up. "Xander isn't a pure-blooded demon."

"That information isn't in our profile," Dad offers tightly.

"We didn't know the queen had a son until recently either," Harper points out. "I think we need to recognize the possibility of new developments when it comes to this particular situation."

Dad sighs on the other end of the phone. "You're right, Harper."

Mom lowers her gaze as she leans against the side of her desk. "This has gone too far already," she says without looking up. "I'm putting a protective detail on you immediately."

My stomach drops. "Uh, no. I don't need—"

Her gaze snaps up. "I wasn't asking, Camille."

I gape at her. "I have Harper."

"Harper hasn't graduated yet," Dad says.

"So move up her graduation. You both know she's worked her ass off and proved herself more times than any other trainee."

"We're impressed with Harper's skills, but this is non-negotiable."

"Then who?" Harper asks the question I'm dreading.

There's a beat of silence before Dad clears his throat. "I'll speak to Noah when we hang up and get him on the next flight to Seattle."

"No," I say immediately. "Absolutely not." The thought of him being assigned to essentially become my shadow makes the hair on the back of my neck tingle as my chest tightens.

Harper nudges me. "It's not the worst idea," she offers under her breath.

I turn to her. "Uh, yeah it is." Looking back at my mom, I add, "I understand why you want to do this, and I won't fight you on it, so long as you find someone other than Noah."

My mom exhales a heavy sigh, pushing away from her desk and walking around it to sit back down. "Scott?"

"I'll handle it. Keep me posted on everything there." His voice softens before he adds, "I love you, Camille."

Relief flickers through me. This situation is far from ideal, but at least I escaped getting stuck with Noah.

"Love you too, Dad."

"We'll talk soon," Mom says before ending the call and leaning back in her chair.

Each breath I take feels shorter. My lungs refuse to fill with air and the room starts closing in on me, cranking the temperature of my body up as I glance between my mom and Harper.

"Camille—" Mom starts.

I get to my feet and blurt, "I have class." I walk to the door as Harper jumps up to follow me. "Please stay." I tell her. "Fill my mom in on anything I missed. I-I need to get out of here."

Mom stands behind her desk. "You need to go straight home after class. There's enough of a hunter presence on campus to be safe there, but I don't want you going anywhere else without a detail."

I bite my tongue to keep from reminding her I'm not a child and she doesn't get to decide what I do. It won't do any good to argue, and I suppose I should just take the win that she hasn't used this whole thing to strong-arm me back into training.

"Okay," I finally say, giving Harper one last look before hurrying out of the office.

I slip into the lecture hall just before my professor starts her lesson and steal a spot near the back of the room. Scanning the room, I frown when I don't see Phoebe. It's not totally unlike her to show up late—even later than me today—but she usually lets me know.

Once it's clear she isn't coming, I send her a text.

> Still wrecked from the weekend?

When she doesn't answer, I spend the rest of the lecture trying to be rational and stop myself from overthinking the situation. And when I can't, I slip out of the room at the first opportunity, calling Phoebe. My stomach sinks when it goes straight to voicemail, and a sick feeling trickles in when I check my text and don't see the delivery notification.

I try Grayson next, my pulse spiking when his line rings. But then it eventually clicks over to voicemail too. "Hey, Gray, just trying to reach you or Phoebe. I think her phone is dead. Can one of you please call me back?"

I hang up and immediately send another text to Adrianna and Harper.

> I can't reach Phoebe or Grayson. Have you talked to them today?

Adrianna

> No, sorry. I haven't talked to either of them since we left the lake house yesterday.

Harper

> I'm calling you in two minutes.

The tendrils of dread in my chest expand, and I chew the inside of my cheek until I taste blood as I pace the length of the barren garden outside the lecture hall. The air is cool, but the panic crackling in my veins is making me sweat so much the phone nearly slips through my fingers when it starts vibrating with an incoming call.

"Harper." My voice is pitchy. "Have you heard from them?"

"Where are you?"

I frown at her forced-level tone. "Campus. I left class after Phoebe didn't show, and I've been trying to get ahold of her ever since. Either her phone is off or dead, because it went straight to voicemail. Grayson isn't answering either, and Adrianna also hasn't heard from them." I suck in a breath.

"I think you need to come back to HQ," she says in a low voice.

In the space of a heartbeat, my head goes to the worst case scenario. "What's going on?"

"Grayson and Phoebe were taken by demons, Cami."

My hand flies to my chest as I choke on the dryness in my throat when I try to take a breath. "What? No. How is that even—*No.*" I stumble toward my car, the edges of my vision darkening as my pulse races and my head spins. I shake my head, struggling to get my key into the lock, then drop behind the wheel. "How are you sure?" Starting the car, it takes a few seconds before my phone connects to the bluetooth, and I pull out of the student parking lot.

Harper exhales a heavy breath. "Because," she says, "the demon who took them is well-known to the organization. He's one of Lucia's inner circle, and he was caught on CCTV around the dorm right before they went missing."

I curse, gritting my teeth and gripping the steering wheel until my knuckles are white and press harder on the gas to make it through a yellow light.

"We're going to get them back," she vows, but despite the fierceness of her tone, I can't bring myself to believe it. This isn't some low-level demon we're dealing with. This demon is connected to Lucia, which means he's part of her plan.

I lock my jaw as bile rises in my throat, and I flick the blinker to turn right, the safety of my car feeling far more suffocating than normal.

"Are you on your way?"

I hesitate. "I'm...saving a step."

"You're saving?—Cami, *no.*"

"He knows where they are, Harper. He has to."

"I don't care. You going to him alone is reckless and won't get the result you're looking for, so please, don't do this."

I swallow past the lump in my throat. "Whatever happened to them is because of me. Because Lucia wants to get to me."

"They were taken because *Xander* knew who they are to you," she points out. "He must've told Lucia."

All I can say is, "I won't let them get hurt for being my friends."

Thinking about Xander being involved with Phoebe and Grayson going missing has my blood pressure skyrocketing. I don't want to believe it. Lucia could have other demons keeping tabs on me—a thought I don't let myself get stuck on because *that* is terrifying—but Xander feeding her the information is the most obvious answer.

"Fine," Harper says in a tight voice, "but don't go alone. Please."

I shake my head even though she can't see me. "I have to. If I bring an entourage of hunters, there's no way I'll convince him to let them go."

"And you think he will if you, what, *ask nicely*?"

I wince at the harshness of her words. "You didn't see him the other night. There's a part of him that doesn't want to be the monster Lucia is forcing him to be."

There's a beat of silence and then, "You really believe that?"

"Yes." *I have to.*

There's a stretch of silence on the line and then, "I don't like this."

Turning onto Xander's street, my pulse ticks faster. "I know."

"Are you absolutely sure about this?"

No. "Yes."

"Are you lying to me right now?"

Yes. "No."

By some stroke of luck, I find a spot on the street outside his building and shift my car into park.

"Keep your phone on. Your location is still shared with me, so if I don't hear from you within fifteen minutes from right now, I'm sending a team. Got it?"

"Yes. Thank you," I repeat.

Harper sighs. "Fuck, I really hope you're right about him."

"Me too." I end the call, staring out the windshield as I fight to get a grip on my pounding heartbeat.

Part of me must know this idea is stupid. Even still, here I am, hoping Xander will surprise me. That he'll care enough about me, about my friends who he's spent time with on more than one occasion, to help me get them back.

Before I can talk myself out of it, I get out of the car and walk into the building. The concierge glances up when I approach—it's a different person than the one I spoke with last time I was here, but I still get a polite smile.

"I'm here to see Xander."

The man nods. "Name?"

"Camille."

He checks his computer, humming softly before returning his gaze to me. "Go on up, Ms. Morgan."

"Thanks," I say, walking to the elevator. I press the button for Xander's floor and exhale a shaky breath as the door slides shut.

A hand stops it at the last minute, and my back straightens against the mirrored wall as Blake steps inside, blocking the exit until the door slides shut. The corner of his mouth tugs up as he stares at me, his eyes sparkling with delight.

"Hey, hunter girl. Cat got your tongue?"

My eyes narrow. "I'm not a hunter."

He shrugs. "Hunter adjacent, then. Whatever." He takes a step closer, and I stiffen on instinct.

"What are you doing here?" I blurt, glancing at the rising floor number on the panel beside him. We're almost to Xander's floor, and I'm not sure that will bring any relief to the tightness in my chest, but I also don't want to be stuck in this elevator with Blake.

He arches a brow, giving me a conspicuous once-over. "I could ask you the same thing."

"Oh, you didn't hear? Xander is betraying his mother so we can run away together. Guess you guys aren't as close as you thought."

Blake chuckles, leaning against the wall opposite me. "I enjoy your humor, Cami."

I scowl. "My name is Camille. Only my *friends* call me Cami, and we are not, Blake."

Before he can respond, the elevator stops and the door slides open. He swings his arm out, gesturing for me to walk ahead, but I offer a humorless laugh, shaking my head. Blake steps off the elevator ahead of me, walking down the hallway as I trail after him, my nerves buzzing with energy. Him being here adds a layer of complication I really don't need, but I'm not going to let that deter me. Phoebe's and Grayson's lives could very well depend on it.

Blake stops at Xander's door, pulling a key out of his army green joggers and lets himself in. He leaves the door open, so I follow him inside, closing it none too gently.

I'm immediately enveloped in Xander's scent, and my next breath gets caught in my throat as I push forward and walk into the open concept kitchen and living room space. My eyes land on him immediately where he stands at the kitchen island pouring coffee from a French press. There are two mugs on the counter in front of him. He must've been expecting Blake. His eyes shift from his friend to me, and a bit of surprise flickers in them.

"Camille—"

"Where are Phoebe and Grayson?" I demand, not giving him a chance to say more than my name before cutting him off.

Confusion passes over his features, and he shakes his head.

My eyes narrow. "A demon took them," I clarify in a biting tone, and Blake whistles under his breath, dropping onto the couch in the living room and pulling out his phone. I focus on Xander. "Where. Are. They?"

He sets the French press down. "What makes you think I know where your friends are?"

"Are you telling me you don't?" I push.

"I'm not telling you anything. I'm asking you a question."

"And I'm not playing this game, Xander. Tell me where they are."

He drums his fingers against the counter. "Say I do know where they are, and I even go so far as to tell you where that is. What will you give me in return?"

The blood drains from my face. "You've got to be kidding me."

He shrugs. "Your friends are alive. I'll even have them brought here."

"And what is it you want in return?" I ask in a forced level tone.

"I'm gonna give you guys a minute," Blake chimes in before slipping through a door that appears to lead to a balcony I hadn't noticed last time I was here.

That feels so long ago.

"Dinner," Xander says, and my gaze snaps back to him. "Just the two of us."

I open and close my mouth twice, grappling for a suitable response, but I've got nothing. "If my friends are harmed in any way, I will kill whoever took them," I vow, surprised at how steady my voice comes out.

"Spoken like a true demon hunter," he says casually.

"Screw you, Xander," I snap, moving away from him. Harper was right. This was a mistake.

"Wait," he says, and it sounds much closer than it should.

I turn back and find him standing right there. Pulling in an uneven breath, I mutter, "What?"

A muscle ticks along his jaw. "I'm sorry. That wasn't fair of me to say."

I cross my arms. "Gee, thanks."

"Marcus is a high-level demon who works very closely with my mother," he explains. "It's not safe for you to go after him."

My eyes lift to his. "Now, all of a sudden, you're concerned with my safety?" *How dare he pretend to care?* "He should know how important I am to Lucia's plan and that it would be very stupid of him to hurt me." My tone reeks of mockery.

"Camille," he warns in a soft voice.

"Xander," I deadpan, letting my hands fall to my sides.

He takes a step closer, and I immediately retreat, but in the time it takes me to blink, he wraps his fingers around my wrist, holding me in place. "I understand why you won't believe me, but I don't want you to get hurt."

I tug on my arm, to no avail. "No, you just want me to betray my family and let demons take control of the human world."

"That's what Lucia wants," he says in a low voice.

"What about you? What do *you* want, Xander?" I challenge, though I've stopped fighting his grip. It's useless anyway.

Something akin to pain flashes in his eyes as they darken, and all it does is feed the confusion growing in my chest. Xander appears torn by my question, by how upset I am.

I can't help the physical pull I feel to him. Even worse, I hate how I can't stop thinking about kissing him even as the pain of his betrayal still burns in my chest. I lift my free hand and cup his cheek, my fingers grazing slowly across the stubble there.

"I hate how badly I still want you." The words taste bitter on my tongue, like unsweetened coffee.

His eyes flick to my wrist as if he can hear the quick beat of my pulse beneath the skin. He turns his face to press his lips against it, and my breathing halts. "I know." His words solidify what I already know. He craves it—my surrender.

Hell, maybe there's a part of me that craves it, too.

Xander slips a finger under my chin and tilts my face up, tracing his lips over mine in a whisper of a kiss.

"We can't," I say, even as I move my lips against his.

"Tell me to stop." His words against my lips taste dangerously sweet.

"I won't." *I can't.*

He pauses. "Camille..."

"Is this what you want?" I breathe. "Because you deserve the life you want, same I do. So choose that over what Lucia has planned. For once, choose *yourself.*"

He cups my cheeks in his hands, and the air gets caught in my lungs as he leans in until his bottom lip brushes mine. "You have no idea how badly I wish it was that simple." With that, he pulls back, and I'm left with a cold pit of defeat unfurling in my chest.

EIGHTEEN
CAMILLE

The campus library is quiet when I arrive the next afternoon with the intention of burying myself in schoolwork and pretending yesterday's interaction with Xander didn't happen.

After I left his apartment, I texted Harper that it had been a waste of time—intentionally leaving out the part about the kiss.

I hate that I can still feel the tingle his lips left on mine, made worse by the fact I haven't been able to stop thinking about it.

Why can't I walk away from him?

He's done nothing but trick me from the moment we met. *Was any of it real or just part of his and Lucia's plan to turn me into a pawn?*

I can only imagine how complicated the relationship is between Xander and his mother—his *queen*. I was stupid to think there'd be a world where he'd defy her, even if part of him wants to. It's not enough.

My phone buzzes on the table in front of me, and I peer over at it, frowning at the screen.

Talk about complicated parental relationships...

I've been ignoring my parents' calls since I left headquarters yesterday and only responded to texts so they'd know I was safe. Apparently, my protection detail is being finalized and will be at my apartment by the end of the day.

I shove my phone into my bag and blow out a breath, tying my hair back and refocusing on the textbook I'm desperately trying to study.

Ten minutes later, I've accomplished nothing but reading the same sentence a dozen times. There's a dull pounding in my temples, threatening a headache, so I close the book with a sigh and collect my things before walking out of the library.

The student parking lot is pretty barren, and I make my way toward where I parked my car.

"Camille!"

I pause, turning toward the unfamiliar voice to find a redheaded girl who looks around my age approaching. She has long, loose curls and dark makeup, and I have no idea who she is—or why she's smiling as if she knows me. She's wearing dark jeans and a washed-out band T-shirt under a leather jacket. Pressing my lips together, I'm increasingly aware of the discomfort creeping up my spine, making the back of my neck tingle.

"You're a hard person to track down," she says with a laugh, stopping a few feet from me.

I shake my head, gripping my keys a bit tighter as I slink back a step, peeking around the parking lot as subtly as I can. "I am?"

She grins, and unease blossoms in my chest. It isn't friendly. If anything, it's predatory. "Hmm, not really actually."

I blink at her. "Sorry, do I know you?"

Her grin fades a little, triggering the alarm bells in my head. "Oh. No, no, of course not."

My brows scrunch closer as I stare at the girl. "I'm confused. Who are you?"

"That's the last thing you should worry about." Her tone takes on a snarky air, and her moss green eyes fill with endless black in the time it takes me to blink.

Reeling backward as I choke on a scream, my back hits a solid wall of muscle. Before I can whirl around or call for help, my head explodes with a sharp pain so intense it steals the air from my lungs. I'm falling as my vision blurs and everything sounds far away. Darkness engulfs me, and I lose consciousness before I hit the pavement.

Noise slowly reaches me while my eyes remain shut. I can't remember how to open them at this exact moment, and the throbbing in my skull won't allow it, anyway.

"I did exactly as you asked."

I wince inwardly at the sound. I want to cover my face, my ears. Everything is too loud, too bright.

There's a soft, melodic laugh, and then a voice as smooth as butter speaks. "I see that."

"Are you pleased?" It's the girl who ambushed me in the parking lot, and she sounds...nervous?

"I am. Well done, Madeline. You are dismissed."

"But—"

"*Go.*"

Madeline nearly whimpers. "Yes, my queen. Of course. Thank you." There are hurried footsteps and a moment later, a door clicks shut.

There's a beat of silence and then, "Will you continue this ruse of sleep, sweetness?"

My posture goes rigid, even slumped in the chair, and I grit my teeth as pain floods through me, reminiscent of my earliest days of hunter training. I pry my eyes open, blinking quickly at the sudden intrusion of light. When my vision rights itself, slowly coming into focus, my throat goes dry as I meet the queen of hell's piercing blue gaze.

Lucia is the most beautiful person I've ever seen.

She exudes pure darkness and unbridled power, and it takes every ounce of willpower I have not to tremble before her.

Her soft brown hair hangs slightly past her shoulders—it's shiny, with hints of gold when caught right by the light above. Of course, her complexion is dewy and free of blemishes. Her makeup is simple. Glittering gold eyeshadow with dark, thick lashes and sharp brows. Paired with a floor length black silk dress, Lucia fits the royal persona to a T.

I sit up, wincing at the sharp pain behind my eyes, and scan the room in an attempt to get my bearings. The space is bigger than most of the rooms in my apartment combined. The walls that aren't made of windows are adorned with rich, textured maroon wallpaper, and black crown molding frames the room, adding to its subtle opulence. A massive black marble fireplace is the focal point of the space, though currently unlit, it sits below a massive mantel that holds an intricate art piece I recognize from an elective I took last year as being inspired by *Paradise Lost*.

If I wasn't so screwed, it might be funny.

In front of me is a circular, glass coffee table with a few art history tomes on top as well as a burning candle that fills the room with the scent of sandalwood. On the other side of it is a black couch that matches the wingback chair I'm in. Beyond the sitting area, there are several completely full bookshelves. There's a turntable set up between them, playing a soft piano melody that does nothing to calm my racing thoughts or jumpy nerves.

My gaze snaps back to my demon captor as she takes a step closer.

Lucia moves with such an elegant grace, I can't help but get lost in a trance of watching her approach. She grips my chin before I can consider turning away, tilting my head back to look into my eyes. My pulse thrums and my jaw clenches, but I don't fight her grasp. It's a losing game, and I'm not naive enough to think otherwise.

Her crimson stained lips slowly curl into a faint grin as the subtle scent of smoky lavender invades my senses. "It is a pleasure to finally meet you, Camille."

"Can't say I agree," I say through my teeth as I fight the bile rising in my throat. "Your *Majesty.*"

Her eyes glitter with amusement. "How delightful your sharp tongue is. I see why my son is so taken with you."

When she frees me, I fall back against the chair. "What am I doing here?" I demand in what I hope sounds like a firm voice, because quite frankly, I feel about two seconds away from bursting into tears.

Lucia straightens, clasping her hands behind her back as she stares down at me. "I thought it was time you and I met."

My eyes narrow, and I swallow before saying, "So you had me knocked out and brought to you?" I frown at the view from the windows across the room. There's nothing but forest for as far as I can see. "Where are we?" I ask in a lower voice, forcing my gaze back to Lucia.

"Just outside Portland." She exhales a breath, as if my response to the situation is irritating, which doesn't make me feel better about it. "You can relax, Camille. I am not going to hurt you. That would be such a waste."

Wasted potential.

Noah's words come back to haunt me, and I sit up straighter, squaring my shoulders. "I know you're planning to use me to get to the organization, and I'm not going to help, so you're wasting your time."

Lucia glides around the coffee table and lowers herself onto the couch, perching in an eerily graceful way in the middle of it. "You will not even wait to hear me out?" The air of amusement in her voice reminds me this is just a game to her, a form of entertainment while she schemes to get her way.

"No," I snap, despite not being in a position to deny her. This woman—this *monster*—holds my life in her hands, so even though there's no chance I can give her what she wants, I should be pretending that I can and that I will.

She purses her lips, a dangerous glint in her eyes. "Not even if it could save your friends' lives?"

My lips part in a silent gasp and my voice cracks when I finally force out, "What?"

She smiles cooly. "I thought that would get your attention."

I narrow my eyes, shooting to my feet before I can stop myself. My temples throb, and I grit my teeth against the pain. "What have you done with them?" I demand, my hands balling into fists at my sides.

She crosses her leg over the opposite knee, folding her hands in her lap. "Not much—yet. How things proceed really depends on you, Camille, so you would do well to listen to me."

I shake my head, the glare I'm shooting her way cold as ice. "You—"

"You speak far too much for someone in your position. I will make this short and simple for you. I need someone with close connections to the hunters. That is where you come in."

"No—"

"You are going to rejoin the organization," she continues as if I haven't spoken. "They already trust you, which is precisely what I need."

My stomach tightens with knots and waves of nausea. "You want me to be your spy."

Some of the harshness in her expression smooths. She seems pleased I've come to that conclusion. "That would be lovely. You see, once you have infiltrated the organization, you can inform me on its top-level missions and plans to hunt my kind."

I blink at her. "You...are insane." I step back, swallowing hard. "They're not just going to give me all the information you're so desperate for. It would take *years* for me to reach the clearance level for that." Not to mention, I told them Lucia's plan to use me. They wouldn't believe me if I tried to dive back into training now. This plan is impossible, but I'm not about to tell her that, because if I'm no longer part of her plan, I'm dangerously expendable.

Lucia nods thoughtfully. "I understand things take time. I am a patient woman to some extent, Camille. However, this is not something for which we have the luxury of time. You see, there has been some chatter among my people about abolishing my reign. Therefore, I am determined to show anyone considering turning against me that defiance is not an option if they wish to continue breathing."

Staring at her for several beats, silence stretches between us, and I fight the urge to cry. I'm not sure if it's more from anger, fear, dread, or an awful mix of all three. "Do you know me? At all? Has Xander told you *anything* about me?"

Lucia cocks her head to the side. "Why do you ask?"

"I left—no, I *fled*—the organization five years ago, after my sister was killed by a demon. My parents have been doing everything they can since then to convince me to go back. Nothing they've done—no amount of pleading or manipulation—has worked. And now, you think I'm going to do exactly that as some secret informant for you?" I shake my head, exhaling a disgusted sigh as my eyes burn. "Go to hell."

She laughs softly. "You humans truly are selfish things. You would go so far as to sacrifice your friends to avoid becoming the pride and joy of your parents?"

I blink quickly, fighting back tears. If I agree to her completely insane plan on the condition she lets Phoebe and Grayson go unharmed *and* she vows not to hurt my parents or Harper...and then she figured out I was never in a position to keep up my end of the deal, I can only imagine the bloodshed that would follow. She'd be sure to punish me for my disobedience, and it has tension and nausea coiling tightly in my stomach as I grasp at a plausible response. "That's not—"

"Fair?" she cuts in with a cruel smile. "Very well. Allow me to sweeten the deal for you. To show you I can be generous. Do as I ask, and I will release Xander from the power I hold over him as his queen. You will have the opportunity to have a life with him free from my influence."

I don't speak for what feels like a short eternity, because what. The. *Fuck?* For the life of me, I can't make sense of what Lucia has just presented me—much less consider my future with Xander, if there even is one at this point. If I *want* one.

My head is spinning so fast, I wish I was still sitting, because my legs are getting shakier by the second. But if I drop into a chair now, that will show weakness I can't afford to let Lucia witness. It's bad enough she can hear the race of my pulse and the thunder in my chest.

She exhales a sigh. "Here I am thinking I am making this easy for you." She glances upward for a moment before meeting my gaze, her eyes narrowing. "Should you refuse me, you will watch me destroy everyone you love, and then my son will destroy you."

My stomach plummets and my legs move back without conscious thought. Inwardly, I'm screaming and crying and begging for someone to save me. Outwardly, though, my expression is frozen. I briefly consider that I might be going into shock. I'm so out of my element here, my body has shifted into survival mode without me even realizing it. Everything is starting to feel so detached, as if I'm watching this entire exchange from outside of my body.

Lucia purses her lips, as if she's ensuring her lip color is still even. "It would be quite a shame if that came to fruition, Camille. You see, my son...Xander does not want to hurt you. You might not know how you feel about him, but he does care for you. He battles with it constantly—I can feel it. It is his biggest weakness. He is torn between what he feels for you and the part of him that clings to the demonic nature to serve me. Killing you will hurt him, but I have accepted that."

I clench my jaw so tight, my molars grind and my temples throb in protest. I'm willing the bile in my throat to recede so I don't vomit all over my feet. I'm torn between wanting to scream and sob, and not being able to do either is making my chest feel as if it's about to explode. I stare at her wide eyed and horrified. "You would do that to your own son."

It isn't a question, but she doesn't miss a beat in answering.

"I would, and he would come to understand why."

I shake my head. "If he cares for me the way you say he does, I wouldn't be so sure he would."

Lucia shrugs and somehow makes even that look graceful. "No matter. The choice is yours, Camille."

I continue shaking my head. "You can't be serious."

She smiles, a slow, wicked twist of her lips that makes my blood run cold. "Allow me to show you just how serious I am."

Before I know what's happening, Lucia whistles sharply, and the double doors behind me swing open. Two impeccably dressed men storm in, grabbing me by the arms, and drag me out of the room. A scream tears its way up my throat, and I start fighting, trying to break free from their grasp. It's instantly clear my captors are demons, which means there's no chance I can overpower them. They haul me down the hallway, barely fazed by my kicking and screaming as I try to dig my nails into their skin. I whip my head back at the sound of Lucia's melodic chuckle, then quickly turn away as hot tears burn my eyes.

A moment later, one of the demons opens a door, and I'm thrown into another room. This one has no windows, just dark wallpaper and gold sconces that casts the space in soft, warm light. There's nothing in here, save for a large area rug and two chairs in the middle of the room with—

I choke on a horrified gasp when my eyes land on Phoebe and Grayson slumped over in the chairs with their shoulders pressed against each other's. At first glance, they look unharmed. No visible injuries, nothing beyond slightly disheveled appearances.

I start toward them, but the demons hold me back with infuriatingly little effort as Lucia waltzes into the room past me at an easy pace and comes to a stop at my friends' backs.

"Let them go," I say, my teeth chattering as I shake with a debilitating combination of white-hot anger and bone-chilling fear.

No amount of hunter training would have prepared me for this moment—this *nightmare*.

When Lucia rests her hands on each of their shoulders, they stir, stiffening in the chairs they're sitting in unsecured. She's not worried about them escaping.

Phoebe looks up first, her terror-filled gaze slamming into me. The blood drains from her face, leaving it pale, and her chest rises and falls quickly as she breathes shallowly. She opens her mouth as if she's going to speak, but nothing comes out.

"Let. Them. Go," I repeat in a shaky voice.

One of the demons holding me releases my arm and stalks toward my friends, while the other keeps me from going to them myself. My eyes swim with tears, the heavy weight of helplessness making it hard to breathe as my eyes dart back and forth between my friends and the queen of demons standing over them.

She holds the power, and she fucking knows it. The smug glint in her eyes and the twist of her dark red lips says as much.

The weight on my shoulders, the defeat blanketing me, only adds to the pain filling my entire body. Because whatever happens, whatever I decide, I lose. It's just a matter of *who* gets hurt in the process of my choice that is somewhat within my power. I can say without an ounce of doubt Lucia crafted it that way to ensure the maximum amount of suffering.

"You don't have to hurt them," I say. I am not above begging her to spare them.

She offers a soft laugh, walking closer to me, while one of the demons who led me here takes her place. He trails his fingers along Phoebe's collarbones before crouching in front of her and gripping her chin to make her look at him.

"No—" I try to take a step forward, but the other demon's grip on my arm tightens, biting into my skin until I yelp. I clamp my jaw shut, unable to tear my eyes away from my friend as hers fill with unbridled panic. Her gaze goes vacant, her eyes filling with tears that roll silently down her cheeks, and then she lets out a bloodcurdling scream.

Grayson startles out of the daze he was in, falling off the chair and scrambling upright. He sways on his feet before catching his balance, his eyes whipping around the room, taking in his surrounding before his gaze swings between the demon and Phoebe, then to Lucia, and finally to me. He shakes his head, confusion and panic contorting his typically soft, charming features.

"What the hell is going on?" he shouts, grabbing for the demon, who swats him away without so much as glancing in his direction. Grayson lands with a loud *thump*, smacking his head on the wood floor so hard his eyes roll back.

My eyes dart between him and the demon standing over Phoebe as he wraps his fingers around her throat. She gasps for air, pleading with the demon as he blocks her from my view. And when my name leaves her lips in a strangled cry, I suck in a breath and turn my attention to Lucia.

"Make him stop! He's going to kill her!" My voice cracks, and the demon holding me cackles in my ear as I struggle against him, fighting to break free.

Lucia licks her lips, casting an uninterested glance in their direction. "Yes," she says simply, "he is." With that, Lucia leaves the room, renewing my vigor to fight my captor.

I slam my elbow back, catching him in the ribs, but he only barks out a laugh and tightens his grip.

I have to fight harder. I can't let them win, can't let—

When Phoebe's whimpering gasps go quiet, I freeze.

No. Please, no.

The demon in front of her huffs out an irritated sigh and shifts away.

A sob gets caught in my throat when my eyes land on her face. It's blanched of color, her eyes bloodshot and empty and her cheeks wet with tears. She's unnaturally still, and blood drips from both of her nostrils, spilling over her lips and chin.

I can't look away. I'm waiting for her to blink, to *breathe*, but she doesn't. Phoebe is *gone*.

I shake my head, tears rolling down my cheeks. When Grayson stirs on the floor, I finally look away from Phoebe. Grayson groans in pain as he struggles to sit up, appearing more dazed than before. Until his eyes fall on Phoebe.

"No," he whispers, shaking his head, as if he's trying to dispel what he's seeing.

"Gray," I cry, "I'm so sorry."

He's on his knees, staring at her as tears fill his eyes. Minutes pass, or maybe it's only seconds. Time doesn't make sense anymore—nothing does. Grayson finally looks at me, and the confusion mixed with agony in his eyes punches a hole right through my gut. "Cami..." My name on his lips sounds like a prayer, as if he believes I can save us.

"It's going to be okay," I lie through my teeth, through the fresh tears gathering in my eyes.

The demon moves in a blur, and in the space of a heartbeat, he snaps Grayson's neck.

There's an awful, high-pitched shriek that fills my ears, and too much time passes before I realize the sound is coming from me. It rattles through me until my throat is raw and tears are streaming down my cheeks.

"Why?" I scream through the tears.

"Remember this moment the next time you consider defying our queen," the demon speaks low in my ear, then releases me. "This is simply a taste of the pain she can inflict upon you if she doesn't get what she wants."

My mouth falls open as the other demon drops Grayson's body, as if it's a piece of trash he's disposing of. The demons walk out of the room without another word, and the door slamming shut behind him echoes through me, as if I'm completely hollow.

I can't breathe. I can't breathe. I can't breathe.

Gasping for air as I choke on a sob, my face heats and black spots dot my vision. My stomach floods with nausea as tears roll down my cheeks, and I feel myself falling. Time stretches thin, and I can't hear anything over the ringing in my ears.

I should be running, trying to escape this hell, but the panic consuming my entire body makes it impossible to move, to think, to *breathe*.

Collapsing in between the bodies of my friends, the world goes dark, and I fall into oblivion.

Nineteen
Xander

I slam the empty shot glass onto the counter, grimacing at the brutal tightness in my chest. The liquor was meant to act as a distraction from the foreign sensation, but the burn igniting a path from my throat to my stomach is dull in comparison.

"What's the matter with you?" Blake asks, arching a brow as he refills my glass.

We've been sitting at his bar for over an hour. I've lost count of the shots I've swallowed, and Blake doesn't stop pouring them. I exhale a quiet sigh, glancing around while he types a message on his phone.

Blake has owned this place for a few years, having opened it to cure his boredom at the time.

The atmosphere is subdued, and with no windows, the only light comes from exposed bulbs hanging from the wood-paneled ceiling. It feels more like an old-fashioned tavern than a bar, which is probably why I don't mind spending time here. As an added bonus, it's hidden from street view. You'd have to know it was here to find it.

Behind the wooden bar we're sitting at, several glass shelves span the counter to the ceiling, filled with dozens of liquor bottles. Round tables and plush booths sit throughout the bar, offering secluded corners for those seeking a bit of privacy from the rest of the room. There's a young couple having dinner in the far corner, speaking in hushed voices, and a few older men sit around one of the tables, grumbling about work as they toss back their beer. Soft rock music filters through the room and the smell of stale alcohol permeates the air. It's the middle of the week, so the place is quiet enough to hold a conversation, though that's the last thing I'm looking to do.

"Nothing's the matter with me," I grumble, because Blake won't understand the emotions warring in my chest. Frankly, I can't remember the last time he genuinely gave a damn about anything. Most demons don't, which is likely why Lucia sees my human side as a deficiency she wants to erase.

Blake shoves his hands into the pockets of his magenta windbreaker with a dramatic sigh. He tilts his head to the side, his bright pink hair falling across his forehead. "Is this whole pity party about that human girlfriend of yours?"

I rake my fingers through my hair before dragging my hand down my face, groaning inwardly. I'm not sure I can call her my anything anymore, though my hackles raise at the thought. The monster in me wholeheartedly believes she is mine. Which is slightly complicated when I think, at least now, she'd vehemently disagree. Though I can't help but recall our last interaction.

You deserve the life you want. For once, choose yourself.

I've played her words over in my head to the point of a migraine more than once since that night. I can't fathom a world where it could possibly work, despite the part of me that wants it.

It doesn't matter, I remind myself. So long as my mother sits on her throne, determined to eradicate the hunters, what I want is irrelevant. And that makes it very difficult to care about anything, to fight the voices in my head that whisper at me constantly to let go of my grip on my humanity. But I can't. It's the only thing I have that, try as she might, Lucia can't destroy.

Blake whistles softly. "Shit. You've got it bad, huh?"

A muscle feathers along my jaw, and my fingers itch to reach for the bottle between us. "It doesn't matter."

He nods. "Who are you trying to convince?"

"It doesn't matter," I repeat, "because Camille is never going to agree to Lucia's demands. She'll fight with everything she has to protect the people she loves."

"I hear the disappointment in your voice," he points out, lowering his voice. "You want to be one of those people."

I shrug, tapping my thumb against the side of my empty glass as I meet his gaze. "I can't be."

Blake's brows knit, and he shakes his head, exhaling a heavy sigh. "Fuck, Xander. I don't know what to tell you. I'm...sorry." The sincerity in his voice is rare. I'm used to a flippant, uncaring demon when I talk to my friend. It's been a long time since we've had this type of conversation, the kind that left unchecked, could turn dangerously vulnerable.

So I swipe the whiskey and pour us both another shot.

The street is quiet when I leave Blake's an hour later with a decent buzz. He tried to convince me to crash at his place above the bar, but the urge to get outside was nagging at me. The music and chatter of conversation around the room was getting more irritating by the second.

I slip out the door while he's grabbing bottles from the stockroom, and my phone vibrates in my pocket a minute later. I pull it out to find a message from Blake and fight back an eye roll.

> Where the fuck did you go?

> I'm going home. I don't need a babysitter to walk six blocks.

> Your mother will rip off my testicles if she finds out.

I shudder, shaking my head as I round the corner and type a response.

> Thanks for that image, jackass. I can take care of myself.

> Are you almost home? Text me as soon as you get there and fucking keep to yourself. There are hunters scouring the streets for your dumb ass.

> Take the night off from worrying about me.

> As fucking if. What are you up to?

I shove my phone back into my pocket without responding. The monster is banging against the bars of the cage. I've gotten fairly skilled at keeping it shut tight. Tonight, though, all I can think about is quieting the noise in my head and the pain in my chest. Giving in to my most carnal need is the only surefire way to find a reprieve from the human emotions plaguing me, but I know how dangerously addicting it is. Which is why Blake has had to pester me about feeding more and more these days. Because the more I feed, the easier it is to let the darkest parts of me take over. They call to me now as I prowl down the street, pushing my senses outward to keep tabs on my surroundings.

I pass a pizzeria with its front doors open to the street. Music and casual conversation mixes with the savory smell of bread and cheese.

I briefly consider walking inside, but there are too many humans to choose from. While some demons are able to feed on an entire room of people, that is not in my skill set.

Turning my head, I catch sight of a young woman jogging on the sidewalk across the street. She looks to be around my age, with golden blond hair haphazardly tied back and a matching animal print workout set that Blake would most definitely approve of. Studio headphones cover her ears, playing an upbeat tune, and her gaze is focused, her breathing measured with each inhale and exhale.

I'm moving before I can overthink it, stalking behind her but keeping enough of a distance to stay conspicuous to any onlooker. Until she approaches the mouth of an alley between two storefronts. That's when I strike. I move faster than any human can see, snatching her off the sidewalk and dragging her into the alley, clamping my hand over her mouth before she can make a sound. The surrounding stores are closed for the day, the sun fully absent from the sky, but I'm not taking any chances of getting caught. Not when I'm so fucking starving. You'd think I haven't fed in weeks with how eager my demon side is to get my claws in her.

The music continues playing in her ears, and her eyes bulge out of her face. The fear in them has the corner of my lips twisting up as I hold her against the brick exterior of the building. I don't even need to project fear into her subconscious—she's terrified of me already.

She shakes in my grip, her heart hammering in her chest as a sheen of sweat covers her face and chest. Even still, she tries to fight, to push me away. Her screams are muffled by my hand, and they only grow louder, more desperate when a shudder ripples through me, turning my eyes black as I lean in to devour her fear. I inhale deeply, letting the power of her terror feed the worst parts of me as tears stream down her cheeks. Blood drains from her face, leaving the girl white as a sheet. Within seconds her knees buckle, and she slides down the wall until she's sitting on the ground. She's still conscious, but she has stopped screaming. Her head tips back against the building as soft whimpers escape her lips.

"Pl-please," she croaks, peering at me through her tears as she shakes her head back and forth, shivers racking her body. "Let...me go."

I cock my head to the side, crouching in front of her as I pull her headphones off. "I will," I offer in a smooth voice.

More tears slip down her cheeks. "Why are you doing this to me?"

I press my lips together for a moment before sighing, reaching toward her and tucking a bit of hair that escaped her tie behind her ear as she continues shivering. "Because I don't have a choice."

The fear radiating from her fills my veins with a jolt of energy, and the monster in me makes a sound of delight, a soft, growl-like rumble in my chest. It feels like waking up from the most restful sleep. The dull ache in my muscles melts away and the throbbing behind my eyes fades, allowing me to see everything in such detail it's almost overwhelming.

I'm fairly certain the human has gone into shock. She isn't fighting me or screaming anymore. If I had to bet, she has completely disassociated. I don't blame her—it's pretty much what I'm doing too. At least, the human part of me is. The demon part revels in the power I take from my prey, and as I straighten and back away from the woman, I'm filled with a conflicting mix of satisfaction and remorse.

My boots echo off the pavement as I walk away from the alley, tuning out the broken sounds coming from the human I left on the ground. She'll likely report the attack to the police, but the hunters will step in before it can make it to the media. Keeping secret the monsters that hunt in the shadows, just as they have for decades. But not for much longer, if Lucia gets her way.

At some point, I resigned myself to whatever outcome will arise. This is the most destructive plan she's had in my lifetime, and whatever threat the hunters believe me to be, I have no power when it comes to this fight. Because I will follow Lucia's orders, do what she expects of me. And it will be the last time.

TWENTY
CAMILLE

The next time I open my eyes, I find myself staring at the ceiling in my bedroom. The darkness gives way to a blurry haze, and I have about ten seconds of relief where I trick myself into believing the horror I endured was nothing but a terrible, twisted nightmare. And then it all comes rushing back.

I bolt upright, gasping for air, as if my lungs have forgotten how to breathe. *I can't breathe.* Same as when I watched my friends die.

"Camille."

I whip my head toward the sound of Harper's voice. "What happened?" I force out, my voice cracking. "How did I get here?"

She frowns. Her eyes are bloodshot and dark circles cast shadows beneath them. "You were dropped off at HQ. The back service entrance, where you couldn't be seen from the street. The security team spotted you on one of the surveillance cameras and sent a few hunters after the demon who left you there. We carried you inside to get you checked out before your mom and I brought you home."

"Did they catch her?" I ask in a small voice.

She nods. "They, uh, found her getting into a vehicle, and Phoebe—" Her voice breaks, and she stops talking as her eyes well.

My own eyes burn, and my vision blurs with tears. "Phoebe and Grayson," I whisper, unable to erase the memory of watching them...I choke on a sob. "I couldn't save them." I shake my head, as if that will change what happened. As if that will bring back our friends.

Harper nods and swallows hard. "I know." She glances away. "Your mom is still here," she says hoarsely, then clears her throat and looks at me again. "She thinks you should visit your dad for a few days."

I exhale a shaky breath. Instead of responding to that, I ask, "What happened to the demon?"

"She was captured and interrogated. We found out her name was Madeline. Seems like she was trying to work her way into Lucia's inner circle. She was tasked with returning you and...*disposing* of Phoebe and Grayson." Her voice shakes with a mix of anger and grief, her jaw working as she struggles not to start crying.

I close my eyes against the burn of more tears, my stomach coiling tight. "What's going to happen to her?"

"Exactly what she deserves," Harper says firmly.

Lucia gave Madeline a task she knew the demon wouldn't survive, and she did it without hesitation. Because the only thing that mattered to Madeline was gaining her queen's approval.

I nod absently. "Where's my mom?" I'm not sure I'm ready to face her, but I also want to get it over with.

"Living room. Want me to get her?"

"Sure." I lean back against the headboard, reaching for the glass of water on the nightstand, and down half of it.

Harper slides off the bed and slips out of the room.

A minute later, my mom walks in and closes the door behind her. She's dressed in all black and her auburn hair is in a slick bun. So, she either came directly from training or a mission. She approaches with an expression that brings the tears back to my eyes. The softness in her typically cool blue gaze isn't a common occurrence.

"Hi, Mom," I say, messing with the sheets for something to do with my hands.

She perches on the side of the bed, placing her hand over mine. "I'm very sorry for your loss, Camille."

I hold my breath, waiting for her to dive into the recruitment speech she must have memorized by now, but she doesn't, so I nod silently.

"I spoke to your father on my way here," she says.

"Harper told me."

Mom nods, looking away when her breath hitches. She sniffles, and I struggle to keep the shock off my face when I see the tears in her eyes. "I don't know what I would have done if you had—" She stops herself, shaking her head as she squeezes my hand. "I understand you don't want to be surrounded by hunters, and I want to respect your wishes, but I refuse to allow what happened to your friends happen to you. You can be angry with me if you need to, but I have assigned a team of hunters for your protection. They will guard your apartment even when Harper is home. At least two of them will accompany you to class and wherever else you need to go."

I blink at her, and the familiar sensation of struggling to breathe starts to creep in. "A team, Mom?" The thought of having my every move tracked, of having a shadow everywhere I go, threatens to break the levee on my barely-contained anxiety.

"Until this fight is over, one isn't enough. Especially when the queen thinks she can use you against us."

"But—"

"I'm not going to let you get hurt again, Camille." She blinks quickly, her eyes glassy as she holds my gaze. Her grip on my hand is growing uncomfortably tight, but I don't try to pull away. "I won't lose another child to those monsters. I *can't.*"

My throat clogs with emotion, and all I can do is nod, resigning myself to the reality that this is how things have to be, at least for now.

She sniffles, wiping her nose with her other hand before clearing her throat. "What do you think about going to New York for a while?"

I curl my fingers around hers and squeeze her hand. "Yeah, I...want to go."

She doesn't attempt to mask her surprise. "Really? I thought for sure I'd have to argue with you about it."

My gaze drops to my lap, and I lick the dryness from my lips. "No. I need to get out of here."

"Do you want to talk about what happened?" she asks.

I shake my head without looking at her.

She leans in and kisses the side of my head. "Pack a bag, and I'll get you on the next flight."

My dad is waiting at arrivals when I land at JFK. He pulls me into a hug the moment we meet, and I wrap my arms around him, clinging to him as if he'll be able to keep me together. We don't talk on the drive to his condo on the Upper West Side. I stare out the windshield at the cars and brownstones, while he taps his fingers against the steering wheel to the soft rock song on the radio.

After passing through a security checkpoint, Dad pulls into the underground garage and turns the car off.

"Those guards," I say, "they're hunters, aren't they?"

He nods. "I have a team that keeps an eye on things around here. The job your mother and I have has always been dangerous, but we're in new territory now. These precautions are necessary to protect everyone."

"So they're here to keep you safe?"

"Exactly. There are also guards stationed who look to any human like normal building security guards. I also have a guard outside my suite for the duration of your visit."

My brows lift at the same moment my stomach sinks. "Is that really necessary?"

"If you think he isn't keeping tabs on you, you need to be more realistic, kiddo."

"That's not—" I stop myself as we get into the elevator, because things with Xander is the last topic of conversation I want right now. "Never mind."

We step off the elevator into the entryway, and sure enough, there's a guy who looks a few years older than me. He's dressed in all black, standing against the wall next to the front door.

"Mr. Morgan," he greets Dad before turning to me. "Ms. Morgan."

"Brody, this is my daughter, Camille."

I offer an awkward wave. "Hey."

Brody cracks a warm smile. "Nice to meet you."

Nodding, I give him a quick once-over. Despite being a skilled demon hunter, Brody gives me giant teddy bear vibes. He has curly, brown hair and hazel eyes. I feel tiny as we move closer to him. This guy has to be at least six feet tall and is *seriously* built.

Dad unlocks and opens the door, and I walk inside ahead of him.

I drop my bag in the guest room before curling up on the couch in the living room, snagging the quilt off the back of it. It's one my grandmother made years ago, and wrapping myself in it provides a semblance of comfort. I angle myself to look out the floor-to-ceiling windows across the room, taking in the view of Central Park. The trees have started turning, providing a warm mix of colors. There's less variety inside Dad's apartment. Everything is muted tones of gray and black and white. The high ceilings and dark hardwood floors give the space a sophisticated feel, but nothing about it feels personal. He's never had an eye for design.

I wonder if it's because he doesn't spend much time here.

Dad comes into the room with a mug in each hand, handing me one. "It's lavender tea," he says as I wrap my fingers around the mug and lift it to my nose, inhaling slowly.

"Thanks," I murmur.

He nods, setting his cup on the coffee table and sitting in the chair across from the couch. "I read your mom's report on the incident your friends were involved in, but do you want to tell me anything?"

I take a sip of the tea before setting the mug down. "I don't know what to say," I admit.

Dad offers me a sympathetic look. "I'm not asking in any official capacity. And if you don't want to talk about it, that's okay, too."

I press my lips together for a moment before exhaling an uneven breath. "I wasn't there when Danielle died, but watching Phoebe and Grayson being killed by a demon...It felt like I was reliving Dani's death. I've never felt so helpless, Dad." The tears are back, and I make no effort to hold them back. They roll down my cheeks, and I sniffle, wiping my nose with my sleeve. I inch closer to a panic attack, the anxiety simmering just beneath the surface. And no matter how many deep breaths I take, the suffocating sensation refuses to dissipate.

"I understand, kiddo. I wish there was something I could say to make you feel better, but if nothing else, I'm glad to give you a break from Seattle. You know I love when you visit me. You're welcome here anytime."

I manage a watery smile. "Yeah. Thanks, Dad."

Once we've had dinner, I leave him watching a hockey game in the living room and crawl into bed. I send a quick check-in text to Harper and my mom before setting my phone on the nightstand. Rolling over to face the window, I curl onto my side and pull the blankets up around me. After a day of travel, I'm grateful when sleep finds me quickly.

Dad is gone when I wake up the next day. He left a note stuck to the coffee machine, letting me know he'll be at work until later. I rummage through the kitchen and settle on a bowl of oatmeal with blueberries and eat on the balcony.

After getting dressed, I head out to explore the city.

Brody is in the same spot outside the front door, sipping from a to-go cup as I step into the hallway.

"Morning," I say.

"Hey there," he replies. "Heading out?"

"Um, yeah. I can't stay cooped up all day. It's too nice out." Plus, the whole idea of this trip is to be a distraction from what happened in Seattle.

He nods, glancing at his watch. "I'm supposed to accompany you if you leave the building."

"No offense, but I don't really want company. I don't suppose you'd look the other way?"

Brody offers me a smile.

I exhale a sigh. "Of course not."

I spend the morning walking around Central Park, sipping a chai latte and nibbling on a jumbo pretzel as I try to ignore Brody.

He keeps his distance, but I know he's there, keeping his gaze trained on my every move.

Still, I pretend my life is someone else's, smiling at tourists and locals alike as they pass me by. I vaguely wonder if I look like a tourist or a local myself as I pause at the Bethesda Fountain, staring at the *Angel of the Waters* sculpture atop it. Getting lost in the intricate details of the angel's wings, I take a deep breath and glance skyward, allowing myself to enjoy the warmth of the sun against my face.

I lose track of time wandering the paths and eventually take a break when the late morning sun streams through the trees, leaving the back of my neck damp with sweat. I grab a bottle of water from a vendor and find a bench in the shade, listening to the sound of birds chirping. Closing my eyes, I try to center myself. I inhale slowly for four seconds, hold it for seven seconds, and exhale for eight seconds. It takes repeating the action twice more before I finally reach a semblance of feeling relaxed. It's something my nerves aren't familiar with these days.

After taking a long drink of water, I screw the cap back on as my phone vibrates in my jacket pocket. I lean back and pull it out, frowning. It's a message from an unknown message.

> You look like you belong here.

I freeze, my pulse kicking up as my throat goes dry.

Someone is watching me.

My brain immediately goes to Xander, but he wouldn't bother texting me from an unknown number. I have half a mind to consider Blake, though he doesn't seem like the type to send a cryptic message instead of just popping out of the trees to say hi in person.

I chew my thumbnail for a few seconds, reading over the message again, and then type out a response.

> Who is this?

I glance around the park but don't see anyone I recognize or anyone on their phone. I consider getting up and going to Brody, but before I can move, another message comes through.

> Now you look freaked. Shit, I didn't mean to scare you.

My head whips up and my gaze immediately meets Noah's. I scowl, trying to calm my racing heart. "What the fuck, Daniels?" I grumble. "Are you stalking me now? And what's with the creepy texts? How'd you even get my number?"

He chuckles softly and sits beside me without an invitation.

Despite my annoyance, I can't help but notice how good Noah looks out of hunter attire. The casual dark jeans and gray long sleeve definitely suits him.

"I thought it'd be funny," he says. "Your dad told me Brody was keeping an eye on you today, so I hit him up to see where you guys were. Scott gave me your number." He adds in a wry tone, "In hindsight, my message probably wasn't the best entrance."

I shoot him a dry look. "You think? What do you want, Noah?"

"What are you up to?" he asks instead of answering my question.

"Oh, you know," I say breezily, "questioning the last several weeks of my life while trying to erase the image of my friends dying in front of me. Normal stuff."

The smile curling his lips fades. "I'm sorry about what happened."

I sigh, crossing my arms as I lean against the back of the bench. "Look, can we not do this?"

Noah cocks his head to the side. "What should we do instead?"

I nearly choke on a humorless laugh. "Nothing. We aren't doing anything. I know my dad is worried about me, but I don't need a babysitter."

"Maybe I do," he offers.

"I don't doubt that, but it's not going to be me. Take Brody."

His lips twitch. "When was the last time you were here? In NYC?" he asks.

I think about it for a minute before shrugging. "I don't know. It's been a while."

"Why don't we do a little sightseeing? Grab some lunch and—"

"You don't want to spend the day with me."

"I don't?" he asks, frowning faintly.

I shake my head. "I'm not in the mood to socialize." And I'm *really* not in the mood to keep up the ruse of strength, which I've always felt the need to do around him. To impress him or something, I don't know. It's ridiculous, and I hate how he makes me feel like I'm sixteen years old again. Noah is the type of childhood crush who turned into the most annoying, arrogant—

He drops his hand to my knee, and my thoughts scatter.

My gaze follows his hand and I press my lips together at how *not* weird it feels to have him touching me. I should pull away or knock his hand off my knee, but I don't do either.

"I'm off today," he says. "Why don't I take over for Brody and show you around the city? There's something I think you'd enjoy."

I swallow twice before I can speak. "I don't think I can enjoy anything right now."

"Give me an hour? It just might make you feel better."

I arch a brow, and despite the pit in my stomach, I can't help it—my curiosity is piqued. I exhale a heavy sigh. "Okay, fine. *One* hour."

I stare at Noah after we get out of the cab, my brows halfway up my forehead. "Axe throwing? Are you sure you want to put a weapon in my hands?"

He laughs softly, nodding. "Trust me. Throwing sharp objects can be surprisingly therapeutic." He nudges my shoulder, offering a faint smirk. "Especially if you manage to hit the target."

"Okay, then," I grumble as we walk toward the building. The inside resembles something between a bowling alley and a gym. It has the faint scent of wood and an interesting combination of liquor and fried food.

We check in and sign a waiver that basically says we can't sue them if we lose a limb. Then I follow Noah over to our section.

"Have you ever done this before?" he asks, a glint of excitement in his eyes.

I prop my hands on my hips. "Does it look like I have?"

"Absolutely not. I just thought I would give you the benefit of the doubt by asking."

I roll my eyes. "I'm assuming you've done this before. Why don't you show me how it's done?"

Noah steps up and grabs a hatchet-sized axe with his dominant hand, testing the weight of it before he steps up to the red line, focusing on the target across the room. He inhales slowly and lifts both arms above his head, holding the axe steady, then lets it fly. It slams into the target about five inches above the bullseye.

I can't help the curl of my lips watching him. Before I can stop myself, my gaze goes to the muscles in his forearms. It's undeniable how attractive Noah is, but I'm usually caught up in him running his mouth at me. *Not* what that mouth would feel like—*Nope*. Not going there.

He walks back to me, grinning like he's waiting for me to praise him.

"Okay," I say flatly, "so you just throw it at the board?"

He offers a deep laugh. "There's a bit more to it than that. You need a firm grip on the axe and follow through naturally after you throw it. And you want to throw it outward, not up."

"Uh-huh," I say, nodding, as if I'm following his words. I'm surprised by the nervous flutter in my stomach. There's also a part of me that's worried I'm going to completely miss the target and embarrass myself, giving Noah another thing to hold over my head.

His words echo back to me from the day I ran into him at headquarters. *Wasted potential.*

I shake my head, trying to dispel the memory, and take a deep breath.

"You've got this," he says with an encouraging nudge.

I walk over and pick up an axe, stopping at the red line. Inhaling slowly, I raise the axe above my shoulder, trying my best to copy the motion Noah demonstrated. The axe is surprisingly heavy. I'm not entirely sure I'm strong enough for this but I'm not about to back down now. I set my sights on the target, squinting at it as the bullseye taunts me.

Summoning every ounce of strength and courage I have, I swing my arm forward, releasing the axe with a flick of my wrist. It sails through the air, and I hold my breath, waiting for it to land. It sinks into the target with a loud *thud* on the first ring.

"Not bad," Noah says.

I jump at the sound of his voice so close to my ear. A rush of adrenaline sends my head spinning. I whip around to face him, my lips splitting into a grin. "Holy shit," I say, "that was fun."

"I'm not going to say I told you so. I don't think I have to."

I slap him on the shoulder halfheartedly. Leave it to Noah to make this moment about himself.

We throw a few more before wandering over to the food court. Despite not being super hungry, I agree to split a basket of fries.

He also orders me a chocolate milkshake.

My stomach feels weirdly fluttery, thinking that he remembered from when we were younger. "Thanks for this," I say in a soft voice as we leave the building and I find myself wondering how much simpler my life would be if I hadn't met Xander. If I hadn't quit the organization. Moreover, what would've become of my teenage crush on Noah.

He nods, his expression unexpectedly sincere. "I'm glad I could offer a distraction, even if it was temporary. How long do you think you'll stay in the city?"

I shrug. "Not sure. I can't miss much school, but the thought of returning to Seattle..." My voice trails off. "I don't think I can get on a plane just yet."

He nods again. "I'm sure your dad is happy to have you here."

"Yeah, I think so. He's at the academy today, but hopefully he'll be able to get some time away tomorrow."

Noah rakes his hand through his hair. "I'm teaching an introductory seminar tomorrow. You should check it out if you end up needing something to do."

My stomach dips and suddenly doesn't feel so light and fluttery. I narrow my eyes. "I guess I should be happy that we *almost* got through a full encounter without that being brought up."

He frowns briefly. "It was just an idea to keep your mind off things."

"You think hanging out with a bunch of demon hunters is going to help take my mind off demons?"

He raises his hands defensively. "Forget I asked."

I nod curtly. "Already forgotten."

Noah exhales a heavy sigh. "Shit, Cam, I'm sorry. This whole thing was meant to make you feel better. I know you think I'm an ass—"

"I think you're an ass because you *act* like an ass."

"Noted," he grants with a faint smile. "Come on. I'll take you home. Your dad should be done working soon, and I'm sure he'll want to spend time with you."

I nod, not wanting to end what was a surprisingly good time on a sour note—just because I started to overthink what he was saying.

"And if you ever want to do this again," he says casually while meeting my gaze, "well, at least now you have my number."

Is that Noah's way of saying he wants me to use it?

Younger me would be ecstatic at that, but I don't know how to feel right now. After everything that happened with Xander, I'm finding it difficult to trust my gut when it comes to the guys in my life. Granted, I've known Noah since I was a kid and I'm confident he's not lying about his identity, but that doesn't mean he wouldn't hurt me.

So I build up a wall, offer him a polite smile, and decide I'm not going to call him.

TWENTY-ONE
XANDER

Camille left the city. And after what happened to her friends, I don't blame her. The part of me that cares for her is infected with the pain of sympathy mixed with guilt surrounding how they lost their lives. I have no fucking clue how to deal, and drinking with Blake only works to numb things for so long.

I typically consider myself someone with a high level of self control, so I can't quite explain how I ended up booking a flight to JFK. Even once I'm at the airport, standing at the gate waiting to board, I don't fully understand why I'm going or what I'm going to do when I get there. All I know is I couldn't ignore this urge to go, so I left.

I can feel *something* brewing among the demons, which means, no matter where Camille is, she isn't safe. No one will touch her if I'm close, so perhaps part of my reason for going is tied to that. Because everything else aside, and even with the darkness inside me longing to serve Lucia, I won't let Camille get hurt more than she already has.

I don't expect her to be happy to see me. Getting around her father is going to add a layer of complication to this impromptu trip to the Big Apple, because I have no doubt Scott Morgan would kill me on sight, if given the chance. No hesitation or remorse. Hell, it would be justified for what I've done to his daughter, but that doesn't stop me from going after her, anyway.

"What are you doing?"

I glance over at Blake, who's behind the wheel of the rental car. He wouldn't let me take the trip on my own. While I'm not sure it's the best idea having him here, I suppose it's better to have backup. In case I run into the neighborhood watch of hunters on the Upper West Side.

"I think we should tell her we're here," I say, tapping my finger against my phone as I contemplate how to craft that message.

"Why? So Daddy Hunter can come up with a plan to take us out the moment we arrive?"

"No, but I think if we show up out of nowhere, Camille will immediately go on the defensive." And she'd have every right to. I haven't exactly given her any reason to trust me.

Blake sighs, raking a hand through his hair. He hasn't dyed it in a while, so the pink is fading. "I think she's going to either way, my friend."

The tension unfurling in my chest tells me he's right, but I ignore it all the same. There's no turning back now.

"Do you know what you're going to say to her?" he asks as we sit at a red light. He swipes through his playlist without letting any song play for more than a few seconds.

I glance out the windshield at the concrete jungle ahead. The sky is overcast, threatening rain, but the streets are still packed with crowds of people. "Not a fucking clue," I admit, scratching my jaw. "I'm hoping the words will come to me when I see her."

Blake snorts. "That's the most ridiculously naive thing you've said in a long time."

I scowl, leaning back against the headrest. "Yeah, well, what do you suggest I say?"

A lopsided grin curves his lips. "You really want to know?"

Probably not. "Forget it," I grumble.

Half an hour of New York traffic—aka the human world's closest thing to hell—later, we arrive at the St. Regis and check into our suite.

I drop my duffle bag on the end of the bed before sinking down beside it. This tangled web of deceit has escalated much faster than I'd been expecting. While it might've been stupid of me to think I could get through this without growing some form of attachment to my target, it's painfully clear now I haven't escaped it.

I thought it would be so fucking simple. Seduce and persuade Camille to turn against the organization she already hates and give Lucia what she wants. Then I'd disappear for the rest of my life, never having to face the monster who did everything she could to make me one too. And maybe in some ways and to some people I am, but that's never who—never *what*—I wanted to be.

But Lucia took that choice away from me when she decided to use me as a pawn. It's not something I wanted to do to Camille, but it's what

I have to do to break free from the hell I've been stuck in long after I left the twisted demonic realm itself.

"That's quite the pensive look," Blake comments, slinking toward me with a crystal glass of bourbon.

I push my fingers through my hair, exhaling a heavy sigh. I'm at a loss on exactly how to start the conversation. The mounting pressure in my chest is desperate to be let out. Instead of overthinking it a moment longer, I finally settle on, "Do you ever think about getting out?"

Blake cocks his head to the side, peering at me with a glint of curiosity in his gaze. "Getting out of what?"

I clench my jaw, rubbing my hands on my thighs before meeting his gaze, which is shrouded with confusion. "This life. Don't you feel like it isn't your own? For years now, you've been ordered to put my life above yours, no matter the cost. And you have, without failure or even a split second of hesitation."

Any hint of humor or amusement vanishes from his face as his features sharpen into focus and he steps forward. "My life is yours," he says in a deep, level tone.

I shake my head. "That's not—"

"It's *yours*, Xander," he continues firmly, "for many reasons, but most importantly, because I'd be dead without you."

I don't say anything for a short eternity. My pulse ticks unnervingly fast, and the intensity in Blake's eyes makes the pressure in my chest heighten tenfold. If the intention of his declaration is to bring me calmness, it does the opposite. His loyalty, as precious as it is, means I have more to lose. More for Lucia to take from me if I step even slightly out of line.

"You may change your mind after this trip."

Blake cracks a grin and claps me on the shoulder. "Nice try," he says. "You're not getting rid of me. I'm here until the bitter end, my friend."

I exhale a laugh. "Yeah, maybe don't joke about that."

He arches a brow. "Who's joking?" Downing the rest of his bourbon, he smacks his lips. "Now, come on. Let's get you a drink and then you can tell me why you decided it was necessary to follow your whatever-you-want-to-call-her all the way to New York. Despite it being one of the highest populated hunter cities in the world." His tone is casual, flippant, but the lingering concern in his gaze tells me he's completely serious.

"That's probably going be a three-drink conversation," I offer grimly as I stand.

Blake drops his arm over my shoulders and chuckles. "Well, then. It's a good thing you're buying."

We ride the elevator downstairs and find a small table in the quiet corner of the King Cole Bar. It's a sleek, elegant space filled with dark tones and wooden accents. The subtle scents of high-end perfume and expensive liquor mingle with the soft buzz of conversation around us. The patrons appear to be a mix of businesspeople and tourists, and the overall feel is still very upscale yet warm.

Blake and I keep our heads down, leaning close to not be overheard.

"Are you going to tell me what's going on in that head of yours, mate?" he asks, skimming the cocktail menu.

I rub my jaw, catching the gaze of the waiter across the room, who offers a smile that suggests he'll be coming by our table shortly. With a sigh, I turn my attention back to Blake. "You're still keeping your ear to the ground these days, yeah?"

He shrugs. "More or less."

I arch a brow. "Which is it?"

"Hmm...less at the moment."

Before I can respond, the waiter stops at our table.

Blake orders a bourbon while I opt for a scotch.

Once the waiter is gone, I say, "Have you heard any recent chatter about the crown?"

Blake inclines his head. "Whispers here and there. Nothing all that concerning, though, considering who it's coming from."

"I think it's more widespread than you know. Lucia's concerned, which is the reason behind her moving up the timeline with Camille and the hunters."

"And that has to do with following your human to New York, how?"

"Part of my mother's plan is to have Camille double-cross her parents. *My* plan is to have her double-cross Lucia."

Blake nods, mulling it over. "When did you decide this?"

I press my lips together, pausing when the waiter drops off our drinks, then say, "I was initially resigned to following in Lucia's plan to destroy the hunters. I vowed it would be the very last thing I'd do for her and then I would disappear."

He blinks at me, hiding the shock on his face by swallowing a mouthful of his drink. He sucks in air through his teeth. "What—and I cannot stress this enough—the fuck?"

I chuckle, but it lacks any humor. "I wouldn't go anywhere without you, so you can relax. It doesn't matter now regardless, because it's not going to happen."

"You leaving, or Lucia destroying the hunters?"

I take a drink of my scotch before answering, "Neither."

His brows lift. "How do you figure?"

Taking a quick look around, I lower my voice even further. "There's a growing number of demons—especially ones who have been around a long time—that are becoming increasingly wary of her reign. I think this idea that she'll be able to eradicate the hunters, thus eliminating the biggest threat to our kind, is seen differently to most than how she sees it."

"It seems more like a power move than protecting her people to me."

"Exactly. And many agree."

Blake leans back in his chair. "Well, shit. Does *she* know that? I mean, she has to, right?"

I offer him a look.

"Of course she does," he says, rolling his eyes and shaking his head. "I guess her paranoia of being overthrown has manifested into reality, huh?"

"Hmm." I take another drink. "Seems like it."

"Okay," Blake says before emptying his glass and slamming it on the table, earning a few looks from surrounding tables. "So, what's our plan?"

TWENTY-TWO
CAMILLE

Dad, unsurprisingly, got called into the academy on his day off. Which leaves me alone in his condo. I spent the morning reorganizing his bookshelves and watering the few plants he has. By lunchtime I realize I haven't eaten, so I shuffle into the kitchen, still in my sleep shorts and tank top. Once I've pulled a few items out of the fridge to make an omelette, I call Harper on speaker so I can cook and talk at the same time.

"*Heyyy*," she sings into the phone. "How's NYC?"

"It's—" I take a few seconds to craft an answer as I pull a knife from the block on the counter and find a cutting board to chop the peppers. "It's been interesting."

"Wait, really? You've been there for a day. What happened?"

I chop the end off a pepper. "*Noah* happened."

"Uhhh, I'm going to need more than that, Cami."

I keep chopping. "We ran into each other yesterday, and he took me axe throwing. We had some food, and then I went back to my dad's."

"Why does that sound like a date?"

I set the knife down, then crack an egg into a glass bowl, tossing the shell into the garbage. "It *wasn't* a date," I say firmly.

"Damn. Twelve-year-old Cami would've died for a date with Noah Daniels. And here you are...denying you had one."

"Yep," I say, dragging out the word before moving on to chop a red onion, adding it to the bowl. "It was a nice distraction, but that's all it was. I'm serious, Harper."

Once I've whisked everything together, I find a frying pan in the cupboard beside the oven. Igniting the burner, I grab the bowl of egg mixture and pour it into the pan.

"If you say so."

Instead of responding to that, I ask, "How are things there?"

Silence fills the line, and then Harper sighs. "A little complicated, but we don't need to talk about it. Everything is being handled."

I pause. "What does that mean, Harper?"

Another stretch of silence has my nerves perking up, the back of my neck tingling in response.

"In the last twenty-four hours, there have been a number of fatal demon attacks in several states."

I press my lips together at the sinking feeling in my stomach. "I'm guessing this is out of the ordinary?"

"Yeah," she says in a tight voice. "The reports coming in are triple what the organization is used to. It's unprecedented. Everyone is working doubles. I'm at home right now to shower and then I'll be heading back to HQ."

The tension in my chest worsens. If everyone is being called in to work doubles, this is *bad*.

This is Lucia sending me a message. Reminding me she can hurt anyone. Whenever she desires.

"Harper, please be careful." The worry in my voice is impossible to mask, and I'm no longer hungry for breakfast.

"Of course. Listen, I have to go, but I'll check in with you later, okay? Try to enjoy your time there. And tell your dad I said 'hey.'"

"Okay," I force out. "Talk soon."

After ending the call, I finish making my omelette, flipping it onto a plate and sitting at the breakfast bar. I poke at it, forcing myself to swallow a few mouthfuls and sip the glass of orange juice I poured, despite the unease churning in my stomach.

My worry has me close to texting Noah, but there's nothing he can say that'll change what's happening. Hell, he's probably too wrapped up in it to even answer me, anyway.

Once I've managed to eat most of the omelette, I clean the few dishes I used. Then I head upstairs to shower and get ready, for no other reason than a distraction from my thought spiral. I spend the rest of the afternoon tidying things and even wash the bedding from both bedrooms. I need to keep busy—I can't let myself think about what's going on with the demons.

My phone chimes from the coffee table, and I race toward it, expecting an update from Harper. Instead, it's a message from my dad.

> Going to be late tonight. Let me know where you want to go for dinner, and I'll meet you there at 8 p.m.

I let out the breath I was holding, fighting the urge to ask him about what's going on. It's probably best to ask him in person.

> I like that bistro around the corner.

> Sounds great. See you there.

I chew the pad of my thumb for a minute, then start typing again.

> I spoke to Harper a few hours ago, so I know what's going on. Are you sure you'll be able to get away for dinner?

I hesitate before sending another message.

> I can bring you something if you need to stay there.

Five minutes go by before I get a response.

> I appreciate that, kiddo, but I'll need a break by that point, anyway.

That's...unexpected. Though Dad has always been a bit better with the whole work-life balance thing than Mom.

> Okay. See you soon.

Leaving the condo a few hours later, I smile at the middle-aged, female hunter stationed at the door. We make the short walk to the bistro a few blocks away, and I try to ignore the feeling of being watched as she follows me.

Last time I was in the city, Dad brought me here, and I fell in love with their food—especially the dessert menu. We went nearly every night during my visit. My stomach grumbles as I think about their decadent red velvet cake with mouth-watering cream cheese frosting.

I grab a seat on the patio, wanting to take advantage of the unseasonably warm mid-October weather. I peruse the menu while I wait for my dad to arrive, as if I don't already know I'm going to order the chicken parmesan and kale caesar salad.

He's only a few minutes late, which I consider impressive. I stand as he approaches the table and give him a tight squeeze, noticing the hunter who followed me is leaving now that my dad is here.

"Hey, kiddo," he says, kissing the side of my head.

"Hey, Dad." We pull back, and I shoot him a sympathetic smile. "Just another boring day at the office, huh?"

He chuckles as he takes a seat. "Something like that."

I'm afraid to ask, but the words leave my lips, anyway. "Do you have to go back after this?"

He frowns, and I have my answer.

I nod. "I figured as much."

The waiter comes over to take our order. After he walks away, Dad says, "Noah told me you two spent some time together yesterday."

"Yes, your golden boy took your daughter axe throwing," I say in a light tone, gasping dramatically.

His brows lift. "I'm surprised he gave you a sharp object."

I roll my eyes at Dad's teasing tone, though I can't argue with that. "It was actually really fun. And he was, surprisingly, not the most annoying he's ever been."

The waiter stops by with our drinks, and Dad takes a sip of his beer before saying, "There was a time you viewed Noah as a god."

I swallow a mouthful of my whiskey sour. "Yeah, and then I grew up and realized how full of himself he is."

"He's very talented at what he does."

"That's great," I mutter, because I know. I've known for as long as I can remember. Most hunters aspire to be Noah. He doesn't need *more* praise. His head is giant enough already.

Dad checks his phone, cursing under his breath before catching himself, glancing over at me and apologizing.

"What's up?"

"There's been another attack. This one is in Brooklyn."

My brows knit, the knots that seem to live in my stomach these days pulling tighter. "Do you have to go?"

He types quickly on his phone for a few seconds. "It doesn't appear so. Not immediately, at least."

Once our food comes, we don't speak much. Dad asks about school and work, so I have the super-fun time telling him I lost my job when the café closed. I figured Mom would've told him already. She'd see it as another opportunity to twist my arm into training again, especially after the monetary offer she presented me with.

"I'm sorry to hear that. I know how much you enjoyed that job."

I manage a smile, because at least his knee-jerk response wasn't to nudge me toward the academy. "Yeah. Thanks, Dad."

His phone chimes, and he frowns as he retrieves it and reads the message at the same moment the waiter comes back to our table.

I frown, wanting to ask my dad what's going on.

"Can I get you folks anything else? Dessert or coffee?"

Dad pulls out his credit card and slides it across the table toward me. "I have to go," he says as he gets up, glancing between me and the waiter. He looks as if he doesn't want to leave me here alone, but the call of duty isn't one he can ignore, especially in the current climate of his work. He stands with his back to the waiter, lowering his voice. "Cami—"

"It's fine," I assure him. "I'm going to order a giant piece of cake and be home in less than ten minutes stuffing my face. I'll let today's bodyguard know I'll be there shortly." My voice takes on a wry tone, because even though I understand the reason for the security team, thinking about having one still sometimes makes me feel twitchy and claustrophobic.

He hesitates, a muscle popping in his jaw as he clenches his teeth. The uncertainly is clear on his face. He's torn between my safety and his duty, and we both know he doesn't really have a choice. Such is the life of a demon hunter. Finally, he nods. "Text me as soon as you get home. I'll see you there soon."

I get up to hug him goodbye, squeezing extra hard. "Be careful," I say in a quiet but firm voice.

"Always," he says back, kissing my cheek.

Once he's gone, I take another look at the dessert menu. The waiter leaves to put my order in and get the bill, and I lean back in my chair, taking a moment to center my breathing. As hard as I try not to think of my dad running off to fight the demons, my head immediately goes there. He's a skilled hunter—one of the best in North America, which is what got him the position he's in now—but there's no stopping the worry that fills me, especially now. *Unprecedented* isn't a word you want to hear in the line of work he's in.

I pull my phone out to check for any updates from Harper, frowning at the lack of new messages before setting it on the table. There might even be a tiny part of me that had hoped to hear from Noah again, but I refuse to sit here and analyze that right now.

Someone drops into the chair across from me, and my head shoots up, my eyes narrowing when they land on the prince of hell.

"Are you *insane*?" I snap. "What are you doing here?"

His eyes flick between mine, his mouth hinting at a smile. "That was about the greeting I expected."

Before I can reach for my phone, Xander grabs it off the table. My heart beats faster, and I glance around subtly. We're the only ones on the patio, and this particular street is never very busy with foot traffic.

"You can relax, *mo shíorghrá*."

There's that nickname again. I tried looking it up after the first time he spoke it, but I must've butchered the spelling, because I couldn't find any translations that made sense.

"Not likely," I mutter, crossing my arms over my chest as I stare at him, waiting for him to explain himself.

The waiter chooses that moment to return with the plastic to-go container of cake. He glances at Xander, his brows lifting slightly, probably surprised to find someone new sitting across from me. "Good evening, sir. Can I get you anything?"

Xander keeps his eyes on me. "No, thank you. We're good here."

"Ma'am?" the waiter asks, and I look at him again.

"Just the bill, please," I force out in a level tone.

The uncertainty in his eyes makes me nervous, because if he continues to hover, I have no idea what Xander will do. All I know is that I don't want to find out.

"Of course." He pulls the slip out of his apron, handing it to me before the card machine. The payment goes through, but the waiter doesn't walk away. "Are you sure there isn't anything else I can get for you?"

I nod. "Thank you very much."

He hesitates, shooting another glance in Xander's direction.

Walk away, I desperately want to say, but that would likely only make him more wary of the demon sat across from me.

Finally he leaves the table, and I exhale, returning my focus to Xander, who is still looking at me. He hasn't taken his eyes off me since he arrived.

"I don't suppose you're willing to share?" He inclines his head slightly toward my cake.

I blink at him in surprise. *How is he being so casual right now?* "What are you doing here, Xander? If my dad had seen you..." I trail off, not wanting my thoughts to go there. I've always been good at jumping to the worst-case scenario, and this is no different. The idea of my dad fighting Xander makes my stomach churn, especially with the uncertainty of the outcome. Would Xander kill him? Would my dad, if he could, defy the order to detain the prince of hell and instead kill him?

"Which is why I waited for him to leave."

"That doesn't answer my question," I say tightly.

Xander nods. "I needed to see you."

I clench my jaw at the dip in my stomach. I shouldn't feel it. I don't *want* to feel it. Xander's gaze and his words shouldn't have this effect on me anymore, and I hate that they do. That I can't make it stop. "You needed to see me," I echo. "Why?"

"You know why."

"No." I shake my head. "That's not good enough. Tell me why you're here. Did you have something to do with the attack in Brooklyn? Or any others, for that matter? You have to know what's going on right now."

"I know what's going on," he agrees, drumming his fingers on the table, "but I have no part in it."

"I don't believe you," I snap.

"That's fair." He glances toward the restaurant before looking at me again. "Perhaps we could take a walk? It's a lovely night."

"I'm not going anywhere with you," I say without missing a beat, not bothering to add that there's a hunter at my dad's waiting for me to get back. Hell, he probably already knows.

Xander tips his head to the side. "Not even if I say *please*?"

I clamp my jaw shut to keep from gaping at him. "Your mother killed two of my best friends." I stand, and my chair scrapes across the patio. Grabbing my bag and to-go container, I offer him one last look that I hope projects the malice swirling around my chest. "I mean this with the utmost sincerity—go to hell."

TWENTY-THREE
Xander

The fire in her eyes calls to the darkest, most twisted parts of me. It feeds on the hatred emulating from her, and the strength of it directed at me has the demon half of me purring. Because behind that fiery hatred is a thin veil of fear. It's spicy, like a cinnamon heart candy, and I crave the taste far more than I care to admit. I won't feed on it—on *her*—no matter how fierce that desire is.

"You don't want me here, and I understand that. But there are much bigger things at play right now. It's not safe for you to be out in the open like this, and frankly, I'm surprised your father left you alone." We aren't far from where he lives, but after the ordeal of Camille being kidnapped, leaving her without protection is a risk I didn't think Scott would take.

Her eyes narrow as her pulse quickens. "I can—"

"Take care of yourself?" I challenge. The doubt in my voice certainly won't win me any points with her, but she has to know how dangerous her simply being here is. So as much as the sight of me brings fury to her usually soft features, I'm not going anywhere. I stand, stepping closer to her. "I'll walk you home." My tone doesn't invite an argument.

Still, she stares at me defiantly, arms crossed and expression filled with determination.

What an inappropriate moment to realize just how hard I've fallen for her.

Something on my face must give away the all-too human emotions flooding through me, because her breath hitches.

Her eyes widen slightly before she recovers, throwing up a wall—a mask of indifference. It fills her expression and feels like a cold, hard punch to the gut.

"What do you want from me?" she says in a low voice.

I bend slightly, putting us eye-to-eye, and speak the truth, because there's no sense hiding it now. "Everything."

Camille's lips part in a silent gasp, her cheeks flushing pink. She shifts behind her chair to keep it between us. "That's not a real answer."

The corner of my mouth kicks up as I lean closer, considering my amended answer for a moment, before I murmur, "I want *you*."

Her heart is a storm of thunder in her chest, and she grips the back of the chair until her knuckles turn white. When she speaks next, her voice is low and uneven, as if she's fighting back emotions. "You *had* me, Xander."

I exhale slowly, shaking my head. "I lost you the moment you found out what I am."

She swallows hard. "And yet, you're still here."

I move faster than her eyes can track, moving the chair and wrapping my fingers around her wrist before she can back away.

"Xander—"

"You're not safe," I warn in a hushed voice. "You think Lucia is going to stop these attacks because of a little pushback from the hunters?" I pull her closer, speaking into her ear. "She won't stop until you give her what she wants."

Camille tugs on her wrist, gritting her teeth as she fights my grip, but I hold her easily.

"Let go of me," she practically growls, glancing around to check if anyone is watching us.

The patio is empty. I tighten my grip and draw her closer.

She grabs the front of my shirt, thoroughly wrinkling the cotton between her fingers.

I'm no longer sure she actually wants me to release her. It's the last thing I want, but there's also a twisted part of me that enjoys her reluctance and the way she challenges me.

"Are you sure?" I offer, my lips brushing the shell of her ear, and I delight in the way she shivers against me.

"What?" she breathes.

"Are you sure you want me to let you go?" I slide my thumb over the racing pulse in her wrist. "You're still holding onto me, *mo shíorghrá*."

She reels back, wrenching her hand away from my chest as if it burned her, and scowls as I release her. "You need to leave me alone. I *mean* it, Xander."

Before I can respond, Blake saunters through the door of the restaurant, glancing between us. "Uh-oh," he says in an annoyingly amused voice. "Trouble in paradise, lovers?"

"Fuck off," Camille snaps at him.

He whistles. "And here I was, hoping you'd be happy to see me, love."

"In what world?" she shoots back without missing a beat.

I can't stop the twist of my lips, because despite the fear rippling off her in dark waves and the way her heart continues pounding in her chest, she refuses to back down. Her strength is one of many things I've come to admire about her.

Blake holds his hands up in a gesture I think is meant to be calming, but it only acts to irritate Camille further. "Believe it or not, Cam Cam, we're here to do the opposite of hurt you."

She folds her arms over her chest. "My *heroes*," she remarks dryly, the distrust clear in both her tone and her icy expression.

My friend grins, his gaze shifting toward me. He arches a brow, as if to ask how I want to proceed.

A muscle ticks along my jaw as I clench it. It's not going to be easy to get Camille to come with us, and I'd rather not force her into the back of our rental car. But the conversation we need to have can't be overheard.

"Camille," I say, stealing her attention from Blake. "We need—"

"No," she cuts in firmly, shaking her head. She grabs her to-go box and moves away from the table. "I don't care what *you* need. I can't be here—with you. This isn't..." Her voice trails off, and she shakes her head again. "I'm done." She turns her back on us, walking toward the patio exit to the street at a hurried pace.

"Are you going to stop her, mate?" Blake checks, shoving his hands into the pockets of his jacket.

I exhale a sigh and start walking in the direction Camille fled. Blake is beside me, and I debate sending him away so I can talk to her alone, but ultimately decide it's best to have him close in case we run into someone. Whether it be one of Lucia's lackeys or a squad of hunters looking to make a name for themselves by catching me.

This organization-wide hunt for me is proving to be a real pain in the ass. I'm still not sure how they connected me to Lucia, though it doesn't really matter at this point. Every hunter in that damn organization knows who I am and what I look like.

It doesn't take long for Camille to realize we're following her. As much as she'd never admit it, I think there's a good amount of instinct lingering from her training days.

Good. That will help keep her alive.

She whirls around, stomping toward us. "Stop. Following. Me." She enunciates every word, her voice filled with venom.

"Or what?" Blake taunts in a cocky voice I know is not going to help our case.

I shoot him an icy glare that clearly says, *enough.*

"What will it take for you to talk to me?" I ask her.

She blinks at me, her cheeks flushed and her hair windswept from the cool breeze. "I don't...Why?"

"Because," I say in a low voice, "we need your help."

She chokes on a laugh, which dies off when she realizes I'm not joking. Arching a brow, her voice is full of suspicion when she says, "My help for *what*, Xander?"

There's a brief silence that hangs in the air before I say, "To send my mother back to hell."

Twenty-Four
Camille

I have no idea how long I stand there staring at him. Time ceases to exist as his words play on a loop in my head. There's no way I heard him correctly—right?

Otherwise, there's no way he could possibly be serious.

"I think you broke her, mate," Blake comments under his breath.

I shake my head, pushing through the shock induced by the weight of Xander's words. "I don't understand."

He nods, stepping forward, and when I don't pull away, he grips my chin, tilting my head back until our eyes meet. "I know you don't trust me, but I need you to at least listen. Then, if you decide you never want to see me again, I promise you won't."

Should that make me feel better? Relieved, at least? Because that promise—the thought of never seeing Xander again—feels like a kick to the stomach. I glance between the demons standing in front of me, so entirely out of my element, it's not even close to funny. "Why now?" I demand. "Why are you so suddenly ready to fight the monster you've been loyal to your entire life?"

"It's not a simple answer," Xander says, and the rigidness of his posture isn't lost on me.

I stare at him for a moment before finally saying, "I'm listening."

Something akin to relief passes across his face, but it's gone too quick for me to fully decipher it.

"Perhaps we should take this off the street?" Blake suggests. "What we need to discuss isn't something that should be out in the open."

I push my fingers through my hair, exhaling a heavy breath. "My dad got called into work because of an attack in Brooklyn." I can't help the sharpness of my tone, considering the demons I'm speaking to are the same kind of monsters my dad is actively fighting.

"No way," Blake chimes in, smacking Xander in the shoulder. "We're not about to walk right into the den of—"

"Let's go," Xander cuts in, as if Blake hadn't spoken.

I look at Blake. "He won't be home for hours. Most likely, he'll sleep for a few hours at Ballard and then go back into the field." I pause. "But there's a small complication of the hunter guarding my dad's front door. I'll have to distract her so you guys can get in." Getting them out might be a little tricky, but one step at a time.

Blake keeps his hands in his pockets, shaking his head. "I trust you and your father as much as you trust us and Xander's mother, so..." He trails off.

I shrug. "Great. Then you can stay here."

His eyes narrow. "I'm not letting Xander walk into that place alone."

Rolling my eyes, I mutter, "It's a condo on the Upper West Side, not some dangerous hovel."

"We have a room at The St. Regis. We should go there."

They're staying at a hotel? How long have they been in the city?

"Or, here's an idea," I say brightly, "You let me go home and enjoy my cake in peace, and you two work out whatever you've got going on *without* me."

"Camille," Xander says in a smooth voice, snaring my gaze once more. "Please."

I huff out a sigh. The anxiety creeping into my chest triggers me to attempt easing the tension threatening to suffocate me. "Fine. I'll go with you, but we're ordering drinks, and he's paying for them." I jab a finger in Blake's direction, and he shrugs.

I huff out a sigh. The anxiety creeping into my chest triggers me to attempt easing the tension threatening to suffocate me. "Fine. I'll go with you, but we're ordering drinks, and he's paying for them." I jab a finger in Blake's direction, and he shrugs.

After a short drive from the restaurant, we get to the hotel and ride up to their suite. The air of sophistication makes it clear we're in one of the nicest places in the city, but my reason for being here doesn't leave space to enjoy the opulence.

On the way up, I send a quick message to the hunter outside Dad's place and tell her I'm going out with Noah. It's an easy lie—too easy—

and one I know won't be questioned. And then I send a message to my dad, telling him I made it home safe. That lie feels even heavier in my gut, and I hope to any higher power listening I won't regret it.

The moment the three of us step inside the room and the door clicks shut, I whirl on them. "Start talking before I come to my senses and get out of here." It goes without saying that following two demons into a hotel room alone wasn't the smartest move. But if they wanted me dead, they wouldn't have bothered with the pomp and circumstance of getting me here. I would have been dead a long time ago.

Xander and Blake exchange a glance, before the former rubs his jaw. "Maybe we should sit down?" he suggests, gesturing toward the small seating area around a glass coffee table.

His tone triggers the unease in my stomach to spread through my chest, making it harder to breathe normally. His tone is smooth and deep, but there's a flicker of desperation there that catches me by surprise. It's what has me following them instead of walking out the door.

As we move through the suite, I scan the impeccably clean space. The lighting is soft, inviting. Tasteful art pieces, no doubt intentionally curated for the room, decorate the neutral walls. The windows offer breathtaking views of the city skyline, and the faint scent of citrus fills the air. There's a small kitchenette to my left and a set of double doors to my right, which I can guess leads to the bedroom portion of the suite.

Exhaling slowly, I take the black loveseat, while Xander and Blake take the matching armchairs across the table. Setting my to-go container down, I have an awful feeling I won't be hungry for the dessert inside following this conversation.

Xander clears his throat. "My mother—Lucia—needs to be stopped before more people are harmed. Before she can enact her plan to destroy the hunters' organization."

My pulse jackhammers. I can't agree fast enough, but his suddenness to act on it begs about a hundred questions. "What exactly do you expect me to do?" is the first I can put words to.

He still hasn't told me why this is happening *now*, and I'm not going to leave this room until I get an explanation. Though part of me worries the answer won't provide anything good. And just because I agreed to hear them out doesn't mean I'm jumping on board with whatever plan they've crafted. I'm here to get information. What I do with it will depend on what it is and if—a big fucking if—I can bring myself to trust Xander, which I'm still struggling to do.

Blake drags a hand through his hair that's now a faded pastel pink. "Basically, we're going to open a portal to hell and drag her back there, making sure she can't get out."

I blink at him, the pressure in my chest becoming tighter as the seconds tick by. There's a faint ringing in my ears, and a tingle at the back of my neck that warns of an impending panic attack, the anxiety simmering just beneath the surface. It has me getting to my feet, because sitting still only makes it worse. "Absolutely nothing about what you just said sounds *basic*. I also don't see where I come in."

"We need you to expose a weakness in her. Crack the facade."

My brows knit. "How do you think I'm going to be able to do that?"

Xander glances away from Blake, focusing his attention on me as he stands as well. "If we convince her you've surrendered to us, that you'll fulfill her demands, we'll be more likely to catch her off guard. That should give us a window of opportunity then to overpower her and take her down."

I shake my head, flicking a brief look between them. "Let me get this straight. You'd like me to double-cross the queen of hell?"

Blake grins, but it appears forced. "Exactly. Easy peasy."

"Easy pea—Are you insane? She'll never buy it." Shaking my head adamantly, I add, "I'm not going to risk my family and friends." I meet Xander's gaze. "She'll kill everyone I've ever so much as looked at if she finds out." I choke on the lump in my throat. "It won't work," I say in a low voice.

Blake shrugs. "I'm willing to try it."

My gaze swings to him, morphing into a glare at his blasé attitude toward what is sounding more and more like a suicide mission. "What about your loyalty to your queen?" I ask, my tone effortlessly condescending.

His eyes flash black as a growl rumbles in his throat.

Before I know what's happening, Xander grabs my wrist and pulls me back, putting himself between me and his friend as he jumps up from his chair. "Blake," he says gruffly, and it sends a shiver through me as he keeps a firm grip on my wrist. "Knock it off."

The demon blinks a few times, a muscle ticking in his jaw, and grumbles, "I'm fine."

"If you can't control yourself when I so much as question your loyalty, how do you expect to actually betray Lucia?" I challenge, trying to step away from Xander.

"It's not going to be easy," Blake says cooly, "but we will manage it." My brows lift. "*We?*"

Xander turns to me, releasing my wrist. "This is bigger than just us, Camille. There are other demons who have been against Lucia's reign for some time."

I struggle to hold on to my composure, to keep the shock from showing on my face. If other demons want to stop her, that would at least mean we wouldn't be going against her alone. I exhale an uneven breath, suddenly wishing I was still sitting, because the way my head is spinning makes me feel like I'm going to collapse.

"Camille," Xander says, sliding his fingers from around my wrist to cup my elbow, as if he senses how unsteady I am.

I turn my head until our eyes meet. "Do you truly believe this can be done?" I hate the way my voice sounds so small. *Scared.* I want this to work, but the hope that is trying desperately to ignite in my chest also makes me rigid with fear.

No doubt Xander and Blake can feel it—the dark cloud threatening to consume me from the inside.

The possibility that either or both demons I'm sharing a room with might feed on that fear fills my thoughts. I've never been fed on, but I've heard different stories on how it feels. Both sickeningly awful and blissfully numbing depending on the scenario. I'm not prepared to find out myself.

Xander nods. "It can be done, which is why she's concerned about the demons turning against her. She knows if she doesn't secure their loyalty by any means necessary, she can be overpowered. That said, it's going to take precise planning and near-perfect timing to work."

What he's saying objectively makes sense, but it has my head spinning as I try to sort through the emotions at war in my chest.

"If we do this and something goes wrong, a lot of people are going to die," I say, swallowing hard to force the bile down my throat.

"If we *don't* do this, a lot of people are going to die," Blake points out, and I don't have a rebuttal, because he isn't wrong.

I want to shoot down this plan, to demand an opportunity to come up with something else. Unfortunately, though, time is not on our side, which leaves me very little choice but to trust Xander enough to get on board with this plan.

"There's no chance just the three of us can pull this off. I want to talk to Harper about it and see what she thinks. If we can get some hunters to help, that will at least increase our odds of success."

Blake's brows lift, but before he can say anything, Xander chimes in, "We won't refuse their help, so long as we can come to some sort of understanding that allows both sides to trust each other for the purposes of this...mission."

I nod. "If Harper—or any hunter, for that matter—is going to be involved, they'll want to be part of hashing out the specifics."

"Yes," Xander agrees, "and we'll have that conversation once you've had a chance to speak with her."

Silence stretches between us for several beats before a sigh escapes me. "Okay," I find myself saying, pressing my lips together for a moment before I lock eyes with Xander and finally ask the question that's been dying to escape since he told me about sending Lucia back to hell. "Why are you doing this?"

His brows inch closer and his expression softens so briefly, I almost miss it. But the flutter in my stomach confirms what I saw. "It's what needs to be done. Lucia has been completely consumed by her power."

I nod along, pulling away from him. The pit in my stomach tells me that wasn't the answer I was hoping for.

You wanted it to be about what he feels for you, an annoyingly familiar voice at the back of my head says, and I hate that it's not wrong.

"And I'm helping," Blake chimes in again, "because the danger of potential brutal, violent death is such a rush."

I arch a brow at him. "I don't know how to respond to that."

Xander coughs on a laugh. "Blake is helping because as much as he'd love for everyone to think he doesn't give a shit about anything—"

"Hey now," Blake cuts in, pouting childishly. "I never said I don't give a shit about *anything*, just that very few things are interesting or entertaining enough to earn my attention."

"So you're just unbelievably arrogant?" I offer dryly.

He shrugs. "I care about Xander. He says he needs help sending his crazy-ass mother back to hell. I'm going to be the first one to put my life on the line to make it happen."

"Really?" I question without thinking, and I can't keep the surprise out of my voice.

Blake nods, his expression completely serious and his tone confident when he says, "He'd do the same for me."

I lick the dryness from my lips and glance between the demons. After a deep breath, I say, "I think it's time for that drink."

The car is deafeningly silent as Xander drives me back to the Upper West Side. I stare out the windshield, my hands clasped in my lap and my head still spinning with all the possible outcomes of this plan to send Lucia back to hell.

He pulls up to the curb outside the condo. I'm not surprised he knows where it is despite my lack of direction, but the thought of any other demons knowing where my dad lives makes me uneasy. I fully believe he's skilled enough to defend himself, but that doesn't lessen the worry in my chest.

I turn to Xander when he shuts off the car. "Are you sure about this?"

"About which part?" he asks.

I frown, unbuckling my belt so I can angle myself toward him. "I don't know," I admit. "This all seems so sudden. One day you're saying I need to join you on the dark side or whatever, and now..." I trail off. "I'm trying to understand what changed. What has you in a place where you're now willing—eager even—to betray your queen? Your *family*."

Xander nods, turning to face me. "I have no delusions that Lucia cares for me as anything more than a pawn in her twisted game for power and control. The longer it goes on, the harder I find it to follow her with blind obedience. I struggle with that pull to serve her, but my own desires are getting stronger every day."

I lower my gaze to my lap, pressing my lips together when my cheeks fill with warmth. My breath catches when he reaches over and slides his fingers along my jaw to cup my cheek, tilting my face back up.

"I understand I've done nothing to deserve your trust or your forgiveness for deceiving you when we met, but I'm going to do everything in my power to earn it." His thumb brushes over my bottom lip. "Can you trust that?"

"I want to," I whisper.

The corner of his mouth tugs into a faint smile as he leans closer. "I'll take it."

We stare at each other for a few beats, my pulse pounding as I struggle to put words to the mess of emotions tangling in my chest.

"I'm sorry." The words fly out of my mouth before I can rein them in, and confusion flickers in his gaze. I continue, "I'm sorry you never had the opportunity to meet your father." I'm not sure if it was Xander's comment about knowing Lucia only cares about the power he can bring her, or having dinner with my own father earlier, but I'm reminded that Xander doesn't have that option. He has no connection to his human family. No ties to his humanity—none except me.

He rests his forehead against mine, closing his eyes as a soft sigh escapes his lips. "*Mo shíorghrá.*"

He's called me that several times since the night we spent together, and I never could find a proper translation. I finally ask what I've wanted to for a while. "What does that mean?"

Xander opens his eyes, pulling back just enough to look into mine, and there's a beat of hesitation before he murmurs, "It's Irish for *my eternal love.* Of the very few details I've been able to gather on the human side of my family, my ancestors immigrated to the United States from Ireland over a century ago."

I slide my hand up his chest, curling my fingers around the back of his neck and brushing my lips against his. "Xander," I breathe, my heart thumping wildly.

He dips his face, sealing his lips over mine before I can contemplate what a bad idea this is. In a matter of seconds, our kiss becomes feverish, desperate, as if we're both using it to say what we can't seem to aloud.

This fight goes far beyond us. It's about Lucia and her horrific plan to eliminate the hunters, which I have to think would lead to unleashing hell on earth, because why else would she do it? I can't see her wanting a place for demons to live peacefully when they thrive on chaos and strife.

There's no happy ending for humans if Lucia wins.

Xander pulls away first, pressing a kiss to my forehead, and his lips linger there as we catch our breaths.

There's a new pain, a startling realization that fills my chest and digs unforgiving claws into my heart.

I don't want to lose him.

THE DEVIL'S WALTZ

As we sit in silence, holding onto each other as if we're both equally terrified to let go, my resolve hardens.

This plan to stop Lucia, to send her back to hell—it has to work.

TWENTY-FIVE
XANDER

The hotel suite is quiet when I pry my eyes open sometime in the morning. I slept like shit, on and off through the night, and the lethargy clinging to my muscles tells me the sleep I did get wasn't restful.

I roll over and swipe my phone off the nightstand, finding a message from Blake.

> I'm picking up breakfast at the coffee shop down the street. Take a shower and get dressed before I come back. We have people we need to meet with.

He only sent the message a few minutes ago, so I figure I still have enough time before he gets back and curses me out for not being ready.

I haul my ass out of bed and into the en suite, cranking the shower as hot as it'll go. Once steam fills the room, I undress and step under the water, where I scrub my hair and skin until everything is tingling and red. I get out and grab the clothes off the vanity that Blake must have laid out for me. Black dress pants and a navy button-up dress shirt. There are multiple hair products and even an expensive bottle of cologne.

By the time the keycard beeps to unlock the suite door, I'm sitting in the wingback chair in the seating area, spinning my phone between my thumb and finger. I'm fighting the urge to check in with Camille after last night, after hearing her say she wants to give us a fighting chance. Beyond that, I find myself *wanting* to make this work. To come up with all the ways I'm going to make it up to her for how we met and the things I've done.

Unfortunately, none of those ways matter if all of us are dead. Which is a very real possibility if Lucia catches on to what we're doing.

Blake walks in with his typical upbeat swagger, carrying a brown bag and a tray with to-go cups of coffee, by the smell of it. He sets them on the coffee table between us and drops into the chair across from me.

He frowns at me. "I know, I look ridiculous, but the demons we're meeting with today likely wouldn't appreciate my normal attire."

Now it's my turn to frown. Blake has never let what others think of him dictate how he lives his life. The fact he's changing such a huge part of himself only speaks to the magnitude of what we're attempting.

"Eat." He nods toward the table. "I got you a bacon, egg, and cheese bagel. Oh, and a chocolate croissant because they looked fucking amazing."

I lean forward, opting for the coffee first. "Thanks, Blake." After taking a sip, I reach for the food. "You didn't get anything for yourself?"

He snorts. "I ate mine on the walk back. I was starving, mate. Wasn't going to wait for your sleepy arse."

I chuckle as I unwrap the food. "Fair enough." My stomach grumbles at the aroma-filled steam that escapes.

As I devour my breakfast, Blake reads off the list of names—our potential allies. Most of them I recognize, and the ones I don't know, Blake does, so they can be trusted.

"A couple of them live elsewhere but are here on business and have agreed to meet with us."

Swallowing the last of my bagel, I wash it down with a mouthful of coffee. "Have we coordinated a meeting place?"

Blake leans back, crossing one leg over the other. "Several. First, we're going to pay a visit to my mate, Will, and his partner, Steven, in Brooklyn. They're well known among the demons around here and will be an asset for us to get messages out quickly."

I nod, taking another drink of my coffee. "Let's get moving then. Every minute we're working against Lucia is—"

"A gamble with death," Blake cuts in with a grim smile. "Yeah, yeah, I know."

We get up, and I pocket my phone on the way to the door.

"You talk to your girl yet this morning?" Blake asks in the elevator.

Your girl.

I push past the newly familiar tension in my chest and shake my head. "I figured it was best to give her space after we ambushed her."

"Do you regret it? Coming here?"

I glance at the panel of buttons as we descend to the lobby. "No."

His eyes narrow slightly, as if he doesn't believe me. "Your pulse is all over the place, mate. What's going on in that head of yours?"

"Too fucking much," I offer as the elevator dings and the door opens.

We're silent as we walk to the car, and it isn't until we've been driving for a while that Blake speaks again.

"Are you still thinking about leaving Seattle after Lucia is gone?"

I open my mouth, but the words die on my lips. "I don't know," I finally admit. "I haven't let myself consider what her going back means for me."

"You've spent your life under her thumb," he says in a serious tone, keeping his eyes on the road. "It makes sense to be uncertain what you'll do once you finally have the freedom you've dreamed of for years."

It's an overwhelming idea, what I'll do once I'm free of Lucia. Of only one thing, I'm sure. "I'll go wherever Camille is."

Blake blows out a breath. "What if she doesn't want to see you after all this is over?"

I stare forward, squinting at the tension building behind my eyes. "If she decides she never wants to see me again, I'll leave." The words taste like poison on my tongue.

"Really?" He hums. "You've got it bad, huh?"

I scrub a hand down my face, scratching the bit of stubble growing along my jaw. "Can we talk about something else?" I grumble.

"Don't need to." He turns onto a residential street and pulls over, shifting the car into park. "We're here."

We get out of the car and walk up the driveway. I arch a brow at the sleek mustang. "Remind me again how do you know these guys?"

"I met Will at a rave in Portland about a decade ago. We've partied together a lot over the years."

That tracks.

Stopping at the front door, I face Blake and ask a question I should have earlier. "What about that experience makes him trustworthy?"

Blake chuckles. "Besides the fact you know I'm excellent at reading people? He put his life on the line to save mine when the warehouse we were partying at a few years ago was raided by hunters."

I frown. "How come I didn't know about that?"

He shrugs, reaching past me to ring the doorbell. "You didn't need to. It all worked out fine."

Before I have a chance to say anything else, the door swings open. We're greeted by a tall, lanky demon with short, white-blond hair and hazel eyes. They bounce between us before landing on me.

"If it isn't the prince of hell, standing on my doorstep." He doesn't appear impressed. If anything, he seems inconvenienced by our presence.

I give him a once-over. He's probably a few years older than me and dressed casually in jeans and a gray crewneck sweater. The fuzzy slippers are a bit of a surprise, though.

"I'm here too, Steven," Blake points out.

The demon's gaze doesn't waver. "I suppose you should come inside." He shifts back, and I cast a sideways glance at Blake before stepping inside.

We follow the demon down a long, narrow hallway into a living space. It's furnished with a black leather L-shaped couch, oak coffee table, and a TV mounted on the wall above a white marble fireplace. Crackling flames fill the space with warm, and soft jazz music plays from another room.

"Will, your company is here," Steven calls out, crossing the room to a bar cart in the corner and pouring himself a glass of amber liquid. "Can I fix you gentlemen a drink?"

"I'm fine, thank you."

"Yeah, we're good," Blake adds, raking a hand through his hair as the demon I presume is Will enters the room and grins at him.

Our host is a dark-skinned demon with a sharp jaw and moss-colored eyes. If I had to guess, he's in his mid-thirties, and he's dressed impeccably in black dress pants and a matching polo under a maroon dress jacket.

"Blake *fucking* Taylor. How the hell are you?" His voice is deep but friendly, and the two hug, slapping each other on the back before breaking apart.

"Keeping busy, mate," Blake says, then turns to me. "Will, meet Xander. Xander, Will."

Will steps closer to me, holding out his hand in greeting. "Good to meet you, Xander."

I nod, shaking his hand. "Likewise. Thank you for meeting with us."

"Given an excuse to take part in the downfall of your mother's savage reign, the pleasure is ours," Steven chimes in, drumming his fingers against his thigh.

My brows lift, and I say, "Right."

The four of us move to sit around the coffee table, and Blake doesn't waste any time with small talk.

"We need to keep this absolutely silent until the exact moment we want people to know."

"How big is your network?" I ask.

Will exchanges a glance with Steven before shifting his gaze to me. "It's big enough," he assures me, "and it spans the entirety of North America. If you need to get a message out, we're the ones to do it."

"I have to ask," Steven says, glancing toward Will before returning his attention to me. "What's the plan if things go sideways?"

Blake laughs, but it's void of any humor. "Run."

I shoot him a look before saying, "My mother is already concerned about demons acting against her, so an attack of any kind won't come as a surprise. Of course, that makes our plan more dangerous and every detail critical, but it also means her suspect pool wouldn't be a small one."

Steven nods. "So long as you're not asking us to fight."

Will reaches for him, as if on instinct, and laces their fingers together, while keeping his gaze on me. "We're happy to provide assistance with communication, but that's the extent of our participation."

"Understood," I say, looking between them. "Thank you both."

Will's lips curl into a slow smile. "Now that the business chitchat is out of the way, are you sure we can't get you both a drink?"

"I wish," Blake says with a sigh. "We have to get back to the city for another meeting."

"Once this shit show is over and the dust settles," Will says. "you'll have to come back and let me take you to this new spot in Queens. You're gonna love it."

Blake smirks. "You've got yourself a deal, mate."

With that, Will and Steven walk us to the door.

"Keep us posted," Steven says.

"Of course," I say, extending my hand to him to shake, then do the same with Will.

"We'll be in touch soon," Blake says as we step outside and head for the car.

Once we're on the road again, I pull my phone out to check for any messages from Camille.

There aren't any.

"You know," Blake says in an annoyingly amused voice, "phones work both ways. You can text her as easily as she can text you."

I roll my eyes and deadpan, "Thank you for the unsolicited tech lesson, asshole."

He gasps as if he's insulted, speeding up to pass the car in front of us. "You are so *mean* to me. I'm only trying to help you."

Ignoring him, I pocket my phone again and lean my head back to close my eyes until we return to the city. The sound of traffic around us and the steady movement of the vehicle lulls me to a state of almost falling asleep.

Blake hums along to the music playing, tapping the steering wheel to the beat as I doze off.

No more than ten minutes later, I open my eyes again to see we're back in the city, surrounded by traffic and buildings on both sides of us.

"Where are we going now?" I ask, my voice gravelly as sleep clings to it.

Blake casts a glance in my direction. "Sleeping beauty wakes," he teases, turning his attention back to the road when I shoot him a dark look. "We're heading to Greenwich Village, but I need to get something for lunch before my stomach starts eating itself. There's a deli on the way, and their sandwiches are going to change your life."

We drive the rest of the way in silence. He does a quick scan of the area before we walk into the deli.

It's a black brick building on the corner of a side street, and based on the worn signage over the all-glass storefront, it's been here a long time. There are a few other people inside, a couple eating lunch in the small dining area to the right and an older man at the deli counter ordering a variety of cold cuts.

The sound of a machine rhythmically slicing meat fills the air, and the scent of freshly baked bread wafts from the open kitchen, making my stomach rumble.

"I'll grab us a couple of sandwiches to go," Blake says. "We shouldn't linger too long."

I nod, scanning the chalkboard menu hung on the wall behind the counter. It lists the daily specials in artistic handwriting. Today's is black forest ham on rye with a homemade sauce. I point to the board. "That sounds good." Shoving my hands in my pockets, I add, "I'll wait in the car."

Blake chuckles. "You're going to take another nap, aren't you?"

I shrug, backing toward the front door. "I might."

The bell above the door chimes as I retreat outside and round the corner, walking toward the parking lot at the back of the building.

Something in my chest senses her before my eyes land on Camille. She's sitting on the patio outside a café a couple of blocks up the street—and she's not alone.

My eyes narrow as I move around the side of our car to keep out of sight. I'm not sure how long I stand there before Blake returns with our lunch.

"Ah, shit," he says under his breath. "Of all the fucking places..." He trails off as I keep my eyes locked on the hunter legend, Noah Daniels.

It's obvious he cares for her. Part of me is glad she has him. The other part, though, wants to shred him to ribbons for so much as looking in her direction. They have a history, and she feels safe with him—something I might never be able to provide her—but I can't shake the possessive urge I have to steal her away.

"Jealous is an interesting color on you, mate."

I ignore him, watching with my jaw clenched painfully tight as Camille breaks off a piece of a scone before pushing the rest toward Noah. My stomach twists as he smiles at her, tension coiling throughout my whole body.

Blake punches me in the shoulder.

I hiss out a growl in his direction.

"Focus," he says in a low voice.

"I'm fine," I shoot back, tearing my gaze away from Camille and Noah as we get back into the car. "Who's next on our list?"

TWENTY-SIX
CAMILLE

My dad drives me to the airport a few days later. After the demon attack in Brooklyn, I was relieved his second-in-command insisted he take a couple of days off. I was expecting him to be wrapped up in work so completely I wouldn't see him for the remainder of my trip. So, it was a happy surprise getting to spend time with him.

We had lunch at my favorite spot in Manhattan yesterday before wandering around the city. Then we window shopped and chatted about post-graduation plans over cups of hot chocolate in Central Park.

Dad cooked my favorite meal last night, and we watched the old sit-com that was constantly on when I was younger. It felt mundane and wonderful, a breath of fresh air in the midst of the storm I've been trudging through for nearly a month. Ever since discovering I was in a relationship—however fake it was—with the prince of hell.

When we finally called it a night, I slept terribly, knowing I'd be flying back to Seattle today. I spent most of the night tossing and turning, unable to get comfortable enough for any restful sleep. Maybe it's anxiety about traveling. But it's more likely about knowing Lucia is waiting for me back home.

Standing outside the departure doors, Dad wraps his arms around me so tight I struggle to get a breath in. But I don't complain—I need this as much as he does.

"Take care of yourself, kiddo," he says in a thick voice, and when he finally pulls away, his eyes are glassy.

"I will," I promise him. "You too, Dad."

He nods. "I better hear from you at least once a week."

I can't help but smile at him. "You got it."

"I want you to know how proud I am of you." His voice is steady even as his bottom lip wobbles and his gaze takes on a glassy sheen. "You're chasing your dreams with a determination that demands admiration. And you've faced adversity with such grace and strength. I am the luckiest man on earth, being able to call you my daughter."

My eyes burn with a sudden onslaught of tears, and I can barely force out, "Thank you, Dad."

"And I'm going to talk to your mom about laying off the training talk. She needs to accept you've chosen a different path for your life. She'll just have to be okay with that."

An announcement over the loudspeaker interrupts before I can respond. The lump in my throat would have made it too difficult, anyway. My chest feels like it's seconds away from exploding from an overwhelming mix of relief and shock.

"You better get in there," he says, and I nod. He hugs me one more time, planting a kiss on the top of my head before handing over my duffel bag.

I sling it over my shoulder and toss him another smile as I walk to the door. "I'll let you know when I get home. Love you, Dad."

"Love you too, Camille. More than you will ever know."

I turn away at that point, my vision blurring with tears I try to fight back, but as soon as I'm through the doors, I let them fall.

After so many years of begging my parents to understand my inability to rejoin the hunters, I've finally made a small amount of progress. With one of them, at least. That's more than I ever thought I'd get, and I'm not about to take it for granted.

I move through the airport until I reach my gate, and soon enough, it's time to board. I'm not sure what lies ahead when I return to Seattle, but there's a renewed strength burning in my veins to face whatever it might be.

I haven't heard from Xander since he dropped me off at my dad's place, and I haven't stopped thinking about the kiss we shared. It felt different, as if it meant more somehow, and that terrifies me.

He and Blake stayed in New York a bit longer in the hopes of reaching some contacts who might help us.

The day after I get home is the memorial service for Phoebe and Grayson. I wake up before my alarm, having tossed and turned nearly all night, and stare at the ceiling, bleary-eyed and physically and emotionally exhausted.

Shortly after nine, there's a soft knock on my door, and I roll over as it opens, and my mom pokes her head inside.

"Hi," I say, the surprise at seeing her clear in my voice as I sit up, the blankets pooling in my lap.

"Morning, honey," she says, closing the door and approaching the bed. "How was your trip?"

"Good." I watch her warily. "What's going on? Why are you here?"

"I wanted to check in on you before the service today. I know it's going to be hard for you after everything that's happened."

My brows knit. "I don't really want to talk about it."

"You could have been killed," she says anyway, sitting on the side of the bed. "Your friends—Phoebe and Grayson died. And I am so, so sorry for your loss."

I press my lips together and wait for it. For the guilt trip about it being my fault for not having been prepared. *If you had kept up with your training, you might have been able to save your friends' lives.*

It doesn't come, and that alone makes my eyes burn with tears.

I open my mouth, finding that I'm seconds away from exploding. "Mom." My voice cracks, and her face fills with concern as she reaches for me, wrapping her hand around my knee.

"What is it?"

Swallowing hard, I say, "I think...I've fallen for the prince of hell."

Her face pales. "Camille—"

"His father was human," I rush to remind her, as if that'll make it better. Easier to swallow.

She frowns. "I know you said that, which I can assume means it's something he told you, but have you considered the possibility he lied about that, too? We haven't been able to find any information to confirm the validity of his claim to be part human."

Mirroring her expression, I say, "Of course you haven't. Lucia wanted to hide his identity from the hunters, but also the part of him she sees as a weakness." A tool she wouldn't hesitate to use to her advantage, but a failing, nonetheless.

She seems to consider that for a moment. The silence that stretches between us sets me on edge as doubt clouds her expression.

I shake my head, tension coiling tighter in my gut. "There's humanity in him," I insist. "I've seen it, Mom. And I have to believe it, because the alternative isn't something I can—" My voice cracks, and I swallow the lump in my throat. "I have to believe it," I repeat quietly.

My mom presses her other hand to her forehead. "I don't know what to say, Camille." She shakes her head, the fear in her expression something I haven't seen in a very long time. "But if he truly cares about you, why were your friends killed?"

My stomach plummets. "He didn't know about that until after it happened," I say in a low voice. "It was Lucia. She was punishing me for not conceding to her. And I..." I look away. "I couldn't help them." My words are low, heavy with the guilt of their deaths.

The hard facade I've grown to associate with my mother's position of power in the hunter world fades into something...softer.

"Oh, sweetheart." She wraps her arms around me tightly, and I let myself fall apart in her embrace.

When I calm down enough to pull back and wipe my cheeks, exhaustion still clings to my muscles, but the unbearable weight on my chest has lessened ever so slightly. I needed that.

"Let me help," she says. "You shouldn't have to face this alone. We've known the queen was planning to act against us for some time, but to find out she was planning to use my own daughter to do it..." Her jaw clenches. "I won't let her hurt you, Camille."

I exhale a heavy sigh. "Okay," is all I'm able to say. The thought of telling her about Xander's plan to send Lucia back to hell pops into my head, but I keep my mouth shut. Until I know more, I'm not ready to involve my family.

Mom squeezes my knee gently before standing from the bed. "I'm heading into HQ for the day, but let me know if you need anything, okay?"

"Sure. Thanks, Mom."

After she leaves, I force myself out of bed and into the shower so I can get ready for the service.

Harper and I ride over to the funeral home together, both dressed in simple black dresses with stockings and heels. Harper opted to curl her hair, while I blew mine dry. We did our makeup in silence, and I bit my tongue to keep from spilling about what happened with Xander while I was in New York. I'm going to tell her everything, but not until we get through this.

Today needs to be about Phoebe and Grayson.

Soft piano music fills the reception hall of the funeral home when Harper and I step inside. Adrianna greets us with a watery smile and a hug, and I squeeze tighter when I catch a hint of alcohol coming from her.

The three of us walk around the room, looking over the photo collages set up on poster boards. A few of Grayson's soccer trophies and Phoebe's watercolor paintings are also on display.

Phoebe's parents and Grayson's mom chose to do a combined memorial, knowing how much their kids meant to each other, so the room is packed with people from both families. The actual service is tomorrow and is for immediate family only, which explains why this visitation is so well-attended.

The space is lit from the chandeliers hanging from the ceiling, and the faint aroma of roses hits me each time we pass one of the arrangements set up around the hall.

After an impossibly long hour of listening to stories about my friends and trying desperately to stop crying, I seek solace in a quiet corner of the room. I just need some time away from the crowd. My eyes burn, swollen from crying, and the guilt is still there, unabated.

My stomach drops when Phoebe's parents approach, their grief-stricken expressions a punch to the gut. They each take a turn hugging me tightly, and thank me for being a good friend to their daughter throughout the years.

All I can manage is a choked, "I'm sorry."

They will never know what actually happened to her, the same as Grayson's mom will never know what happened to him. The story they were fed by authorities—influenced by the organization—was a fatal car accident, with enough proof to back up the lie.

Once they move on to speak with another group of mourners, I force myself to cross the room and pay my respects to Grayson's mom. She is a blubbering mess, losing her only child less than a year after divorcing her husband. Her life is full of loss.

My cheeks are wet with tears when I walk away from talking to her, and I hurry to find Harper near the entrance of the room so we can go. We say goodbye to Adrianna, and get in the car to leave.

Exhaustion clings to every ounce of my being when we walk into our apartment, and I fall onto the couch with a defeated sigh. Harper follows, stretching her legs out and leaning her head against my shoulder.

I close my eyes against the lingering burn in them. "There's something you should know."

Harper leans away from me. "What's going on?"

I blink my eyes open, meeting her gaze. "While I was in New York, I, um...I saw Xander."

She stares at me. "You *saw* him."

I nod. "And Blake."

Her brows draw together. "Those motherfu—Did they follow you there? What happened?"

Taking a deep breath, I explain everything to her, sparing no detail—including the kiss Xander and I shared when he dropped me off. By the time I stop talking, her face is ghostly pale and her mouth is set in a tight line. I knew this wouldn't be an easy sell, but if we're going to pull this off, we're going to need help. Strength in numbers, especially those trained to fight.

Without a word, Harper gets off the couch and walks toward the bar cart on the other side of the room. Snatching up some tequila, she twists the cap off, taking a swig directly from the bottle as she returns to the couch and offers it to me. I take a large sip, cringing as it burns down my throat, pooling warmth in my stomach as it settles there.

Harper takes the tequila back when I pass it her way, taking another deep swig before setting it on the coffee table. "I don't like this, Cami," she says, shaking her head. "You might trust Xander enough, but I sure as hell don't. And that friend of his seems even less trustworthy."

I can't argue with her there. Blake is...unpredictable.

"Are you saying you won't help me?" I ask.

"I'm not saying that at all. But I think we need to loop in some backup. There is no world in which the four of us can overpower a demon of Lucia's power. Especially when Xander and Blake are going to find it very difficult physically and mentally to act against their queen."

I rehash the part of the plan where they are recruiting other demons to help, and she balks.

"If they're doing that, I think we need to bring in more hunters than just me."

I shake my head. "I don't want my parents to know about this. If they find out, they're going to do everything in their power to keep me out of it, and I can't do that."

She takes another shot. "Okay, so we don't tell Rachel and Scott. I don't like that, but I suppose I can work with it."

I arch a brow at her and hesitate before asking, "What are you planning, Harper?"

"I have friends in the organization that I trust with my life. Also, one hunter in particular I wouldn't exactly consider a *friend* but is extremely skilled. He would be an asset to this mission you've gotten us wrapped up in."

The uneasy sensation that unfurls in my chest tells me I know exactly who she's talking about, but still I ask, hoping I'm wrong. "Do I even need to ask who you're talking about?"

She offers me a knowing smile, and my groan fills the room.

Twenty-Seven
Xander

Camille returned to Seattle yesterday for her friends' memorial service. Despite the insistent part of me that wanted to go, to be there for her, I didn't have much of a choice in the matter. It wasn't as if I could attend the service with her. Or that she'd even want me there, considering her friends would still be alive if I hadn't come into her life.

Blake and I are going home tomorrow, but before we leave New York, we're meeting with a few more potential allies.

After a much-needed run in the hotel gym, I shower and get dressed in another annoyingly formal outfit.

"Dress for the job you want," Blake had said with a wolfish grin when he pulled it out of the Saks bag earlier. "At least, the one you want people to *think* you want," he'd added with a wink that made me roll my eyes, because what job would that even be? It's not as if I'm running an election campaign to take my mother's place on the throne.

That said, and as annoying as having Blake dress me was, I couldn't be genuinely mad at him if I tried. He was doing it—all of this—for me. Without Blake, I can honestly say I'm not sure how I'd figure everything out.

I walk into the main space of our hotel suite and find Blake unpacking a brown bag that smells like Thai food. He gives me a once-over, nodding in approval before dropping into one of the dining chairs.

"Let's eat, then we need to head out."

I join him at the round table in front of the floor-to-ceiling window and reach for one of the to-go containers. "Thank you for doing all of this, Blake."

He pauses, glancing over at me. Recognition flashes in his eyes as he grasps the full weight of my words, then nods. "Of course. You know I've got you, mate. Which is why you're not going to bitch at me when I tell you we're going hunting after this. Your strength needs to be at its highest when we return to Seattle."

The argument dies on the tip of my tongue. He's right.

We eat in silence for a few minutes before I say, "Steven made a good point asking about the plan if things go sideways. I think we should figure out a backup—and a backup to our backup."

Blake groans around a mouthful of noodles. "One impossible plan was hard enough to craft. *Now* you want to come up with contingencies?"

"I want the people we care about to make it out of this alive."

"Well, fuck, when you put it like that," he grumbles, though I'm fully aware the number of people Blake gives a damn about is far smaller than mine. He'll have my back, regardless.

"If Lucia discovers our plan to double cross her and lock her up in hell before we can pull it off, none of us will be safe." I lean back in my chair, folding my arms over my chest, as if that'll stop Blake from being able to hear how quickly my heart is beating.

He nods in agreement. "She'll immediately start slaughtering everyone she suspects is involved."

"I know. It'll start a war we're not prepared to fight. Which is why you'll need to get everyone far away from Seattle."

He blinks slowly, then narrows his eyes. "I don't like the sound of that. Where the fuck are you going to be?"

"I'll be buying you time to run." I exhale a heavy breath. "At that point, we may have no choice but to ask for help from our Canadian friends."

He schools his features, rubbing his jaw. "I have to say, I'm surprised you came to that conclusion on your own. But I'm so fucking relieved you did."

"Let's try to avoid needing to call on them if we can help it, though, okay?" Friends or not, I don't want to be indebted to anyone.

Blake nods again.

I push the food around my plate, swallowing a few bites before my phone buzzes on the table between us.

"Speak of the devil," Blake remarks dryly.

I reluctantly pick up my phone and answer the call. "Mother."

"So formal," she purrs in a voice laced with amusement. "I understand you and Blake are still gallivanting around New York City while your lovely little human has returned to Seattle."

A muscle ticks along my jaw, and I frown at the twitch in my eye. "That's right."

"I was resigned to accept your trip there to keep tabs on Camille, however—"

"Rest assured, I have eyes on her there."

"I do not care, Xander," she scolds cooly. "I want to know why *your* eyes are not on her."

I close my eyes briefly to center myself before responding. "I felt it was important to address your concerns surrounding the loyalty of our kind. I will have more information for you upon our return to Seattle, but Blake and I are ensuring the demons around here understand the only alternative to bowing to you is being reduced to ash."

There's a stretch of silence that has my pulse ticking faster. Sweat dots my brow as I stand, pushing my chair back, and pace the suite as Blake watches. If I were standing before Lucia, I'd be royally fucked. She'd know immediately I wasn't being truthful. She'd see right through me.

"I am pleased you are finally stepping into your role, my son."

Her voice makes me freeze, and I turn away from Blake's gaze. "Yes," I force out, balling my free hand into a fist at my side.

"I look forward to your return."

The line disconnects before I can respond, leaving me feeling utterly empty and nauseous. I drop back into my chair with a heavy sigh, my heart pounding hard enough it pulses in my throat. The bit of Thai food I managed to swallow threatens to make a return, and I clench my jaw, willing the bile to stay in my stomach.

I have to face Lucia sooner than later. If this plan has any chance of working, I need to be better at pretending I'm who she wants me to be.

TWENTY-EIGHT
CAMILLE

The next evening, I get a message from Xander, letting me know he and Blake are back in Seattle.

> How did it go?

He doesn't answer for a few minutes, and I chew the inside of my cheek until his reply comes through.

> Are you home? We should talk.

My stomach churns as I read his text. I walk over to the kitchen counter and show it to Harper.

She's currently stuffing her face with a slice of extra-cheese pizza, but speeds up when she sees the message. She swallows, downs half a glass of water, and wipes her hands on her napkin as she asks, "What are you thinking?"

I shrug. "We should probably see what's going on."

"Okay," she says, sliding off the stool. "I'll call Noah and Elias."

I wrinkle my nose at that. "Are you *sure* we need to involve Noah?" I can just imagine the judgment he'll bring with him, and I'd really rather avoid that. More than that, there's a part of me I can't explain that feels wildly uneasy over Xander and Noah meeting.

"Uh, *yeah*. We've been over this, Cami. We're going to need all the help we can get to make this work. Noah flew in yesterday to help us, so I'm not about to turn him away, especially considering he—by some miracle—agreed to keep this off the record."

"Yeah, how exactly did you pull that off?" Noah has always been a stickler for the rules, to an annoying degree.

She purses her lips. "Well..." She drags out the word. "I explained the situation and also kind of expressed that we were going to do it with or without him. He was the most pissed off I've seen him in, like, *ever.*"

My brows lift. "Because you told him about all the protocols we're completely ignoring by pursuing this without the organization?"

She tips her head back and forth. "Sure."

I pin her with a look. "Harper."

She sighs. "He got all tense and irritable when I told him about your part in the plan. I think—I *know*, actually—the thought of you being in danger really bothers him."

I ignore the dip in my stomach, and instead of responding to that, I ask, "How'd you convince him not to report this to HQ?"

"I told him you asked us not to."

I shake my head. "And he just accepted that?"

"Temporarily. We'll see if it sticks after we get everyone together to discuss the plan."

"Right," I mumble. "How'd he get authorization to travel to Seattle with everything going on?"

"We told Rachel and Scott that after Phoebe and Grayson's memorial service, you came to your senses and agreed that Noah would be the best person to keep you safe."

The heat blossoming in my cheeks makes me want to look away, but Harper knows me better than anyone. Probably better than I know myself in some ways. "Okay," I say hesitantly.

"We needed to get him here without raising suspicion. And we did."

"I know, I know." I remind myself this is about far more than me or my discomfort over my childhood crush and my demon—whatever Xander is now—meeting. Or how Noah seeming to care about what happens to me makes me feel all weird and tingly.

Focus, Cami, I scold myself. Now is not the time to worry about that.

I type a message back to Xander, hitting send before I freeze by overthinking it.

> I'm at home with Harper. She's looping in a group of hunters to help. We all need to meet and finalize the plan for how this is going to work.

> We'll be there in 30 minutes.

Noah's hunting partner, Elias shows up first. I've spent time with him on a few occasions with Harper, and he seems nice enough. I'm pretty sure he's a year younger than us, though the dark brown beard that match-es the color of his floppy curls makes him appear older. And he was good enough to be paired with Noah, which says enough—the guy has skills. He must've come from a training session, because he's wearing all black—cargo pants, combat boots, and a rain jacket. His soft green eyes look tired, but I have no doubt he's taking in his surroundings as sharp as a hawk.

I offer him a smile as Harper walks him inside, closing the door behind him. "Hey, Elias."

"Camille," he says in greeting, nodding. "How are you?"

"I could be better, all things considered. Thank you for coming. I'm not sure how much Harper has told you, but we're glad you're here."

"Of course. I think I'm pretty well up to speed, and Noah's right be-hind me. He's just parking the car. And there are a few others coming as well. As much as we need the numbers, as you can imagine, we had to be careful who we told about this."

"Definitely. I recognize the magnitude of what we're asking, both the danger of the actual mission and the severity of all the rules it breaks by keeping it from the organization. So thank you again." I move aside so he and Harper can walk over to the couch, leaving me as the lucky winner to answer the door shortly thereafter.

Noah stands on the other side in a near-identical uniform to Elias. "I knew you didn't get enough of me in New York."

I've never rolled my eyes so hard. "Thanks for coming, Noah," I grumble instead of the snippy response I *want* to give, because as much as I hate it and will never admit it out loud, Harper's right—we need him, and his being here is a big deal.

His lips twitch as he walks past me, nudging my arm with his elbow.

I can't stop myself from jabbing him in the ribs.

His response is a mix between a grunt and a laugh.

When I turn back to close the door, I suck in a breath when my eyes land on Xander and Blake.

The latter demon looks bored out of his mind as he leans against the doorframe. He's wearing a forest green Pike Place Market sweater with the hood up and gray joggers with his usual combat boots.

My eyes swing to Xander, and neither of us miss the way my pulse kicks up.

He's glaring daggers at Noah's retreating back, and the flicker of darkness in his eyes gives me pause. Is he *jealous*?

I sink my teeth into my bottom lip at the nerves swirling in my stomach. I'm suddenly thinking I was right to be worried about having Noah and Xander together. Them, together, in the same room could prove to be more dangerous than helpful.

My gaze returns to Xander, allowing myself a moment to take him in. His typically neat hair appears disheveled and his eyes are shadowed with a darkness that makes my chest tighten. Of course, he still looks otherworldly attractive, especially in his ensemble of black jeans and a V-neck under his leather jacket.

Before I can speak, Blake says, "Is this the meeting for the suicide squad?" He smirks, pushing away from the doorway and walking inside.

I bite my tongue, figuring it's better to save my breath than to try to put Blake in his place.

"Who even invited you?" Harper quips instead, and I should've known something like that was coming.

"Please," Blake drawls, bravely stepping closer to her. "It's not a party without yours truly, love."

Harper scowls at him, but surprisingly says nothing more before walking away to rejoin Noah and Elias on the couch.

Both hunters' expressions are grim, filled with distrust as they glare at the demons they've reluctantly agreed to work with. Noah's jaw looks sharp enough to cut glass, and the hatred is crystal clear on Elias's face, though neither of them say a word. They don't have to. And if looks could kill, they wouldn't need obsidian daggers to take out Xander and Blake. In fact, the demons would have already been reduced to ash.

Tension crackles in the air, making my breath shallow as I start to question this entire plan. Are these guys going to be able to work together? Hunters and demons *kill* each other all the time. Have we made a huge mistake in thinking they could set aside the decades' old shared hatred for one another?

Xander steps into my path, and my focus shifts to him as I lift my eyes to meet his gaze.

"How are you?" he asks softly, as if we're the only ones in the room. I fight the urge to close my eyes and lean into him when he splays his fingers across my cheek.

"I'm ready to end this," I answer in a hushed voice, my breath catching when my gaze flits to Noah over Xander's shoulder.

He's facing us on the couch, and his eyes are locked on Xander's every movement, narrowing as the demon's fingers warm my skin.

Suddenly, I wonder if Xander might not be the only one who's jealous...I quickly look away from Noah and fight to ignore the flush of heat in my face.

Xander nods, letting his hand fall back to his side. He's as ready as I am. Likely more so, considering Lucia has controlled him his entire life.

We join the others in the living room, and we all sit around the coffee table. I exchange a glance with Harper. We're both thinking the same thing—how wild it is to have hunters and demons together under our roof, with neither actively attempting to kill the other—*yet.*

"Who else are we expecting?" I ask.

Harper exchanges a glance with Noah, who says, "I called in Ezra, Archer, Sophia, and Rylee. They're all from Seattle, so they should be here any minute."

I nod, though the names are wholly unfamiliar to me. But our options are pretty limited at this point. If Noah trusts them enough to bring them into this, that's good enough for me. I'll take whatever help we can get.

As it turns out, Ezra and Archer are twins and hunting partners. They graduated from the academy the same year as Noah and look about as happy to be in a room with demons as Harper and Elias are. They're dressed the same as the other hunters, black from head to toe, and no doubt equipped with several obsidian daggers each. The only noticeable difference between the two is their hair. One has bushy curls, while the other has choppy and straight locks. They both have stunning blue eyes and dark skin. They're similarly built, with broad chests and thick muscles from years of extensive physical training.

Noah makes a quick introduction, and I offer each of them a smile as I say, "Thanks for coming."

"We're not ones to pass up a challenge," one of them—I think it's Archer—says with a lighthearted grin. He says it so casually, as if the challenge he's referencing isn't thwarting the plan of the most powerful demon in existence.

A few minutes later, Sophia and Rylee show up, again wearing the same unofficial uniform of the hunters. Sophia has cropped white blond hair and sharp blue eyes, while Rylee's appearance is softer. Her hair falls in long brown waves and her eyes are a warm golden brown. They introduce themselves to me, greeting their fellow hunters, but virtually ignore Xander and Blake.

I suppose it's better than attacking them—verbally, or otherwise.

Once we're all seated around the living room, I swallow past the anxiety creeping up my throat. "Let's make sure we're all on the same page. Lucia Kane, aka the queen of all demons, is planning to destroy the organization and wipe out the hunters completely. She's hungry for power in the wake of doubt being cast on her reign. Her initial plan was for me to infiltrate the organization and feed her information, but I don't think she's counting on my involvement anymore." I steal a glance at Xander, who confirms that with a subtle nod.

"She's not going to let anything stand in her way," Harper chimes in. "Which is why we need to act quickly before she can enact her plan."

Sophia and Rylee exchange a grim look that fills my stomach with more unease. I scan the rest of the hunters' faces, who all have similar expressions of concern and doubt.

"What's *our* plan, then?" Archer asks, crossing his legs at the ankles and leaning against the back of the couch as he looks between Harper and Noah.

To my surprise, it's Blake who speaks up. "Xander and I know Lucia better than anyone. We know how she thinks and operates. Above all, she craves power—to a self-destructive level. She's blinded by her desire for it, which is exactly what we're counting on." He turns to me. "You'll need to convince her you're prepared to surrender to her."

My stomach plummets, and I can't bring myself to look at Xander despite the pull I feel to meet his gaze. I can feel it on me—Noah's too, but I ignore both. "How do you expect this to work?" I blurt. "I don't think Lucia is going to buy me having a change of heart to betray my family. Especially after she had Phoebe and Grayson killed in front of me."

"We've considered that, and you're most likely correct," Xander says. "That's where I come in. I'll apply pressure and suggest she offer you an incentive for your cooperation."

I frown at him. "What incentive?"

His eyes shift to Harper, and she immediately narrows her eyes at him, muttering, "I don't like that look."

He nods. "I could suggest another of your colleagues, but there's far less of a chance that Lucia will believe Camille surrendering herself to save them. You, on the other hand, have an established relationship. Her being willing to fight for you makes sense."

"It's a good plan," Blake says, kicking his feet up on the coffee table.

"You think I'm okay with putting her in danger?" I aim my icy tone at the flamboyant demon.

"I'm sure she can take care of herself." His tone is confident, but it does nothing to comfort me at this moment.

My friend is strong and skilled, I'm well aware of that. *But so was Danielle.* Harper is not my sister, and this isn't the same thing, but I can't help the fear that latches on at the thought of losing my best friend.

"She can," Noah chimes in with a firm tone, "but that doesn't mean we're going to put her in a position where she'll undoubtedly have to."

"I'll do it," Harper speaks up.

I exchange a glance with Noah that fills my chest with something I can't quite decipher. He must feel it too, because his brows lift, something like confusion passing over his face, though it's gone as quickly as it came.

"Are you sure?" Elias asks her quietly, and she nods.

"I'll deliver Harper to Lucia's compound in Portland, so it appears I've taken her against her will," Blake explains, and my friend snorts at the last part.

There's an unspoken *as if you could.* I'd be more likely to smile at if she wasn't about to put her life on the line.

"I'm going to be the bargaining chip, then," she says.

Blake nods at her, then turns to me. "That's where you come in."

"Once I've suggested she use Harper as a way to force your hand," Xander says, "Lucia will make a spectacle of your surrender. She'll gather her inner circle to watch as you surrender and agree to loyally serve her."

The knots in my stomach twist tighter with his every word, bile rising in my throat as I struggle to keep my breathing level. The thought of having to bow before the queen of hell makes me want to keel over and vomit.

"That's when we'll attack," Harper suggests, determination shining in her gaze.

"With a room full of demons?" Archer speaks up, his arms folded over his broad chest.

"Lucia's most trusted demons are a limited number," Blake points out. "Six, at most. Think you can handle that, hunter?"

"Blake," Xander warns.

His second rolls his eyes in response, tipping his head against the back of the couch.

Harper shoots him an annoyed look. "Okay, so we're all up to speed. I'll go with Blake to Lucia's creepy-ass compound until mama's boy over there convinces her to use me as bait. Once Cami agrees to sacrifice herself to save me, Xander will bring her to meet Lucia. The hunters will follow, and when Blake is told to take me home, the two of us will let them in for the real fight."

Noah leans forward. "So it'll be seven hunters against at least six demons, along with the queen?" His expression is tense, as if he's attempting to determine our odds of pulling this off.

"Seven hunters and five demons," Xander says.

"Five?" I ask.

"We have friends, you know," Blake mutters.

Harper chokes on a laugh. "Right."

He shoots her a look, and she responds by flipping him off.

Xander scratches the shadow of stubble lining his jaw. "Three of the demons in Lucia's inner circle aren't as loyal to her as she believes them to be."

I frown. "What does that mean, exactly?"

Blake glances at me. "It means they're on our side."

Nodding, I say, "That's good. So we really only need to worry about Lucia and five other demons? Shouldn't we consider the possibility she might have more demons at the compound?"

"Lucia has become more paranoid over the last few years, so she's limited the number of demons she allows close to her home. And she'll be reluctant to fight," Xander says in a detached voice. "She fully expects any demon to put their life on the line so she doesn't have to so much as lift a finger."

"Great," Harper pipes up. "Makes her easier to kill."

I shake my head at her, a pang of sadness weighing heavy in my chest. "We're not killing her, Harper. Xander and Blake have a plan to detain her long enough to send her back to hell and ensure she can't get out." I turn to Xander. "Right?"

He nods, his expression void of any emotion, as if we're not talking about his mother. "There are points along particular ley lines in every state where a portal can be opened by spilling Lucia's blood on sacred ground. Most are guarded by hunters. But last I was informed, the location in Olympia currently is not."

"Where in Olympia is it?" Sophia asks.

"Just inside the national forest," Blake answers.

"That narrows it down," Noah remarks dryly.

"Any *skilled* hunter should be able to find it," Blake shoots back. "I thought I wouldn't be a problem for someone with your reputation. Unless you're all talk?"

Harper exhales a sigh, as if she's already tired of their bickering. "Great, so we just need to kill the members of her inner circle, knock her out for a little road trip from Portland to Olympia, then ship her ass back to hell."

"Basically, yeah," Blake says.

"What's the plan once we're inside the compound?" Rylee asks, tying her hair up as she glances around our group.

"I'll make sure the demons on our side are standing at the front of the room closest to Lucia," Xander explains. "The rest are fair game. Noah, I'll let you direct your team."

"How very gracious of you, princeling," he shoots back in a mocking tone. "As if I need permission from *you* to do my job."

I grit my teeth, dreading Xander's response, but he only chuckles.

Noah turns his attention to the twins. "Take out the other demons as quickly as possible. No fucking around. Sophia and Rylee will hang back a beat before joining the fray as the second wave of attack, eliminating the remaining demons."

"What about you?" I blurt, then press my lips together, as if I can pretend I didn't speak. I don't doubt Noah for a second, but I find myself needing to know what part he's going to play in all of this.

He spares me a brief glance. "I'll move in to detain the queen with Harper and Elias. Blake and Xander, we'll have you flank us and make sure anyone who gets the idea to try to stop us doesn't get the opportunity. Got it?"

The demons exchange a look before nodding at Noah.

I bite my tongue, going back and forth on whether I should voice the question plaguing me. When I can't hold it back any longer, I ask, "What is my role during all of this? Considering I'm not a hunter or a demon, I'm not sure where I fit."

"You can drive the car, love," Blake jokes with a wink in my direction.

I scowl at him, but before I can respond, Harper says, "That's actually not a bad idea. We'll need to get in and out quickly, so if you can make sure our getaway is ready—"

"You have got to be kidding me," I cut in.

"Once we enter the room," Noah starts, as if I haven't spoken, "you get the hell out and wait for us in the car."

I blink against the sudden burn of tears in my eyes, dropping my gaze to hide them. I want to say, *way to make me feel absolutely useless*, but again bite my tongue. This is about far more than me. If this is the plan that has the highest odds of working, it's what we need to do.

"Fine," I finally mutter.

"When are we doing this?" Ezra asks.

"We should put it in motion immediately," Xander says. "The less time we give anyone to catch on or suspect something, the better."

"Agreed," Harper says, turning to Blake. "Let's get this over with."

My stomach sinks, and I blurt, "Wait." Harper meets my gaze, and I add, "Are you absolutely sure about this?"

She reaches across Xander and grabs my hand, squeezing it. "I've got you, babe." Turning her gaze to Xander, she narrows her eyes. "You better not fuck this up. If I think for a second—"

"Harper," I cut in, squeezing her hand until she stops shooting daggers at him.

"Okay," she grumbles, pulling back as she looks at Blake again. "Come on, Double Bubble."

Xander chuckles as Blake grumbles something uncomplimentary, tugging the drawstrings on his hoodie. The former shifts closer until our legs touch, snagging my attention, and says to the others, "Can you give Camille and me a few minutes?"

Harper immediately looks at me, and I give her a subtle nod. She gets up, and Blake follows her as he types on his phone. A minute later, the front door clicks shut.

When I turn my gaze to Noah, he's already looking at me.

"It's okay," I assure him, though I'm not entirely sure why I feel the need. It's not as if I need his *permission*.

His eyes shift to Xander, narrowing slightly as he shakes his head. But he doesn't argue. Getting up without a word, he stalks out of the apartment, with the other hunters following him. I watch him go with a frown, but I don't have the mental capacity to explore the weird mix of feelings swirling in my gut.

I understand Noah's blatant distrust of Xander. Hell, I share it to some degree, though less as of late. What I can't figure out is why I feel so weird about what they think of each other. It's not as if I want them to spark a bromance or anything—I have no delusions that could ever happen. But they're being able to work together is important for us to make this plan successful.

That has it to be it. I ignore the pit of doubt in my stomach, pushing away the urge to overthink their behavior. There are more consequential things to focus on right now.

Once we're alone, Xander leans in, lifting his hand to brush the hair away from my face. "If this goes sideways, you need to run. All of you. Even with a few extra hunters and demons on our side, the danger is beyond what any of them will have experience with. I can't stress that enough." His touch lingers on my cheek, warming my skin.

I wrap my fingers around his wrist, holding his hand against my face. "If we want a chance at whatever this is between us, we have to get rid of her." I press my other hand against his chest, over his heart. "I want to be with you, Xander, but as long as Lucia has this power over you..." I drop my hand. "We can never work."

He catches my hand, lifting it to his lips and places a kiss to my palm. "You have no idea how much power *you* have over me, *mo shíorghrá*."

Tears spring in my eyes, and I shake my head, cracking myself open. "I don't want power, Xander. I just want *you*."

His eyes widen, flicking between mine. "How are you real?" he breathes, leaning in until his lips touch my forehead.

A breathy laugh escapes me. "Says the half-human, half-demon prince of hell."

His responding chuckle stirs the hair at my temple. "Fair point." He wraps his arms around me, pulling me against his chest, where I rest my cheek over his heart. "For as long as you want me, I'll be by your side. The gates of hell couldn't keep me away from you."

The weight of his words settles in my chest, mixing with a spark of hope and a razor-sharp worry that we're about to lose everything.

Twenty-Nine
Camille

The apartment has never felt so empty.

Xander left an hour ago to meet with Lucia, and my nerves have only gotten worse as I pace the living room, looking at the clock every thirty seconds. I take a shower to calm down, but even as I scrub myself with a loofa and my favorite eucalyptus body wash, I'm on the verge of a panic attack. Nausea fills my stomach, and the bile creeping up my throat taunts me with the threat of vomiting in the shower. I swallow it down and rinse my hair out before shutting off the water. Stepping into the steam-filled bathroom, I wrap myself in a towel and dry off before changing into something I would have worn to training years ago. Black leggings and a matching form-fitting long sleeve shirt with built-in padding so I can forgo a bra. After tugging on socks, I run a brush through my hair, staring at my reflection in the mirror as the fog dissipates. I try to focus on the determination in my gaze, but I can't miss the fear lingering there, too.

What happens after this?

Sending Lucia back to hell is no small feat. It's sure to change things for the demons and the hunters, but that's not what I keep thinking about. It's what her being gone will mean for Xander. Because once he's free of her hold on him, he'll be able to live the life he wants. Naturally, I can't stop thinking about where I fit in that. Despite everything that's happened, I still want to try. To give me and Xander a chance at a future together.

My heart leaps out of my chest at the sound of someone knocking at the door. I race out of the bathroom and answer it to find Xander standing on the other side, his expression stoic.

"Did it work?"

He nods as he steps inside and closes the door, facing me. "So far. I convinced her you'd trade yourself to ensure Harper's safety. That you'd take her place."

"It's the truth," I point out. Had Lucia been the one to come up with this, I wouldn't have hesitated to sacrifice myself to save my best friend. In my position, Harper would do the same.

"I have no doubt," he says. "We saved some time by having Blake bring Harper with us. It was an easy decision for her. As much as she could force your hand, having you go to her willingly—even like this with your back against the wall—is exactly what she wanted."

"And she has no idea? No suspicion that you and Blake are working against her?"

He shakes his head. "I wouldn't be standing here if she did."

The hint of sadness in his voice has me stepping into him, sliding my fingers through his hair and gently pushing it back. "I understand this is difficult for you differently from how it is for the rest of us. I just...I want to acknowledge that. Whatever you're feeling—it's completely valid."

His lips form a faint smile. "Thank you."

I nod, leaning up on my tiptoes to kiss his cheek before stepping away. "What happens now?"

"Once you're ready to leave, let the hunters know we're heading out, and we'll send them the address."

With a deep breath, I nod.

It's time to send the devil back where she belongs.

When we pull up the long, winding stone driveway to a massive house, my breath hitches. It takes me a few beats to force enough deep breaths to calm the rising anxiety.

I was knocked out the last time I was here, so I never saw the outside. Even in the dark, this place is stunning. The driveway is lined with perfectly manicured hedges and elegant bronze lampposts that light our path to the house. It exudes an air of sophistication that is impossible to ignore, even as my pulse thrums beneath my skin.

The car slows to a stop at the bottom of the stone stairs, and Xander shifts into park, turning off the Camaro. He gets out and walks around the front, stopping to open my door.

I blow out a shaky breath and take the hand he offers me, stepping out of the car.

As we climb the steps, Xander wraps his hand around my forearm, as if he's worried I'll try to bolt. Granted, I very much want to, but I steel my expression and square my shoulders, projecting an air of confidence I definitely don't feel.

Just before we reach the dark mahogany double doors, one swings open, revealing a few demons all dressed in dark gray attire. *They look like uniforms.* The thought comes and goes quickly as they nod at Xander and step aside.

As we move past them, my eyes immediately go to the stunning chandelier hanging from the high ceiling, casting a glow over the marble-floored foyer.

The other demons follow us as Xander leads me down a seemingly endless hallway. My shoes echo against the floor, and I keep my eyes trained forward, taking note of the closed doors on either side of the hall. The walls in between are empty of any artwork or decorative wallpaper, making the atmosphere colder.

Finally, we stop at the end of the hall in front of another set of double doors. I peek over at Xander, but he doesn't look at me. His posture is tall, almost regal.

It sends a chill down my spine as I stand straighter.

The doors in front of us open to a large room. I squint at the light cast by several chandeliers hung from the vaulted ceiling. That's pretty much the only architectural thing I notice before my eyes land on Lucia.

She sits atop a throne-like chair on a raised platform.

If I wasn't so terrified, I'd laugh. This scene is absolutely ridiculous. I'm pretty sure Lucia turned the living room of this place into a throne room. The chair she's sitting in is the only piece of furniture in here and the walls are crimson red. Heavy black velvet curtains, draped from the ceiling to the floor, cover the windows.

Her eyes glimmer wickedly before turning completely black. "Camille," she purrs in a honey-sweet voice, "I am so pleased you could join us." By *us*, she must mean the demon guards lining the room. *So much for a limited number.* There are already more than we expected, but I can't let that send me into a spiral. I have to stay focused.

"Where is Harper?" I demand, wrenching my arm free from Xander's grip. Violently. As if he really brought me here to save Harper.

Lucia sighs. "Skipping the pleasantries, I see. Very well." She waves her hand in the general direction of one of the demons, and he disappears through another door behind him.

I suck in a sharp breath when the demon comes back, dragging a bruised Harper along with him. She's limping, and there's blood dripping from her lip and a cut above her brow.

"You hurt her," I growl, starting forward, but Xander is faster, quickly pulling me back with his fingers wrapped firmly around my wrist.

The queen rolls her eyes. "She is alive," she says in a bored tone.

"I'm here," I say, my voice trembling with very real terror. "Let her go. That's the deal—her for me."

She cocks her head, her endless black eyes staring into my soul. At least, that's what it feels like. "You are surrendering yourself to me?"

I swallow hard and nod. "So long as you promise her safety."

Lucia smirks. "The hunter will remain alive," she grants in an icy, smooth voice. "Even I can show mercy, Camille." Her eyes shift to Xander. "I would not kill one of the few blood relatives my son has."

My eyes pop wide and my jaw drops as Harper makes a strangled sound and shoves away from the demon holding her. "Shut the fuck up," she snarls at Lucia, spitting blood onto the floor. "Stop saying that!" Her puffy, red-rimmed eyes flit to me. "She's lying!"

Lucia chuckles, folding one leg over the other and clasping her hands together in her lap. "You do not wish to hear it, but that does not make it any less true."

"What are you talking about?" Xander demands in a tight voice, stepping toward where Lucia is seated.

Her lips twitch briefly. "You mean you could not sense it?" She *tsks*. "Once more, I am disappointed by you, Xander."

He shakes his head, his expression straining with thinly veiled confusion. "Mother—"

"Joshua Gilbert was the name of your father. He was killed on my order, along with his wife, Helena."

Harper chokes on a sob, her jaw clenched tight and her eyes swimming with tears.

Mine burn as I try to fight back my own. I can't imagine how she must feel learning that her parents were *specifically* targeted by the queen of hell. Of all the scenarios I played out in my head, the possibility of Xander and Harper being half-siblings never crossed my mind. *Why would it?*

Before either can respond, the doors we came through moments ago fly open again, breaking off their hinges and crashing against the floor.

Blake swaggers into the room, his eyes wild. In a flash, he takes out the guards by the door, snapping necks as if it's a sport.

Several more demons flood the room, but in the same moment, Xander hauls me behind him, where I nearly collide with Archer and Ezra, who must've snuck into the room after Blake's obnoxious entrance. Noah and Elias are right behind them, their expressions grim and focused.

Noah looks like a god of death, wielding an obsidian dagger in each hand as he moves with a lethal grace, attacking without hesitation. He takes out two demons in a matter of seconds, ducking just in time to avoid another's attack. Kicking the demon's legs out from under her, she hits the ground hard, and Noah moves over her, slamming a dagger into her chest. Her mouth forms a perfect 'o' as her eyes widen, then turn vacant seconds before she disintegrates into a pile of black ash like the others.

I'm supposed to be running in the opposite direction, but I can't take my eyes off him. I catch sight of Sophia and Rylee entering the room with their daggers at the ready and matching looks of determination etched into their features.

The sound of battle mixes with the blood rushing through my ears as I press against the wall, unable to look away from the carnage. Archer and Ezra tag-team one demon after another, taking them down, while Sophia and Rylee cover them.

"Elias, look out!"

I turn at the high-pitched sound of Harper's voice just in time to witness a demon plunge her hand into Elias's chest. His eyes bulge out of his face, his mouth opening in a silent scream. The demon pulls her hand out, gripping his heart, and smirks as she lets it roll off her fingers onto the floor, his body collapsing to join it.

Fuck, fuck, fuck.

I blink back tears, my heart pounding so hard I can feel it in my throat. The sound that escapes Harper's lips is cold and vicious. Her eyes are sharp, murderous, and her jaw is tight. She and Elias were close, always competing for the top of the leaderboard. There's no chance she was prepared for this outcome.

I see the exact moment she disassociates from the chaos and taps into her most primal instincts, fully giving herself over to it. She moves toward Elias, snatching the dagger out of his lifeless grip and moves faster than I thought was humanly possible. She shows no mercy as she moves through the room, turning demons to ash as they cross her path.

Harper scowls and wipes the blood from her lip. The cut there must've opened as she fought through the crowd. She swings her arm in a deadly arch, burying her dagger in the chest of the demon who dragged her in here, then moves on to take out another.

The room erupts into utter chaos, and I cry out in pain when a body slams into me. I land on my arm, turning my head to see Harper standing over me. "What the fuck?"

"You aren't supposed to be here," she snaps, driving her dagger into another oncoming demon. His ash covers us both, clinging to my clothes as I struggle not to gag.

"I—"

"*Stay down*," she all but growls at me, the cut above her brow dripping blood down her cheek.

Everything is happening so fast, I can barely keep up.

Blake and Xander are inching closer to the throne, fighting back-to-back and taking out each demon that gets close.

Lucia just stands there watching, a faint look of disappointment on her face as our team fights her inner circle while she doesn't lift a finger.

In what seems like a matter of seconds, they've torn through every demon in the room, save for the ones on our side, who are now fighting their own kind.

Finally, Lucia steps down from her throne with a couple of guards flanking her.

My eyes roam over the room in search of Noah, who is supposed to be moving in to detain Lucia alongside Harper, but he's caught up in fighting another wave of demons.

Where the fuck are they coming from?

Harper lets loose a string of expletives and dives back into battle, attacking the demon currently snarling in Noah's face. She grabs the demon from behind, slamming her dagger into his heart through his back and turning him to ash in the span of about thirty seconds.

"Xander." Lucia tuts her tongue as she watches her son snap the neck of a demon. "Look what a mess you have made."

"No," he growls, standing straighter and wiping the blood from his brow. "*You* did this, mother."

She opens her mouth, as if she's going to respond, but then smirks instead as yet another swarm of demons storm the room.

There have to be at least a dozen now. It's impossible to decipher which of them are on our side. Regardless, it's not looking good.

Harper catches sight of me again, her eyes narrowing. "Cami, get the fuck out of here!" she hisses. The *you're only getting in the way* goes without saying—I'm the only human here not properly trained to fight.

The fear clogging my throat finally convinces me to concede, and I slink along the side of the room, my back against the wall. I can't see much through the wall of fighting, but the air is clogged with the sharp scent of blood and sweat, filled with the sound of physical exertion and painful attacks.

Turning my head at the sound of a large crash, I suck in a sharp breath when I see Ezra on the floor. A demon is poised over him, grinning menacingly in his face, his eyes completely black.

I keep inching toward the door as Archer moves in to backup his twin, but before I can see him rip the demon off Ezra, an ironclad grip steals my wrist, sharp nails digging into my skin. I cry out, and terror fills my veins with ice as my head snaps toward Lucia.

She has a vicious sneer plastered on her blood-red lips, and her eyes are consumed with darkness.

"You truly believed you could double-cross me?" She chuckles, making my stomach clench as tension spreads through my muscles. "Stupid girl. You will not live long to see the consequences of your choice, so allow me to share. I am going to rip everyone you love to shreds, agonizingly slowly, until they beg me to end their suffering. And then I will draw it out even longer."

Nausea rolls through me, and my head spins as fear digs its unforgiving talons into me. I open my mouth to, what, beg her for my life? For everyone else's? It doesn't matter, because nothing comes out. I've lost the ability to form words as I stare at the queen of hell.

In the time it takes me to blink, Lucia wraps her fingers around my throat, slamming me back into the wall as she squeezes my airway shut. The battle around us fades as blood rushes through my ears, making everything sound far away.

All I can see is the endless darkness in Lucia's eyes. Her promise of pain and suffering for my loved ones. The pressure in my head builds and builds, my eyes bulging out of my face as she squeezes harder. I claw at her hand, trying with every ounce of strength I have to push her away, to *breathe*. It hits me then, like a brutal punch to the gut.

I'm going to die.

My vision blurs, my chest burning, and I struggle and ultimately fail to pull in a breath. Black spots dot my vision as tears roll down my cheeks, the muffled sound of shouting lost to the pressure behind my eyes. I can't tell who's screaming. All I can focus on is the expression of pure evil as Lucia leans in, her lips twisted into a cruel, cold smile. The floodgates of terror break open, and it seizes me, making my back go ramrod straight, my entire body going rigid.

Too many things happen at once. My legs give out as someone slams into Lucia from behind, knocking her away and sending me flying to the marble floor. My mouth opens to cry out as white-hot pain lances up my side, but the fire licking up my throat makes it impossible for any sound to escape. I struggle through the pain, kicking my legs out and digging my heels into the floor until I manage to use the wall to sit up. Sounds rush back in, overwhelming me as I clutch the sides of my head, blinking quickly in an attempt to focus my vision.

Just in time to watch Xander drive an obsidian blade deep into his mother's chest.

Her eyes go wide, shock filling the darkness there.

My stomach plummets.

"Xander!" Harper screams, and Blake is suddenly beside her, grabbing her arm and pulling her back.

Xander's expression is grim as he twists the dagger in his mother's chest, making her cry out in agony. A similarly painful sound rips from his throat, too.

Lucia blinks slowly, dropping her gaze to the dagger sticking out of her chest. She reaches for it, but her shaking fingers hover around the hilt, unable to grasp it. "What have you done?" she hisses and sinks to the ground at his feet. She blinks once, twice, and then her eyes don't open again. Within seconds, her form disintegrates into black ash, blanketing the room in a heavy silence. No one moves. No one makes a sound.

My eyes swing toward Harper to find her face shrouded in confusion. I'm sure her expression mirrors on my own as I slowly get to my feet, keeping my back pressed against the wall to stay upright.

This wasn't the plan.

Xander stares at her lifeless body, then his shoulders rise and fall with a sigh before he turns to face us—and who's left of his mother's guards. His eyes are completely black. They survey the room, not stopping anywhere too long.

One by one, each demon sinks to their knees and bows their head.

To Xander.

Blake blinks a few times before he does the same.

Xander's eyes meet mine, flickering from black to brown, and for a fleeting moment, they are completely vulnerable. His expression is filled with utter shock, pain, and *fear*. Fear so strong it knocks the air out of my lungs. A second later, he blinks, and his eyes are fully black again. He's still looking at me, but there's no recognition in his gaze. There's nothing but darkness.

I can't stop staring at him. My feet are blocks of cement. I can't move.

Suddenly, an arm snakes around my waist and hauls me toward the doorway we came in through what seems like an entirety ago. Noah's voice is gruff in my ear, telling me we need to go. But I can't.

Xander just killed his mother. And based on the response of the other demons in the room, he took her place on the throne when he took her life.

Xander is the king of hell.

"Come," Noah urges, dragging me away. "You need to move."

The hallway seems even longer now as Harper shifts closer and helps Noah drag me toward the front of the house. Archer and Ezra are in front of us, while Sophia helps an injured Rylee limp behind us. None of the demons attempt to stop us. I think they too are in shock—or dead.

By the time we reach the front door, my feet are sort of working again, but Noah and Harper don't let go of me until we reach Noah's car. They get me into the backseat before he slams the door and gets behind the wheel. His movements are rushed and jerky as he throws the car into drive and speeds away from the house. The others get into another vehicle and follow close behind us.

Harper sits in the back with me, breathing heavily as her injuries continue to bleed. We're both stunned into silence for several minutes before she says, "Do you want to talk?"

I stare out the window, looking at nothing. "He saved my life." The words leave my lips and twist the knots in my stomach, because he chose to put my life above Lucia's. I so badly want to believe his actions show just how deeply he cares about me. That the thought of me dying pushed him to do something so unbelievably significant.

"Yeah," she says hesitantly.

"He killed his queen—his *mom*—Harper," I whisper, finally looking at her.

Xander didn't have a typical or anywhere near good relationship with the woman—simply put, he hated her, and for good reason—but they were still bonded. I can't imagine what that choice is going to do to him.

She nods. "I know, babe."

"Do you think—I mean—Was this his plan all along? To take her place on the throne?"

Harper sighs. "Did you see Blake's face? If this was Xander's plan, it's safe to say he didn't tell anyone about it."

I hiccup as a fresh batch of tears gathers in my eyes. "What do you think this means?"

She reaches for me, lacing her fingers through mine and squeezing my hand. "I don't know," she finally says.

My phone vibrates from the pocket in my leggings, and I fumble to pull it out. "Fuck," I whisper as my eyes burn, and I answer the call, putting it on speaker. "Mom," I say in a tight voice, barely holding back even more tears.

"Hi, honey. I know it's late—I was just going to leave you a message and see if we could meet tomorrow. There's something I need to talk to you about."

I squint as pain pulses behind my eyes.

"Camille?"

"Sorry," I say, "I'm here."

"Should I just call you tomorrow?"

I swallow the lump in my throat, struggling not to choke on a sob. "No," I force out. "What's going on?"

"Your father and I have been having some difficult conversations. You know how much it hurt when you decided not to continue your training. In the world we live in, your father and I were scared you'd be left unprotected without the skills to defend yourself in case of a demon attack. And since you told me about your relationship with Xander, I've worried even more."

Oh god, I can't do this right now.

"Mom—" Wetness tracks down my cheeks, blurring my vision as my temples throb.

"Wait," she says quickly. "Please, just listen for a minute. This isn't what you think, I promise."

I look at Harper, but she shakes her head as if she has no idea what my mom is getting at.

"Okay," I whisper.

"You deserve everything you want, Camille. I know we haven't always been around. We haven't been there for you in the ways you need and deserve. We failed you as parents. As a mother, I failed my child. For that, I will always have regrets. But I hope it's not too late."

I sniffle, blinking as more tears gather and fall. All I've wanted for the last five years was for my parents to accept who I am, that I didn't want to be a demon hunter, that I wanted to be whatever I chose for myself.

"We understand you want something more for your future and we want to make sure you get whatever that turns out to be."

A sob escapes my lips, and I squeeze my eyes shut. "Mom..."

The relief that floods through me is short-lived. The fear and utter confusion over what I just witnessed is still fresh, so close to the surface it's bound to explode any second. I don't have time to be happy that my parents are being supportive. And that's the worst part.

"Camille, your father and I aren't going to fight you on it anymore. It's not something you need to worry about. Whatever needs to be done to deal with Xander and his mother, the organization will take care of it. We accept that you aren't going to continue your training, and—"

"I'm in," I cut her off, the words flying out before I can stop them.

There's silence on the other end, and then a very quiet, "What?" Confusion fills her tone, and I don't blame her. I'm as confused as she is.

Harper is wide-eyed, shaking her head at me. She mouths, *what are you doing?*

Even Noah glances at me through the rearview mirror, his brows stitched in confusion.

My head spins and my stomach churns, but my resolve hardens as I force down the bile rising in my throat. "I'm going to start training again."

"I don't understand," she says in a thick voice, as if she's holding back tears. "That's not what you want."

I think I just lost what I want.

The future is a never-ending, dark tunnel of unanswered questions. My head is spinning and my heart feels as if it's been cleaved in two. I have no idea what's going to happen now, but my gut tells me I'm going to need all the training I can get.

"Can I start immediately?" I ask, my voice marginally steadier than a few seconds ago.

"I...Of course you can, Camille. But—"

"Okay." I lick the dryness from my lips. "I have to go, Mom. Let's talk tomorrow. There's a lot I need to tell you." I end the call before she can respond.

"What did you just do?" Harper asks when I set my phone on the seat between us.

I close my eyes as a new wave of fear threatens to swallow me whole. "I did what I had to."

Exclusive Hardcover Bonus Content

Spoilers for *The Devil's Waltz* ahead.
Read the entire book before diving into these character interviews.
You've been warned!

Interview with Camillelle Morgan

Jessi: Hello, Camille! You're the first character I'm interviewing. Thanks for taking the time to speak with me!

Camille: I'm happy to. It's a nice break from all the crazy going on around here. And please, call me Cam or Cami. We are friends, after all.

Jessi: Right. Okay, let's start off with a basic question. How do you feel about being the main character?

Camille: Oh, um…weird, I guess? I hope readers connect to my story, but not too literally, of course. *laughs*

Jessi: Of course. Here's a fun one. Do you prefer salty or sweet snacks.

Camille: Oooh, definitely sweet. I'm a sucker for desserts. I love them. Red velvet cake especially.

Jessi: Yum! Me too. Are you a dog or cat person?

Camille: Well, I didn't have pets growing up, but if I was going to get one now, it would be a dog. Probably a husky or golden retriever.

Jessi: What's your favorite color?

Camille: Dark green, like the deepest parts of a forest.

Jessi: Are you the type to unpack as soon as you get home from a trip or a week later?

Camille: I'd love to say as soon as I get home, but I'm definitely guilty of letting my laundry sit in my suitcase for days.

Jessi: You and me both. What's your favorite Disney movie?

Camille: I'm going to be super cliché and say Beauty and the Beast.

Jessi: Hey, it's a classic! What's one hobby you've always wanted to try?

Camille: Boxing. It looks like so much fun! It's also a great method of strength training.

Jessi: Very cool. Favorite road trip snack?

Camille: Pretzels. Oh, and licorice!

Jessi: Both great choices.

Camille: Can I ask you a question?

Jessi: Me? Uh, sure?

Camille: Why is it called *The Devil's Waltz*? I mean, we don't dance, and I'm pretty sure Xander doesn't even know how…

Jessi: Ha! Well, it's not meant to be a literal waltz. That said, there was a scene in the original version of the book that was a masquerade ball. It wasn't written into the final version, but I fell in love with the title almost a decade ago when I wrote it the first time and just couldn't part with it.

Camille: Hmm. Got it. The title is sentimental.

Jessi: Exactly. Anyway, thank you very much for joining me and answering all my questions. I'm sure readers are looking forward to hearing from you!
Camille: Thanks for having me. And if I can leave you with one request, please go easy on me in the sequel.

Jessi: *nervous laugh*

INTERVIEW WITH XANDER KANE

Jessi: Welcome, Xander. Or should I say, your highness?

Xander: *chuckles* Did Blake tell you to say that?

Jessi: No, though that's probably because I haven't spoken to him yet.

Xander: Ah. Yeah, he enjoys messing with me.

Jessi: The best of friends usually do. Anyway, thank you for joining me. I appreciate you taking time out of your busy schedule.

Xander: No problem. What questions do you have for me?

Jessi: Diving right in, great. First thing readers wanted to know is your zodiac sign.

Xander: *blinks* I have no idea. And why do they care?

Jessi: Some people think your zodiac sign says things about you. When were you born?

Xander: April 18th.

Jessi: So, you're an Aries. Interesting. Some people believe Aries make strong leaders.

Xander: Next question.

Jessi: Okay then. What's in your fridge right now?

Xander: Hmm. A few take-out boxes, some random condiments, and the staples—eggs, milk, and a variety of greens.

Jessi: Do you enjoy cooking?

Xander: I do. It's relaxing. I don't have to think when I'm following a recipe.

Jessi: What is your favorite thing to make?

Xander: Penne pasta in vodka sauce.

Jessi: Sounds yummy. What song do you have on repeat right now?

Xander: Just Pretend by Bad Omens.

Jessi: Oh, that's a good one. What's your favorite season of the year?

Xander: I enjoy the newness that comes with spring.

Jessi: If we were in the middle of a zombie apocalypse, who is one person you'd without a doubt want on your team?

Xander: *chuckles and glances around* Don't tell Blake, but I'd probably recruit Camille's friend, Harper. She's a natural fighter, so I'd stand a better chance against them.

Jessi: Fair enough. I'd probably pick Harper too. Hmm, or Noah. Though I understand why he wouldn't be your first choice.

Xander: No comment.

Jessi: I figured as much. Okay, here's an easy one! What's your favorite type of dessert?

Xander: I'm a big fan of pastries. Even better if chocolate is involved.

Jessi: Oh yeah, I fully agree. Do you believe in soulmates?

Xander: Hmm, I suppose that would require having a soul, wouldn't it?

Jessi: I...Yeah. One would assume.

Xander: Sure. I don't necessarily think each person only has one, though.

Jessi: Interesting. This is the last question I have for you. If you could meet anyone in the world, who would it be?

Xander: My father. I unfortunately never had the chance.

Jessi: I'm sorry, but thank you for sharing. I appreciate you taking the time to speak with me.

Xander: You're welcome.

Interview with Harper Gilbert

Jessi: Hey, Harper! Thanks so much for being here. I'm looking forward to chatting with you.

Harper: Anytime, babe. Happy to hang for a bit, but I don't have long.

Jessi: No worries! Let's dive right into the questions. If you weren't a demon hunter, what career path do you think you'd want to pursue?

Harper: Something creative. When I was younger, I loved coming up with stories. I'd tell them to my friends and family, anyone who'd listen, really. So I guess I'd want to be a writer.

Jessi: I love that. What are the top three items on your bucket list?

Harper: That sort of relates to the previous question, because I'd have to say publish a book. Travel to at least ten places I've never been. And…make it to retirement. My job's a bit high-risk, so that's no small feat.

Jessi: Fair enough. Would you rather have slow internet or always forget your passwords?

Harper: That's an awful question. Oh my god. Fuck, I'm going with forgetting my passwords. Slow internet would drive me absolutely insane.

Jessi: I would have picked the same. What is your favorite breakfast food?

Harper: Give me a tall stack of pancakes any day. Preferably with a ton of chocolate chips.

Jessi: What's your favorite holiday?

Harper: I love the time leading up to Christmas. The cozy vibes make me really happy. Christmas Day itself is mostly anticlimactic, but the lead up is always amazing.

Jessi: I know you workout to keep in shape for your job. What do you listen to at the gym?

Harper: Depends on the day, but it's usually my gym playlist, which is made up of fast-paced hard rock, or podcasts. I'm really into the true crime ones at the moment.

Jessi: Would you rather be stranded on a desert island alone or with your worst enemy?

Harper: Oh, that's easy. Alone. Blake would be the worst person to get stranded with. I'd kill him on day one out of pure annoyance.

Jessi: You consider Blake your worst enemy?

Harper: Only on days that end in 'y'.

Blake: *in the distance* I heard that!

Harper: Fuck off! This is my interview, jackass.

Jessi: Okayyyy. Let's wrap this up with a final question. What's something you couldn't live without?

Harper: My best friend.

Jessi: Awe, I love that. Thanks again for hanging with me!

Harper: *smiles* Like I said, anytime.

Interview with Noah Daniels

Jessi: Noah, hello! Thanks for stopping by to chat on your way to training.

Noah: Sure. Happy to be here, but I do only have a few minutes so maybe we can do this rapid-fire style?

Jessi: *laughs* Works for me! What's your favorite part about being a demon hunter?

Noah: Fighting for a better world and protecting the people I care about.

Jessi: If you didn't live in New York, where would you want to be?

Noah: Probably somewhere warm. I've considered California and have some family there.

Jessi: Would you rather never step foot inside a gym again or be able to but only wearing high heels?

Noah: *blinks* Neither are ideal, which I gather is the point. Hmm…Well, I don't need a gym to train and if I tried with heels I'd surely break my neck, so I guess never step foot inside a gym again.

Jessi: What's your favorite ice cream flavor?

Noah: Anything with cookie dough or chocolate. Preferably both. I have a major sweet tooth.

Jessi: Who was the last person you texted and what did you say to them?

Noah: *checks phone* I sent Camille a thumbs-up emoji in response to her reminder text about this interview.

Jessi: Do you and Camille text often?

Noah: *shrugs* Sure. Can we move on now?

Jessi: Uh, yeah. Drink of choice?

Noah: Alcoholic? I love a good craft beer. If we're talking coffee, though, I drink it black with enough sugar to put you in a diabetic coma.

Jessi: If you could only read one book for the rest of your life, what would you choose?

Noah: I'm not sure I could pick a single book, but if I had to pick one author, it'd be Stephen King.

Jessi: What would you do with a million tax-free dollars?

Noah: *shrugs* Travel a bit, I guess. Give some to family and friends.

Jessi: Breakfast for dinner. Yay or nay?

Noah: Absolutely yay. Especially if it's pancakes or French toast.

Jessi: This one is a reader request. Are you currently dating anyone?

Noah: *chuckles* No.

Jessi: What's your social media platform of choice?

Noah: I'm not into social media. You only see people how they want you to, whether or not it's accurate.

Jessi: Hmm, fair enough. Okay, this is my last question! What do you like to do in your free time?

Noah: *smirks* It was nice chatting with you.

Jessi: Ah, I got you. *laughs* Thanks again!

Interview with Blake Taylor

Jessi: Last, but certainly not least… Welcome, Blake!

Blake: Hello, love. So wonderful to be here chatting with you.

Jessi: I have to admit, this is the interview I'm looking forward to the most.

Blake: As you should. I am the most interesting of our lot.

Jessi: I feel like I have so many questions for you, but I'm going to try to keep this short. What is the worst fashion decision you ever made?

Blake: *blinks* Have you met me? I'm a fashion icon. Though once I was traveling and the airline lost my luggage, so I had to shop at a chain department store. It was hell. *shudders*

Jessi: Hell. Right. Okay, what do you do to unwind after a long day?

Blake: Do you want the PG answer or the real one? Because the real one is definitely NSFW.

Jessi: You know, I think that answers the question good enough. We can use our imaginations. Next question is why the pink hair?

Blake: Because it's fun. *shrugs* What color do you think I should do next?

Jessi: Oh, um, I don't know. Maybe blue?

Blake: Huh. Blue. I could pull that off. Okay, next question?

Jessi: Would you rather laugh every time someone said something sad or cry every time someone said something funny?

Blake: Definitely laugh.

Jessi: I had a feeling you were going to say that.

Blake: *grins* I am a demon, after all.

Jessi: Fair enough. What are your most commonly used emojis?

Blake: Xander gets annoyed whenever I use it, but the smirking devil one.

Jessi: That checks out. Next question, would you rather be at the beach or in the mountains?

Blake: Mountains. The beach is too people-y

Jessi: Ha. Yeah, I tend to agree. Okay, last one. Would you rather be always cold or always hot?

Blake: Considering I'm always hot, I think that question answers itself.

Jessi: That's not really an answer, but I'll give it to you, because you're not wrong. Thanks so much for taking the time to answer my questions!

Blake: Anytime, love. *winks*

PLAYLIST

I Found ~ Amber Run
What Kind of Man ~ Florence + The Machine
When It's All Over ~ RAIGN
Devil Side ~ Foxes
Walk Through the Fire ~ Klergy, BELLSAINT
Power Over Me ~ Dermot Kennedy
Coming up for Air ~ Signals In Smoke
Giants ~ Silverberg, Ruelle
Poison & Wine ~ The Civil Wars
The Ice Is Getting Thinner ~ Death Cab for Cutie
Where Do We Go from Here? ~ Ruelle
Hearts Without Chains ~ Ellie Goulding
Paradise Lost ~ Hollywood Undead
In The End ~ Beth Crowley
Bad Things ~ Summer Kennedy
Halo ~ Little Dume
Between the Bars ~ Elliott Smith
What Are We Fighting For ~ Jordin Sparks, Th3rdstream
Jungle ~ Emma Louise
Mount Everest ~ Labrinth
Shadows In The Dark ~ Juke Ross
Ashes ~ Stellar
Between Dusk And Dawn ~ alayna
Blood In the Water ~ Joanna Jones as the Dame
The Beast ~ Old Caltone
Day Is Gone ~ Noah Gundersen
Oh Death ~ Noah Gundersen
Dance With The Devil ~ Rachel Taylor
Every Man Is a Warrior ~ Lena Fayre
The Argument ~ Aidan Hawken
Consequences ~ Camila Cabello
Crave You ~ Robinson
Bitter Heart ~ Memi, Staffan Carlén
Islands ~ Sara Bareilles

I Fell In Love With The Devil ~ Avril Lavigne
Bruises ~ Lewis Capaldi
Together ~ The xx
Pteryla ~ Novo Amor, Lowswimmer
Black Parade ~ Gin Wigmore
Wake Up World ~ UNSECRET, Ruelle
Bloodstream ~ Stateless
Hang On A Little Longer ~ UNSECRET, Ruelle
Hold Me ~ The Sweeplings
With Wings ~ Amy Stroup
I Scare Myself ~ Beth Crowley
Down ~ Jason Walker
How It Ends ~ Beth Crowley
Moon Shines Red ~ Jamie McDell
Down in Flames ~ Daughter Jack
Dynasty ~ MIIA
Free ~ Tommee Profitt, SVRCINA
Cruel Summer ~ Taylor Swift
Half A Man ~ Dean Lewis
Behind the Mask ~ Ivy & Gold
The Last Time ~ Taylor Swift, Gary Lightbody
This Is Love ~ Claire Guerreso
Wrong Direction ~ Hailee Steinfeld
Breathe Again ~ Sara Bareilles
Lovers Death ~ Ursine Vulpine, Annaca
Graveyard ~ Halsey
Savior ~ Beth Crowley
Too Far Gone ~ Hidden Citizens, SVRCINA
Into the Fire ~ Christian Reindl, Lloren
Angel in Hell ~ Klergy
The Ghost Who Is Still Alive ~ Beth Crowley

Scan to listen

Acknowledgments

I first wrote *The Devil's Waltz* in 2014. Then rewrote it in 2016. And then I started rewriting it again in 2020 before other projects shifted it to the back burner. Throughout the years, these characters never stopped talking to me. Their story needed to be told, and I knew that. It was just a matter of the right timing. Fast forward to 2023, when I decided it was time—I was going to rewrite this book for the fourth and *final* time. It has been a crazy journey, but I wouldn't change a thing.

First and foremost, thank you to Inimitable Books and its incredible founder, Zara, who read the very first version of *The Devil's Waltz* in 2014 (and again in 2016). Your excitement and support for this project is unmatched. Thank you for believing in this story (in every stage of its existence) and giving me this amazing opportunity. You have my eternal gratitude.

To my early readers, Bethany, Katie, Sam, and Victoria: thank you for helping make this book-shaped thing something I'm proud and excited to share with readers. I am very lucky to have you in my corner.

To Starbucks, Spotify & Pinterest: I couldn't write books without them.

As always, thank you to my friends and family, for your continued support and encouragement.

And finally, thank *you*, the reader, for picking up this book. I sincerely hope you enjoyed it, but also, buckle up, because this is just the beginning...